Pipe
Vision

J.R.Greulich

CHICAGO SPECTRUM PRESS
12305 WESTPORT RD., STE. 4
LOUISVILLE, KENTUCKY 40245
502-899-1919

Printed in the U.S.A.

10 9 8 7 6 5 4 3 2 1

ISBN: 978-1-58374-284-6

Cover Photo: © 2012 Michalowski | Stock Free Images & Dreamstime Stock Photos

*f*or Grandma and Grandpa,
Mom and Dad

&

all of the
special people in my life
who have supported me
in life and on this project.

A portion of the proceeds
from this book will benefit children
with disabilities who are served by the
Kids Center for Pediatric Therapies in Louisville, KY.
I went there as a child and they were
a huge help to me and my family.
Since 1959 they have been
helping over 700 children per year
discover the "ability in disability"
To learn more go to
www.kidscenterky.org.

1

"**G**reat, I hate packing for these trips. Every year we take this trip and every year is worse than the year before. I hate it. I hate it. I don't even wanna pack."

"Well Conrad, if you're going to have an attitude like that you can stay at Grandpa's."

My name is Conrad Dawson Hughes, but everyone calls me Bub, except when I am in trouble, then they pull out the full name and my brain stops wondering what I did and how much trouble I am about to get into. Of course, if I'd known my mom was listening to me I never would have said that out loud. Now I was busted and had to think quick because as bad as this trip was going to be, I knew staying at my grandpa's would probably be one hundred times worse. "Umm, no Mom. I ... I didn't know you were there. I was just kidding around." I hope she buys it.

"You know, your dad works hard every year to put this trip together. We will be leaving soon, so make sure you have everything."

If he worked so hard to put this trip together each year, then why not plan a trip a fifteen-year-old kid would like? You know, a trip that might involve a convertible, sandy beach and girls in bikinis. Instead, we are all piling into a beat-up Ford truck with duct tape on the bumpers and a camper that looks like it should be flattened. The truck was okay, I guess. It didn't smell or have bugs but I did have to share a room with my snoring kid sister.

I threw my stuff on the bed of the camper. While on vacation, Mom insisted that the bathroom and the living room be clean but we did not have to clean our room. I was a slob and it drove my sister crazy. She and I used to fight over the top bunk, but now she gets it because I am too tall for the top. There were

only twelve more hours until I hear, "STOP SHAKING THE CAMPER," every five minutes.

Space was limited in the truck because there were four of us and our dog, Cosby. So, we were not allowed to have much in front with us. We could have one goodie bag and a pillow, and it had to stay on the floorboards between our feet because Cosby had to sit in the middle seat. Cosby was a mild-mannered dog that pretty much followed me around. The following started after school one day when I was in the seventh grade. After begging and pleading for hours, my dad let us keep him. Dad hated that dog for the first year but now loves him as much as I do, although, he would never admit it.

"All aboard!" My dad was trying to make us smile, though it only worked on mom. We knew he was trying too hard to excite us. Dad stood about six feet tall and wore T-shirts that I am sure Grandma bought him when he was in high school. Half of them my sister and I did not understand. Today's shirt stated, "PROCRASTINATORS UNITE, TOMORROW." After thinking about this for a second, I gave up.

"C'mon Dad, try to act normal," I said.

"Like you know what that is," Sissy said, and stuck her tongue out.

"Cosby," Dad said firmly. "Let's go, boy."

"Yeah, put him by Sis so he will throw up on her," I laughed as I got in the truck. "Here starts the worst vacation ever," I thought to myself.

Over the years, we have had many good vacations there. None was like the summer you are about to read about. This summer changed my life. Forever.

2

Across the country, a chubby kid named Seth sat on his bed playing video games. He knew his mom would be coming in soon to tell him that it was time to go. Once again, it was the time of year to go to Kentucky to spend time with a guy he barely knew. His dad.

Seth wanted to stay home and had pleaded for months with his mom to let him stay home. Her response was always, "Every boy needs to spend time with his father."

"If she wanted me to spend so much time with him, then why did she bring me across the country?" he thought.

"SETH!" His mom screamed up the stairs, "It's time to go."

"Okay, Mom. I'll be right down." Snatching his duffle bag and giving one last look of goodbye to his room, he shut the door and thundered down the stairs.

"I am not going to miss that sound," his mother said adoringly, "but I will miss you. Hug me now because I know you won't at the airport."

Reluctantly, he honored her request, hating every painful second of it. "I know you hate this but it is the only two weeks your dad gets to see you. One day you are going to look back on this and thank me for making you go."

"I seriously doubt it," he rolled his eyes.

"Do you have everything?"

"Mom," he interrupted.

"C'mon now let's be sure you have everything. It is a long way back here from the airport and you know that if you forget something your father isn't going to buy it for you. Underwear? Toothbrush? Do you have enough clothes?"

He cut her off, "Mom, let's just go."

The car was quiet on the way to the airport. Seth was ticked off for having to leave his comfort zone. His mom was feeling guilty for taking him out of his comfort zone. As they sat there in sterile silence, their cell phone rang.

"It's Papua," she said while answering the cell. "Hi Dad, how are you?"

"Where's my boy?" His voice blistered through the phone; Seth could hear their conversation from the passenger seat.

"Oh, he's right here, hold on." Seth's mom offered him the phone.

"Hey big boy, you all ready for a great trip with your dad?" he asked. Seth knew his grandpa hated his father but he never spoke ill of him. Seth never knew why, but understood not to say anything about his dad to his Papua because he knew what he would hear: "Now boy, God did not put us on this earth to speak ill of our kin, no matter how much we want to. It takes a big man to not talk bad about another." This was an important life lesson practiced and never forgotten.

Seth never fully understood that lesson. But, as a somewhat chubby kid who kept to himself, he understood what it felt like to be talked about behind his back.

He talked with his grandpa for the rest of the drive to the airport. It was not an important conversation, but it was a typical grandpa to grandson conversation. A conversation with the occasional "behave yourself" and "you know your mother loves you." His Papua closed the conversation with, "Hey boy, look under the seat and call me back."

Seth hung up the phone. "There's something under the seat for me," he said, handing the phone back to his mom. Reaching under the seat, he found a plainly wrapped box with his name written in black magic marker. "What is it?"

"I have no clue," mom said with a sober face. "Open it."

After tearing the box open, he looked at his mom in amazement. "It's a cell phone," he said in a reverent tone. Seth's eyes started to water. He knew his mom could not afford to give him his own cell phone, and out of respect he never once complained or asked her for one. "How did he know?"

"Your Papua is a smart guy. He knows everything, whether you tell him or not."

"Everything?"

"Everything." After wiping a tear from her eye, Seth's mother reached over and stroked his curly blonde hair.

Seth feverishly dialed his Papua's number. When the old man answered loudly, Seth said, "Thanks! How did you know?"

"Well buddy I wasn't sure, but more importantly, if you got into trouble I wanted you to be able to call me or your mother. Be safe and text your friends. You youngsters like that nowadays, don't you?"

"Yes, sir. Thank goodness I brought my friends' phone numbers," he laughed. "Bye Papua, I love you." Hanging up the phone, Seth took a couple of deep breaths.

Seth rose out of the car and lifted out his overstuffed duffle bag. His mom looked at him and said, "Each year this gets harder and harder. One of these days we will be saying goodbye for more than two weeks."

"C'mon Mom," he said, holding up his new phone, "now I can call you every day! Love you Mom."

"I love you too." She stood there for a few minutes until her little boy disappeared into the crowd.

"**B**oy, you have done it. We can't help you anymore. We have tried and tried. Yet, you still want to be a thug, disobey us and run the streets. I got away from that lifestyle. I brought you and your mom out here so we would never be plagued by the streets again."

Looking down at his feet, he said, "I'm sorry."

"Don't lie! No you aren't. I'm sick of this and so is your mom." He smacked Aaron's face toward him. "Look at me when I talk to you boy! We are a black family that beat the odds and now you want to go back to a life that I fought so hard to get away from." He didn't care about being repetitive.

Aaron's dad, Dave, was the Chief of Police in a suburb of Marysville, Michigan. Aaron's parents moved to Marysville after struggling through school and living in the ghetto. They met as high school sophomores and Aaron was born when his mother was a junior. Unlike their friends and peers, they took the pregnancy seriously. His mom worked crummy jobs, waitressing, fast-food joints, temporary secretarial positions, while his dad studied criminal justice. It was a tough fight, but after a ten-year struggle, their dream turned into reality. The happiness lasted until Aaron's fifteenth year.

Frustrated, his father glared at Aaron, shaking his head, "I have worked so hard to give you everything. Yet, you insist on rejecting your mom and me."

"It's not that, Dad."

"Shut up." Aaron was scared at this point. His parents never told him to shut up. "Go to your room and do not come out until I say. No computer, no TV, no phone, just sit on your bed and think."

Earlier that day, Aaron had been caught stealing some beer from the corner gas station on a dare from his so-called "friends" from school. Caught flat out by the store owner, Aaron should have been arrested. But the store clerk knew his father, so the cops were not called. It was the third incident in as many days.

Aaron was a slender, geeky-looking kid and did not have a lot of friends. He was smart, but like most his age, he chose not to use his head.

"What am I going to do with this boy?" Knowing a reaction was required, Dave reached for his phone and mumbled to himself, "I hope this works."

The deep raspy voice at the other end of the phone answered, "Hey man."

"Greg, how ya doing?"

"I'm okay, and you?"

"Well, not too good. I need your help. I am at a loss with Aaron, and I might need your assistance before it gets too far out of hand."

Greg could hear the fear in his brother's voice, "Sure whatever you need, I'm your guy."

"Well, are you still living on the lake in Kentucky and running that campground?" Aaron's father had to ask because his brother was a nomad and went wherever his travels took him. What Dave didn't know is that Greg hadn't moved in some time. The years ran together.

"Yes, I am still here. Planning on being here through the summer, unless you have a better offer," Greg laughed.

"Believe me brothaman, I wish I did. Aaron has gotten himself into trouble and I think time down there doing some work would be good for him. If your campground can't pay him directly, I will pay his wages, but he needs the learning experience."

"Dave, bring his ass on down! I will be glad to take him in … the money will work itself out later. I think it's a great idea."

"Thanks. We'll be down tomorrow sometime. I want to give you fair warning, I am bringing one pissed kid."

"Ey, we will fix that. I can't wait to see the look on his face when he sees my place. It's a trailer with one TV station and no Internet. I do have running water." They both laughed.

"See you tomorrow. Thanks." Dave felt a little relieved. Aaron will be safe and out of trouble for the summer, he hoped. And boy, is he in for a big surprise.

4

"**W**e hate you!" the angry crowd shouted. "Go back home!"

Mitchell Anderson was the Speaker of the House and was hated by most Americans capable of critical thought. "I know some of you do not like me or my policies," Anderson said, pushing his fist in the air and resting on the podium, "but, you do have to understand the common goal is to keep our freedom and have a stable economy, where all Americans can live the life they choose. The goals of our founding fathers were Life, Liberty and the Pursuit of Happiness. It is my job, as well as the folks in Congress and all arms of government to ensure the first two, but the Pursuit of Happiness rests solely on the shoulders of each and every single American citizen. With hard work, we will all prosper and we will be successful."

"Blah, blah, blah," thought Jaime. "Here we go again, another summer of boring speeches and traveling around the country in armored cars."

Jaime was Congressman Anderson's only daughter. Her parents travelled around the country giving speeches and lobbying for bills that most kids her age, including her, could care less about. Jaime was stuck in the middle of an entourage of security guards and tutors. She was unable to attend school like other kids due to the press constantly following her and zealots wanting to kidnap or hurt her.

As the speech came to a close, her daydream ended. She heard the loud, stern voice of her father say, "Together we can transform America to the way it was meant to be, but it will be a long hard fight. I assure you that the prize at the end, freedom, will be worth it. Join me down this road." There was a mixture of cheering and booing as Anderson waved, glad-handed and briefly chatted with his supporters. While he was walking off the platform, he noticed his little girl sitting near a group of people with an empty look on her face.

"Hey, how did I do?" He always asked this after a speech.

"Great, as usual, Dad," she said, giving her standard answer, while smiling and sticking her thumbs in the air. "Can we do something fun now?"

"What? This isn't fun for you?" he laughed.

"No Daddy, it isn't, and I really don't want to spend another summer traveling from city to city being shuffled around and always having to hide."

His face sunk with embarrassment. What kind of father was he? "Well, what would you like to do for the summer?"

"I want to spend it at the lake house," Jaime said.

"But no one will be there to take care of you and you will be alone all summer, Sweetie. I don't know that Mom will go for that."

"Try. What about Betta? She'll be there, won't she?"

"Well, yes. But …" he was speechless. They were supposed to spend the summer travelling around the country, seeing sights while he made speeches. He was deliberating running for president and was spending the summer break touring the country. So far, it wasn't working out well. It turns out that most voters outside of his state hated him. "Okay. If that's what you really want, then I will see what I can do."

Jaime knew her mom would probably not go for this, but she had to try. Each second she thought of spending the summer with tutors and caretakers on the road sent her into a deeper depression. She was a loner and didn't want to be one. She wanted to be like other girls her age, dreaming about famous boys and talking on the phone about life.

All of her so-called friends were in situations just like hers, but they were too afraid to say anything to their parents. Jamie didn't care. She wanted to grow and be her own person. She could not do this. She was watching from afar as her dad and mom discussed her fate.

"Absolutely not," she read her mom's lipstick-covered lips. "We can't."

Jaime rushed over to her mom. "Please, I just want to have one summer of normalcy."

"Location does not give you that dear, being with your family does."

"I don't know, Jessie, maybe our daughter is right and we are wrong. What harm would it be to let her go to the lake house for a few weeks? She can always come back if she gets scared. She has her cell phone and we can talk to her every day. Besides, we will be down there in a few weeks."

Her mom's face changed and Jaime knew she had gotten her way.

"Oh my God, you mean it?"

"Yes. You can go but you must do what Betta tells you. One call from Betta and you will be right back on the road with us. Understand?"

$$5$$

We were not fifty miles out of the city when I had to pee. The ride in the back seat was getting to me, but I knew not to say a word. It was two hours before lunchtime and my usually noisy phone was quiet. I knew that no one in my crew was awake yet. Most of the time we took turns playing video games at one another's houses. We would stay in one place until one of our parents would say, "Hey, why don't you kids go ride bikes?" Boy! Parents these days did not understand what it was like to be a kid.

"When I was a kid, we were kicked out of the house in the morning, allowed back in at lunch and then had to be back by supper time. If we stayed around the house, we were given chores and we were not paid for them. It was your duty as a member of the family to help out." I could hear a parent saying to us in my mind. But not this week, this week I get to be lazy and do what I want, pretty much. I mean, I still have to mind my manners but if I want to play video games and be lazy, I can. What else is there to do on a vacation? If I had a dollar for every time my dad and mom said this, then I would never have to work.

We were a good crew. We never got into much trouble, and when we did get into trouble, we knew that what we were doing was stupid and we just didn't care. We all had to mow our family lawns once a week, but we teamed up and did each yard together. I was the oldest in the neighborhood and had lived there the longest, but none of that mattered because we cared about each other.

All of the neighborhood kids were home though, and I was going to have to spend the next week alone with my parents and my stupid sister. Dad didn't even know how to turn on a video game, much less how to play one. He was a carpenter by trade and when he was not at work, he piddled around the house or watched TV.

It seemed each mile was going slower and slower. The trailer bogged down the car and every bump rattled though us, making us shake like Jell-O. Pushing against my right side, my sister was acting as if she were asleep, as if anyone could sleep through the freight train pulling the metal hotel room behind us.

"Are you really that bored?" Mom said to me, as I let out a painful sigh.

"Whatever. Leave me alone." I joked with her.

"If you are that bored, why don't you read some of your school books," Mom said, turning and smiling at me.

My mom and dad had enrolled me in a private school and this was the summer before my freshman year. I wasn't really excited about it, since it was an all boys' school and I was the only kid from my middle school attending. So, friends were going to be scarce. My mom always told me to be positive. I was scared.

"No, I can't read in the truck. Mom, you know I get car sick." This was kind of true but it seemed to work.

"I hope you ain't planning to stay in the camper all week playing them games," said my father.

"Use correct grammar around the kids," snapped my mother.

"You can do that at home. We aren't traveling all this way for us to sit in rooms."

"Yes, sir." I smoldered. I knew it was best not to argue, but I was pretty sure this was going to be the worst summer of my life.

I was wrong.

6

"**W**ake up, son. You have twenty minutes to pack for the summer. You're going to Kentucky to spend time with your Uncle Greg. He needs your help."

"Dad, I'm sorry! I'll be good! Just give me one more chance. Please!" Not yet awake, Aaron knew he was in trouble and there was no getting out of this trip. His dad was stubborn and when a decision was made, that was it.

"It's too late Son. You had your chance. I have no choice but to get you away from this crowd. Pack shorts, T-shirts, swimming gear and books. You won't need your video games at all, and probably not your computer or cell phone. But, if you don't give me too much lip, I will let you take them."

Aaron gave the only acceptable answer: "Yes, sir."

Twenty short minutes later, Aaron watched from the red vinyl seats of Dave's white Crown Vic as his mom walked out of the garage door wearing her bathrobe and slippers with her arms crossed. "Boy Dave, he is really pissed at us."

"Yep."

"Do you think he will be all right, Babe?" Annissa asked, as she watched Dave toss his duffle bag in the already open trunk.

Dave slammed the trunk lid and stared at his boy, who was looking straight out the windshield, avoiding eye contact with Dave and Annissa. "He'll be fine," Dave replied, sighing as he walked to the driver's side and sat down.

Giving up on trying to hide his pain, Aaron's cheeks streaked with tear lines. "This is going to be the worst summer ever."

"It will be with that attitude," his mom said, as she leaned in and kissed him goodbye. "I love you. Listen to your dad and uncle. You will have fun and might not want to come home."

"Huh, I doubt that. I love you Momma and I'm sorry." Aaron looked over at his dad and asked, "Is there anything I can do to get out of going?"

"Nope."

The car sped off.

Aaron sat silently in Chief Davis' car. He watched the stripes on the road go by as he rested his head on the window of the undercover police car. His dad would smile at him every now and again and Aaron would sigh, roll his eyes and turn the other way. He didn't know his dad could see him through his sunglasses.

"You know, Aaron, when I was your age," his dad paused, knowing only select words he chose would be listened to, "I thought it was cool to smoke, steal and act like the other older kids in the neighborhood. But as I watched them have babies, drop out of school and do drugs, I began to see that I wanted no part of that life."

Aaron gave no response. He gave his father the cold shoulder, put his earphones in and fidgeted with his CD player. Feeling closeness with no one, Aaron turned to music; this got him out of countless conversations, but, unfortunately, not this time.

"I know you don't want to hear this," said the Chief, pausing to pull the phones out of Aaron's ears and wrapping the cord around the player, "but you are going to listen to me."

"Dad, please, you don't know what it's like these days."

"What? You think I'm stupid, Boy? Out of all your friends' parents, A, I am the only one who cares about his kids and more importantly, B, I am a cop and I know exactly what's going on these days."

"Why don't you just let me do my *thang*?"

"Because your *thang*, Aaron, is going to get you killed and leave me without my only son, and I won't have that."

The sun was bright and the heat was unavoidable. The air-conditioning in the car was at full speed but it could not keep up with the high temperature. Aaron could feel his legs sticking to the blue vinyl seats. He was uncomfortable but refused to let it show.

"Shoot I ain't gonna get kilt. I'm smarter than half those thugs."

"Yeah, you're so smart, huh? You ain't gonna get *kilt*, arrested or none of that?"

"Nope," Aaron said proudly.

Before he could do anything he felt the whack of his dad's hand. "Boy, you cannot be this damn stupid. You got caught stealing, and you say you're so smart and ... and think you know."

"That wasn't my fault!" It was a poor choice of words but they came out too quickly.

"Whose fault is it?"

Knowing he was set up, Aaron decided at this time that his best defense was to keep his mouth shut and just look at the road.

"What? You got nothing to say for yourself?" The Chief took his eyes off the road to look at his son.

"Boy?"

Silence.

"Son?"

Silence.

"Look at me."

Aaron could see his father tensing up with anger.

"No." Aaron finally said, attempting to stand up to his dad, knowing he was putting his life in danger.

"What?"

"No, Dad, just leave me alone. I don't wanna talk right now."

Aaron looked down, hiding his tears. He really didn't want to disobey or be cruel to his father, who was once his best friend. But, no one understood him any more. Aaron didn't even understand himself. He just didn't know what to do.

The brakes of the car squealed as the Chief slammed them, yanking the car to the right. Their bodies flopped with the motion of the car as it stopped in an empty rest area.

"Oh crap," Aaron thought, "I'm in deep now."

Not saying a word, the Chief got out of the car, nearly ripping his arm off with the seatbelt as he ran around the front of the car. The passenger door was flung open, almost hitting his dad in the face. Aaron's eyes bulged and he began to tremble. His dad yanked him out of the car and tossed him to the dirt.

"GET OFF ME!" He was twisting and turning, trying to fight the weight of his father.

"You wanna fight me son? I'll let you! You won't win but I'll take your challenge." The Chief had no intention of fighting Aaron. He just had to win some respect and get his son's attention.

He grabbed both of his son's wrists into one of his hands, pressed them against the boy's chest. He ripped Aaron's sunglasses off and bent down so that they were nose to nose.

"You listen to me and you listen to me good," the Chief hissed. "Right now you're a nobody, a know-it-all little nobody."

"Get off of me!"

"NO!"

"You don't love me! What kind of dumb father does this to his son on the side of the road?" Cars were whizzing by at 80-plus miles an hour. They were both yelling over the sound of rubber on asphalt. "What kind of father calls his son a nobody?"

"I love you more than anything … you've got to see that." Aaron could smell the coffee that his dad had at breakfast and he was blinded by staring up at the sky.

"Whatever."

"Look … "

"Get off of me," Aaron interrupted. The gravel and concrete were pressing against his back, the weight of his father was unbearable. "Nope."

"Yeah, get off of me."

"Not until you listen to me."

"I'll listen, I'll listen," Aaron cried. "Just get OFF OF ME!"

Aaron could not take one more second of that gravel penetrating through his clothes and pressing against his back.

In one swoop, his dad got up and in a singular motion sat his son in the passenger seat, legs hanging out and barricaded by the car door, his father squatting in front of him.

"Look, I know you got a lot of hormones and emotions brewing in your body right now. You are going through a pretty major change. We all did at your age, but you got to understand respect isn't given by stealing and acting thuggish. It's earned by treating others with respect and being the better man when bad situations arrive."

"But all my friends do this … "

The Chief interrupted him before he could finish. "Man, those aren't your friends. Don't you see, Son? No good friend would support you stealing something and then tell on you for doing it."

"It wasn't like that, Dad."

"So your two friends didn't dare you to walk into the store, put a candy bar in your pocket and grab a 12-pack of beer while they distracted the clerk?!" The Chief was yelling and spit was flying onto Aaron's face.

Aaron silently sat and wiped his father's spit off his face.

"Don't you have anything to say for yourself?" The Chief's knees popped as he stood up.

"I guess I see your side, but all these kids I am growing up with are changing and I feel like if I don't change with them I will lose them."

"You might lose them, temporarily or permanently. Only time can answer that question but no matter what happens, you will always have your memories." Aaron's dad looked him in the eye. "No one can ever take those

away from you. Now, can we act like adults, get out of this heat and get you to Uncle Greg's?"

The Chief rose, pulling his son toward him, "I love you and nothing you do will ever change that; but, as long as you're my responsibility, you will behave properly. Understood?"

"Yes, sir," Aaron told his dad, but not really understanding why his parents were so disappointed in him. He sat there and thought quietly to himself as Dave continued driving down the road. After thinking and watching the miles pass, he pulled his phone out of his pocket to call his mom.

After a couple of rings, "Hello," Annissa said.

"Mom, I am sorry for my behavior. I am going to take this time with Uncle Greg and show you and Dad I can behave.

"Good. We love you and just want what is best for you."

"I know."

He paused for a couple of seconds and said, "Mama, I love you."

"I never doubted your love, I just want you to be good."

"Yes ma'am." He hung up the phone and put it in his pocket.

Dave smiled and rubbed Aaron on the head as they continued their trip to Kentucky.

7

Staci's mom and my dad were second or third cousins, I wasn't sure exactly. Basically, we were not related but every summer we stopped to see them on our way to the lake. Aunt Millie always tried to talk to my sister and me like we were her best friends, but the reality was that we had nothing in common. She was country and we were as city as city could be. Last year, when we pulled into their driveway, which is a mix of gravel and grass, there was a little frog sitting in the sun. I never saw it, but Staci reached down and scooped it up with her bare hands. To this day, I get chills up my spine when I think about it.

Staci was portly and had long blonde hair that, when in a ponytail, hung almost to her waist in stringy sections. Every time I saw her, she was wearing cut-off jeans with a white T-shirt. She was six months younger than I, but acted like she was two years younger. She always wanted to go with us, but before my dad could pull out of the driveway, my sister and she were killing each other and my dad would take Staci back in, shaking his head.

After begging my dad for miles to pull over, we finally arrived at my aunt's house. I blitzed out of the car and headed straight for the restroom.

"You're going to ruin these kids' internals," my aunt said.

"No, the boy needs to man up."

"Well, I think he is man enough." She turned to my mother, "Hi Sweetie, it's been another year. We always tell ourselves we won't let another year go by. Yet, here we sit again."

"What's new with you?" My mother was great at acting like she cared.

"Oh, not a lot. Just trying to keep my little girl out of trouble during these teen years. I think it might kill me. The only thing I have going for me is that I

live in a remote area and there aren't many kids around. SHEEEEEEW! Now, during the school year, that's a different story." As my aunt grew more excited, her accent became more southern. "But," she took a long pause as she started pouring iced tea that none of us really wanted, including my cousin who kept eyeballing our cooler, "I can only do so much."

They lived in an old-style aluminum trailer, what would now be called a modular home. This poor trailer looked as if it were going to crumple if a bird landed on the roof. When I walked in to use the restroom, the scent of sour clothes mixed with funeral home enveloped me. As I made my way across the dirty carpet, the floors creaked.

I wanted to get out of that house as fast as I could. There was something eerie about it. There was a presence there. My body started to tingle and my vision began to close as if I was looking through a telescope. As I flushed the toilet, I heard a loud bang and fell to the floor. I fought to get back up, but was forced back down to the dirty linoleum. My body was tingling like when an arm goes to sleep, but it was my whole body. I don't know what it was, but as fast as the power came it was gone and it left me exhausted.

The screen door creaked as I pushed it open to the outside. I was mystified and confused. I had never experienced such a feeling before. The house wasn't haunted. It couldn't be.

I swiftly walked down the deck and tried to avoid my aunt. I could hear them jabbering about their lives and how they haven't seen each other in years. My aunt grabbed me and pulled me against her chest, giving me a hug that no amount of force could avoid.

"We need a good, strong man like you around here to help do some chores for a week or so. Maybe we could get this here place cleaned up."

"Oh, hell naw," I thought to myself, but before I knew what happened …

"What did you say boy?" thundered my dad.

Much to my surprise, I hadn't thought it, I had actually said it aloud.

"Um, nothing. I didn't say anything," I lied.

"I'm pretty sure you said something," snapped my dad before I was done with my lie.

"Oh, it's okay," my aunt said. "I can understand. Who wants to be away from their family doing free manual labor for an aunt and a cousin that they see once a year?"

Thanks Aunt Millie, I owe you one.

"You know, I would be glad to help anytime," I said, lying again, but I was still kinda freaked out about the bathroom incident and my dad was already steamed at me so I figured it couldn't hurt. We'll see.

Aunt Millie stood there wearing a red paisley bandana over her greasy hair, flip flops and her 1970s tank top, which was too short to meet the waistband of her shorts. Staci was dressed in an equally disturbing manner, except her hair was pulled back in a tight ponytail. They could pass for sisters.

"Did you have a good school year?" Mom asked Staci.

"Ah, it was okay. I passed. I really don't care much for the school here. All the kids are snobbish and don't much care for locals like us."

They lived in a rural area and were surrounded by million-dollar horse farms. The only other people that lived in the county were the stablehands and the ones who could not afford to move away after the car-radio factory closed and moved overseas. Staci knew she had no choice but to leave this town to make a better life for herself.

"Well, she's done more than pass! My baby girl made straight A's and didn't miss a day," crowed Millie, looking with pride at Staci.

"Mom!"

"What are you embarrassed for, Sweetie?" inquired mom. "You should be proud. See," she said pointedly to me and my sister. "You come from the same genes. If you worked as hard as Staci did, you could make A's."

She went on and on about how great Staci was and her stupid straight A's. I could care less. I wanted to find out what had happened in the bathroom.

"How much longer are we going to be here?" I snapped, interrupting her sentence mid-stride.

"Oh, I don't know. We'll leave here shortly," Dad said, "Why don't you to go find your sister."

"Hey Staci, wanna go with me?" I knew this would freak out all my family, but there was no point in making her suffer by herself. Plus, I could quiz her about my episode in the bathroom.

"Yeah, let's go find her," Staci said.

As we walked down the road toward where we thought Sissy would be, I yelled for Cosby. He was already behind us.

8

Seth was no longer in view and tears streamed down his mother's face. The tears were a mix of joy and sorrow.

In the security line, Seth stood playing with his new toy. It wasn't one of those slick phones that you could surf the net on, but it was his. He was flipping it open and closed, acting as if he were a big star talking on his cell phone with his shades on in the airport. He felt important, which was a great illusion, until he was checking in at the gate.

As it was midday, the security line seemed crowded, but was moving quickly. It was the first time he did not need a dopey chaperone to tell him what to do. He was an adult. He had 35 bucks in his pocket and was ready to go.

Once through the security, he finally felt free. No one was in front of, or behind, him. He was ready to get to the gate, call his buddies and give them his new number. None of his friends had their own phones.

"Seth, here is your ticket. Come with me and I will get you situated until it is time to board," the ticket agent said, while coming around the counter and starting to lead him.

"Wait, wait! What are you doing?" Seth was confused.

"What's wrong, Sweetie?" She looked puzzled, tossing her blonde hair and thin body around to face him.

"When my mom booked the ticket, the agent told us as long as I was 14 at time of flight, I didn't need a chaperone." He was fighting tears.

"Oh, I'm sorry. You have a chaperone ticket and I can't change it."

His heart sank as he lowered his body and followed the young agent with the peppy walk.

The gate was packed, and he was parked in the corner by the boarding door. He plopped down in the chair and allowed his backpack to fall between his legs.

"Claim check in my wallet, so I won't lose it," he said to himself. He dug a black composition notebook out of his backpack and thumbed through the pages. "Where is it? Hmm, let me just try to dial it."

He called several friends, but the call Seth was most excited about was to Bub. They had known each other for years. They had met Seth's first summer at the lake and they hit it off immediately. Always picking up a conversation right where they left off. For one week each summer, they were not separated by two time zones. Being pen pals was great but it was not the same as the week each year that they saw each other during the lake trip. Even though they were near each other during this week, it was still difficult for the two to hang out. Bub's parents had vacation plans with the family, and Jeff, Seth's dad, well, he was unpredictable.

9

Dad's phone rang in my pocket. Not wanting to be bothered with it, he let me carry it around for a while. "Don't know that number," I said to Staci. "To voicemail it goes," I said, acting like I did this all the time.

A few seconds later, "1 NEW VOICEMAIL" popped up on the screen. I held the phone to my ear. Staci was still rambling on about her grades and how much she hates the area where she lives. Walking in a circle, I notice nothing but white and black fences and horse farms as far as the eye can see. Yeah, I would be miserable here, too. I tried to roll my eyes to show that I understood, but I am not sure if it worked.

The voicemail finally came over the earpiece. It was Seth. "Hey man, I am getting on the plane now. Hopefully be at my dad's tonight. See you when I see you. Oh yeah, by the way, this is my new cell phone number. You can call me anytime you want without going through my mom!" Seth's voice sounded different, like he had aged. We only saw each other once a year at Land Between the Lakes. His father was a park ranger there.

We met a few summers ago when my family was on vacation and we really hit it off. He, an only child, and I, an only boy, found a brotherly solidarity that neither of us had experienced before. It seemed that even though we saw each other only once a year, and sent the occasional letter back and forth, we were connected. Brothers.

I saved his number into dad's phone. Staci was still rambling on about whatever she was talking about, and Cosby was out enjoying nature.

Interrupting Staci mid-thought, I said, "Something freaky happened to me in your bathroom. It's never happened to me before. I, like, blacked out and heard voices. Is your house haunted or something?"

"Connie, are you high?"

"Not that I know of. You know I don't do drugs. I'm not making this up! Has anything like that ever happened to you? Has anyone ever told you about anything weird happening in your house?" I was scared and my entire body was quivering and I do not usually scare easily.

Staci could see the fear in my eyes and in my body language. I don't think she knew how to respond. Hell, I didn't know how to respond. Was I going loco?

"Look, until we get this figured out, let's not tell our folks about this. You don't want them to worry and send you to a doctor or something. Because, I have to be honest, you are talking crazy." Staci raised one eyebrow and examined my face for any perceptible signs of whether I was joking.

"Well, duh! You think?"

"It will be OK."

I don't know why I trusted Staci on this. We never really got along and I always gave her grief when I was around. If I were her, I would want people to think I was crazy just to pay my ass back!

"Connie! Staci! It's time to head back to the house! We need to get back on the road," my mom yelled from the house.

"Want to see something … well, two funny things? Watch the look on my mom's face when you ask to go with us, and watch my dad back this camper out of your driveway. He can barely drive the thing forward, much less back up," I said with a snort.

Staci smiled, "Why do you want me to go? How do you know I will? You know we never get along. What makes you think this time will be any different."

"A hunch."

"A hunch?" Staci said, tilting her head with curiosity.

"Yup," I said, kicking the grass with my feet. My hands were in my pocket and I was looking at the ground to avoid eye contact.

Staci grabbed my chin and turned my face toward her. "Why should I believe you?"

I looked at her and decided to take a chance and tell her about the vision I saw in the bathroom. "Because when I was in your bathroom, I saw a vision of us at the lake together sitting at a picnic table. My mom was laughing and saying, 'This will be a trip we'll never… '"

"Never forget," we said in unison while staring at each other, amazed. I now knew that Staci had similar experiences. I was not alone in this weirdness. My head was reeling.

As we started walking toward the house, I was curious. "When you had your visions Staci, how did it feel?"

"What do you mean, Bub?" Staci, dressed in her long cut-off shorts and tank-top was moving faster than I and it was hard to keep up.

Pipe Vision

I was getting out of breath, so I stopped and said, "Wait." Bending down to rest my hands on my knees, I explained, "Like, the first time I had a vision, it seemed like I was in a dream and I felt my body become all tingly and the vision was very distant, as if I was looking through a tube. Was yours like that?"

She sat on a rock. The grass around the rock appeared to be flattened, as if it were sat on often. Placing her elbow on her knee and cupping her chin in her hand, she responded, "Mine was quite different." Pausing while she selected her words, she said, "It is like a circle in my vision during life."

"During life? I don't know that I understand." I was scratching my head and kicking the grass.

"Like . . . " Pausing to think, she tilted her head toward the sky. When the words came to her, she exclaimed, "Got it! Like if I am looking at you, a circle would pop up in my vision, like a movie. I can see and hear the future and can see real life around the pipe but real noise, real life, is hard to hear, it's faint."

"Does your body tingle?"

"No, but after it happens, I can't stay awake."

"Wow!"

"Bub, Staci, where are you?" My mom was yelling for us to return the house.

"Ugh," I said. "I guess we should head back."

10

Jaime didn't feel like she was spoiled, but her parents felt that she was. They tended to let her get her way because they were always on the road with Mitchell's political career. A life they never felt they chose.

Early in his career, Mitchell was a trial lawyer. A good one. So good at getting guilty people off or helping to create mistrials that the Governor wanted him to quit practicing law. When a Judgeship became available, he was nominated for it. Reluctantly, Mitchell accepted and quit practicing law.

He was a local judge for a few years but never enjoyed it as much as being a trial lawyer. He had a new wife and a baby girl, who were his world. He had already made his name known throughout the state and, so, he decided to run for Governor.

An easy win again.

All of this came with a price, as success always does. The long hours put a strain on his marriage over the years but they persevered. They had a good idea of what their life would be like when Mitchell became a politician and they made a pact to always be honest with each other.

When Mitchell decided to run for the House shortly after Jamie was born, he swore to Jessie that he would never neglect or betray his family. Jessie wanted nothing but success for her husband but she was afraid of being under constant scrutiny by the media. She had seen so many families destroyed due to being in the public eye. She knew that the press was dirty and if they didn't like you, they would do whatever it took, including lying about your personal life, to destroy you and your career.

They were fortunate in the fact that Jessie did not to have to work and to have three homes: a house in the D.C. area, another in their home state of Indiana, and the lakefront property in Kentucky.

Both victims of failed marriages, Mitchell and Jessie met in their late 30s. It was love at first sight. Jessie knew the night they met that Mitchell would be her husband. Even though they were both excited to find each other, they were cautious and took their time. They married exactly two years after their first date and Jaime was born a year later.

"I am still not sure about this," Jessie said to Jaime.

"Mom, I am 16 years old and I know right from wrong. Betta will be there with me. I won't go out at night or have anybody over."

"I know, but it is hard to explain. You will understand one day when you are a parent." Jessie fully trusted her daughter and was not worried about her behavior. She never exhibited any troubling or immature conduct. Jaime was 16 and very pretty, with golden blonde hair, blue eyes and an athletic shape.

"What do you think, Daddy?" Jessie asked her husband.

Mitch and Jesse were concerned that their public lifestyle was the cause of Jaime's rapid maturity. Jaime was daddy's girl; he always tried to give her what she wanted, while not spoiling her. Hoping to keep his daughter safe while at the lake house and making sure she has her freedom was a difficult mix.

Jessie inherited the lake house from her grandparents, and it had been in their family for years. Spending two weeks there every summer and knowing the area by heart, it was the only place she felt content and relaxed. Since Mitch took office, they spent more time at the lake house than at their residence in Indiana because they could enjoy the quiet time.

Shortly after they started spending time there, Mitch met Greg and hired him to watch over the place. They had a full time bookkeeper who lived on the property, but she could not deal with maintenance issues that occasionally popped up. Greg was the man for that.

Between the two, Mitch knew that his little girl would be safe. If he had a shard of doubt, she would not be going.

"I think we have raised a smart young lady who knows the difference between right and wrong. She knows our rules and expectations and I have no worries about letting her go." Mitch turned Jaime toward him and was holding her shoulders, "Besides, you never know when your mother, myself, Greg, or anyone else might pop by. If you do anything wrong or break any rules, we'll know." Looking back up at Jessie who was standing behind Jaime, he added, "Besides, it is a gated community. What could go wrong?"

Astonishment spread across Jaime's face; she did not know what he meant by that. Was his trust so little that he had to have people pop by and spy?

"You have nothing to worry about, Daddy," Jaime assured her father.

He was scheduled to make another appearance in Henderson, the next town south, before returning to D.C. Jaime was ready and her bags were packed. Betta, her nanny since she was three months old, was ready as well. Joe, the driver at the lake house, had traveled two hours to see Mitch, Jesse and Jaime.

The three walked over to Joe, who was talking to the bus driver. "Joe, do you mind if Jaime and Betta ride back with you?" Mitch extended his hand. "Jaime wants a break from the spotlight and I can't say I blame her."

Joe returned the handshake and replied, "Of course not, sir. Whatever you want. I'll pull the car around to the bus and get Jaime and Betta's bags."

"Thank you," Mitch nodded, winking at Joe and then turning back to his daughter and Betta.

"I think you should get going now so you can get there before dark. We love you very much," Mitch assured his daughter. "Your mother and I will see you in a few short weeks. Call us when you get there and any time you want."

11

After the excitement of the car being pulled over suddenly, Aaron sat in the passenger seat listening to his father's choice in music, classic Motown. He hated it, but he dared not say a word.

His dad reached for the volume and turned it down. Aaron was as close to the door as he could be without being outside the car. It was, most definitely, the most uncomfortable situation he had ever been in. He was trying to keep his cool, but his body language gave him away.

"Life is funny."

Aaron could feel one of those "Yes, sir" conversations coming; you know the type, when the only thing you can say is "Yes, sir." Everything else will be negated, and go unheard.

"We all think we are invincible, immortal and that nothing can hurt us when we are fifteen, Aaron. We think our actions do not affect other people. The truth is that everything, every decision, affects people in one way or another. By running with the crowd that you are in, well, it jeopardizes everything we have. It puts the house, cars, our vacations, everything, at risk. My job is 90 percent public perception of me. You and Mom are attached to the perception, like it or not. Because I am the Chief of Police, we have to be so careful. It only takes one misstep to destroy my career and that could change our lives forever."

His father took his eyes off the road and looked directly at him.

"Nothing and nobody is going to destroy my career. Ever. You understand me?"

Aaron was looking at the air bag casing in front of him.

"Hello?"

"Yeah, man. I understand."

"Look at me when you say that," his father snapped.

Aaron was careful not to roll his eyes or sigh when he turned to his father, "Yes, sir. I understand."

"Okay, I don't want to discuss this the whole trip. I have said my piece. This trip might be punishment enough for you but you have to understand how important your behavior is. As hard as this is for me to say … but I can't let you come home until I know that you will attend school and, most important, not get into any trouble." It killed the Chief to say these words, but he had no choice.

"Dad, are you kicking me out?"

"No, you will always be my son but we live a public life which demands respect. We have no choice. Let's take this to the furthest extreme we can. Let's just suppose that you were busted with drugs in our house. What do you think would happen?"

"I'd go to jail."

"Well, yes, but think big picture, forget about me losing my job, that would be a given. Think about your future. Think anyone wants to hire a convicted drug dealer or user? If they do, what kind of job do you think it would be?"

Aaron knew he had to choose his words carefully. He would rather be listening to The Temptations or The Four Tops right now than having this conversation. Laughing to himself and knowing the last thing he needed to do was smile. He knew the obvious answer but wouldn't dare give his father the pleasure. He carefully composed himself and chose his words finely, "I don't know. A garbage man? I hear they make pretty good money."

The Chief quickly interrupted, angrily.

"Boy!"

Aaron knew he was in deep shit when his father said, "Boy!"

"You can't be serious; you really want to sling someone else's waste for a living?" His voice shook with anger as he said this and the color drained from his knuckles as he gripped the steering wheel.

The Chief was thinking to himself, "This kid has no drive at all! What the hell have we done wrong? Have we spoiled him?" Gaining some composure, he thought, "Okay, when you were his age, what was your thinking?"

He always wanted better for himself. He was raised poor and he hated seeing his parents work so hard and never advance. He didn't want every day to be a struggle. He did without when he was a kid. His biggest fear was that Aaron would not get an education. He wanted success for his son. He wanted Aaron to progress.

Dave wanted Aaron to attend private school. With his job as the Chief of Police, he was concerned that if he sent Aaron to a private school people, in

the community may start to wonder how he could afford it. The public school Aaron was attending was failing miserably academically and not teaching or reinforcing the same values and morals Annissa and Dave had. It was horrible and Dave did not have a solution.

"Well, I don't know Dad," Aaron said. "Who knows what I want to be, but I don't want to be a cop, I want to see where life … "

"Takes you? Can you not see that the path you are on is going to take you nowhere?" He was calming down.

"When did you know you wanted to be a cop?"

"Son, that is an excellent question. I had no idea that I was going to be a cop. I couldn't afford to go to college. They were advertising that you could enter the police academy with a high school degree. So, being out of options and having no desire for factory work, I signed up."

The Chief sighed and examined their surroundings.

"You have choices. You can go anywhere and do anything, because your mom and I have saved our money so that you can get an education."

"Dad," Aaron sighed, "I get it. I know I was bad and I'll change."

The Chief turned and looked at his son, "Only your actions will show us if what you say is true."

12

Seth hated going to see his father with a passion. It was a pain to get from Los Angeles to the Land Between the Lakes. He always knew how much money his dad had by the airport he flew him into. If he was poor, Seth would be flown into St. Louis and either his dad would drive to pick him up or Seth would take a bus. This year, Jeff must have been doing pretty well since he was flying in to Metropolis, Illinois, only about an hour's drive from his father's house, but a more expensive flight.

Seth's parents split up after his dad's fifth affair. He really did not like his father but his mom knew a boy needed his father in his life. So he was required to call at least once a week and see his dad for a week at Christmas and two weeks in the summer.

His father was stuck in the '70s. He spent everything he made on women who thought he was rich. It was an illusion completed with supplies from the Goodwill and a monthly lease for a nice truck. Jeff was a golddigger magnet, until the women peeled the onion of his life and exposed his lack of education and wealth. Then, they would both move to their next victims.

Seth was thinking about seeing his friend Bub. Not seeing each other since last year, he wondered how much Bub and Sis had changed. He grew more excited with each air mile that passed.

"Are you OK?" the stewardess asked, bending toward him and cocking her head to the side.

"Yes I am fine, but I would like a soda, when possible." Seth said this in his most adult voice, even though the "child in flight" lanyard hung around his neck.

Pipe Vision

"Okay. If you need anything else, just push this button and one of us will be by." She pointed her finger, with chipped polish, to a button so worn that he doubted if it still worked. "This must be the kids' seat," he laughed to himself.

13

Greg's house was an old mobile home, given to him when he was put in charge of Big Daddy's campground, after relocating from Detroit. Like his brother, he knew the street life of Detroit was no place to be, but unlike his brother, he had no desire to stay in Motown. He had arrived in Kentucky with the clothes on his back 10 years ago and had not returned home even for holidays.

Greg was married once but it ended badly. After several short relationships with a couple of different women, he decided the single life suited him best. Greg was happy his ex-wife faked happiness through their marriage, giving the illusion of a happy and loving wife but secretly staying with him until she found another man to replace him. As badly as he was treated, Greg prided himself on the fact that he never speaks ill of her, or of anyone else for that matter.

Between his youth in Detroit and the last 10 years at Big Daddy's Campground, Greg had seen just about everything. He enjoyed spending time with the children and elderly who visit the park, becoming a mentor, giver of advice, referee in disputes, bicycle repairman, you name it. He would not trade it for anything.

Knowing his brother and nephew would be arriving soon, he was feverishly trying to tidy up his place and get Aaron's room ready. He made a mental note to go to the grocery and stock up on kid food. Soda, cookies, candy bars, chips, all the good stuff he never bought because he had never acquired a taste for it, or had the luxury of having it when he was growing up.

He knew Aaron was being brought here to be taught a lesson, but he still wanted him to feel at home. He knew the hot days and manual labor he

planned for Aaron would be enough punishment. He will never go back to street life again, Greg thought to himself and smiled.

"The house is as clean as it is going to get. What do I care? I'm a bachelor and a messy house is acceptable," Greg said to himself.

He decided to sit down and relax for a little bit, turned on the only channel on his ancient TV. He really wanted to get one of those new flat screen jobs, but he just could not see spending the money until his old one died. It was a typical hot and humid day at the lake, where the air outside is sticky and robs your lungs. The air-conditioner runs non-stop and has a hard time keeping up with the heat penetrating through the metal walls of his trailer.

Nothing was really planned for Aaron today. Greg wanted to spend time with him and get to know him. There was a lot of catching up to do, especially since Greg did not fully believe that his brother was a Police Chief. Letters and phone calls are swell, but nothing like good ol' face-to-face contact.

Most of the arrivals and departures were set up yesterday or early this morning. Greg was done with work for the day unless there was an emergency. He was hoping his brother would stay the night and let him take the three of them out for a nice dinner.

"Police, freeze!" yelled a voice through the door.

He knew who it was; the voice could not be mistaken. It was his brother, Dave.

"Oh yeah?" Greg yelled, "What you going to do if I don't answer?"

"I'll bust your damn door down!"

"It wouldn't take much." Greg flung the door open with eager excitement.

Laughter erupted as the two brothers saw each other face to face through the screen door. "Damn, it's good to see you!" Greg said as he hugged his brother. "Been too long, ya know?"

"Well, you came down here and never looked back. I can see why. God! It is beautiful here."

"Yup. I am a country boy now and I love it."

Across the gravel driveway, Aaron sat on a park bench. He was looking at his father and uncle but was trying to do so in such a manner that it would not be noticed. "It sucks here," Aaron thought.

"Hey, Boy! Get over here and come say hi to your uncle!" The Chief seemed more relaxed than he had in years.

Aaron didn't move, acting as if he didn't hear. Finally conceding to avoid confrontation, he let out a sigh and slowly removed himself from the park bench. He really liked his uncle, but he did not care for the circumstances. He knew he screwed up, he knew when he was shoplifting, and it was wrong, but this punishment was the worst.

14

As we walked back up to the house, Sissy was hanging around my mom and aunt listening to their never-ending chatter. When I was within earshot, I heard my aunt ask my mom, "How are the puberty years going?"

I stopped dead in my tracks, "Dad, where are you at?"

Staci looked at me like I was nuts. "What's wrong?"

"I am not going up there and listening to that conversation. No. I am sure Dad needs some manual labor done, or wants to tell me a story which indirectly affects something I did that he doesn't want to talk directly to me about. I am sure there is a shovel waiting to be stepped on too."

Staci laughed, "Oh grow up."

She thought I was joking, but nothing reddens my face more than being in the middle of an adult conversation that has sex or puberty in it. I agree that it is childish, but I am still a kid!

My dad yelled back, "Over here by the truck."

It was so hot that my shirt was glued to my back with sweat and I was dreading the feeling of my thighs being glued to the seat for two more hours. I was sweaty and thirsty and being outside was the coolest option. So there was no way I was going back into the house with no air-conditioning.

Sissy came running across the yard, her chubby cheeks smiling, with her baby-fat arms and legs that were pounding the earth. "Daddy, Bub, guess what?" She was out of breath and grabbing her knees, bent down trying to catch her breath.

"Run much?" I asked, trying not to laugh. Before I could finish saying much more, I felt the thud of my dad's hand across my head. I looked at him, "What? It's an obvious question."

"Be nice," he grumbled.

"Have you caught your breath yet, athlete of the year?"

"Ha ha. Whatever, tubby."

"You two done, yet?" Dad snapped over his shoulder as he fidgeted with the camper lights.

Staci walked over to Mom and whispered in her ear. A smile spread over Mom's face as she listened. Then, still smiling, she responded, "Of course Staci. You are most certainly welcome to go with us. Right, Larry? "

Dad was not as enthusiastic as Mom, but knew it was in his best interest to agree. So, he gave his usual smile and nod.

I had to act surprised, like I didn't want her to come. If I didn't, they would think something was up. "NO!" I screamed. "This is a family vacation."

"She is family," Sissy so intelligently stated while staring at me.

"Not that type family!" I was moving my hands in a circular motion, as if I were buffing an invisible car. "She is not, like, our family. You know, the four of us."

"You hate being with our family," my mom said, walking over from the porch, "So? What do you care? You will be with Seth most of the week. We all know that you two will be joined at the hip. Sissy can have a playmate."

"Where will I ..."

"Where will you what?" My dad commanded.

Silence overcame me, which is unusual.

"Ummm ... sleep." I knew this was a bad thing to say but I was at a loss for words. "It will work out. It always seems to. Mom, you're right. Sissy deserves to have someone to hang out with, too." There, I think I covered my tracks. Sissy's face was blank and I was unable to tell if she was happy about Staci joining us. "Maybe Seth will let me stay with him a few nights," I chuckled.

My aunt jokingly grabbed my cheek, "Oh stop it, Conrad!"

"Sweetie, why don't you run in and get packed," my mom excitedly said to Staci. "Uncle Larry and Connie will clear you a spot in the truck,"

"Hurry guys. We need to get going soon. At this rate, we are going to have to set the camper up in the middle of the night," Dad said, wanting to get back on the road.

While Dad and I made room for our unplanned guest, Mom and Sissy stepped into the camper to fix some sandwiches for us to eat on the road. He wasn't saying anything, but you could tell Dad was a little puzzled, or worried, as to how he was going to get this rig out of my aunt's narrow, fence-lined driveway.

I climbed into the truck and arranged my game station, Cosby's bed, the cooler, the picnic basket and all of the stuff we didn't want bouncing around in the camper or getting wet in the back of the truck if it rained. My phone rang just as I finished making room for Staci.

"Hello?" I was pretty sure it was Seth.

"Hey man, it's me! I'm in Denver waiting on my flight to Chicago. Wanted to check in. You there, yet?"

"Nope, man. We are still at my cousin's waiting for her to get packed."

"Is that the one you bicker with all the time?" Seth chuckled with a snort.

"Yeah, but I think she's going to be cool. She seems different this year." I was trying to think of a way to cover up all the lies and myths I had said during guy talk about Staci when were hanging out together. I really hope that doesn't come back and haunt me this week.

"I'll be in around midnight, I'll text you. See ya," Seth said as I hung up the phone.

"Why don't you kids ever say goodbye?" Dad inquired.

"No need."

After Staci lugged one bag for each day of the trip, five bags in all, out of the trailer, we all piled into the truck. Dad threw her bike on top of Sissy's and mine. Between the old truck, the camping gear and the bikes, we looked like *Sanford and Son* driving down the road. Miraculously, Dad made it out of the driveway with no property damage to the fences or the truck, but for those 15 minutes, we heard words we didn't know existed and my mom must have said, "Oh, Larry" about 95 times.

We were all tired and the truck was quiet.

15

"**W**ow!" Greg looked down at his watch. Dave, Aaron and he had been sitting on the front porch of his trailer telling childhood stories and hearing about the years he missed with his nephew. The weekend duties of a campground manager could not be placed on hold and there was a ton of work to be done! Parking campers, taking out trash and helping guests become familiar with the facilities were just a few of those duties.

"As much as I would love to keep shooting the breeze, it's the weekend and there's work to be done," said Greg. "Aaron, would you like to drive me around on the golf cart and make sure no one needs any help? Also, I have to empty the trashcans that are full."

"Trash?"

"Am I going to spend my summer taking trash out for other people?" he thought.

"Yup, that is one of our tasks here. We do anything, within reason, to make our guests more comfortable. Also, we need to get the grounds setup for tomorrow's bonfire. I want to get that done so the three of us can grab a bite before your pops leaves." Greg looked at the Chief. "Or are you leaving in the ass-crack of dawn and need to go to bed early?"

The Chief hadn't thought that far ahead. He wanted to get home but he did not realize how hard it was going to be to leave Aaron here for the summer. It sounded like a swell idea, but doubt was setting in with each passing minute.

"Why don't you guys go on and do what you need to do. I am going to call your mother and tell her we made it." He looked over at his brother. "Can I borrow your shower and get cleaned up?"

"Towels are in the hall closet," Greg said as he pulled the door behind him.

The Chief was alone with his thoughts. And they were getting to him. He knew he was doing the right thing but he had to keep reassuring himself. "This is for the best," he said to himself.

Sitting down on a throwback couch from the '70s and propping his feet up on a coffee table that looked like it had once been a part of a basketball floor, he dug in his pocket for his phone.

He waited in anticipation for his wife to pick up.

"Hi Baby." Her voice was soothing to his temperament.

"Hey."

"What's wrong?"

"Nothing, just starting to second-guess myself. I'm wondering if I went too far with this punishment or not. I ... "

"Stop. Stop right there. We've done all we can do with him. He's hanging with the wrong crowd. We can't watch him here all the time while we're at work. If we're not careful, dammit, he will get himself killed and I can't handle that."

The Chief could hear the cracks of crying in her voice. He was hiding his emotions, but agreed.

"I know. I know how right you are, but it's just hard."

"We can call him every day and he will make new friends. Hopefully, good, lifelong friends, or so I am praying."

"My cousin is having the same problem with her kids. We are not unique here."

"I know but I thought we were great parents and this wouldn't happen to us. I guess it is just life. Haven't decided if I am going to head back tonight or leave in the morning."

"Stay the night. Spend time with your son and your brother. Life will be here when you get home."

"Love you, Babe."

"Love you too. See you soon."

The Chief lay back on the couch, kicked off his shoes and stared at the ceiling fan. He was blessed to have such a supportive wife when it came to hard decisions like this.

16

S heriff Paul Clifton had a pretty good job. He was the beloved sheriff of Trigg County, Kentucky. He grew up there and never left. He was a second-generation lawman. Being a single guy, his life revolved around his work and fishing the local lakes.

Trigg County thrived on tourism, boaters, campers, and fisherman, all of whom went there for one reason, the outdoors. There tended to be very little crime, the occasional alcohol-related incident, kids trying out pot, and boating accidents. Here lately, meth had become the moonshine of the new century. This stuff was dangerous to make and equally addictive. Paul had seen the damage meth could do to a family, but no one talked until it was too late.

"You fools got nothing," Zake Wahlford would say, standing at the door with his toothless grin.

Publicly, Paul was tired of being shown up. He knew Zake was dirty. He was a criminal, a local producer of meth. As long as Zake was feeding Paul stacks of green cash, he really didn't care what Zake did. It was a small boring town and state and federal folks never came down in these parts and when they did, Paul was the first to know. Finding out that they were coming was followed by a simple call to Zake and then by a stack of cash in his pocket Cameras were at the end of Paul's driveway so he could see every visitor before a knock on his door. His property was fenced off and there was no other entry and was just up the road from Zake's.

Paul spent most of his days either in the office or visiting local attractions to make sure there wasn't any trouble. He also had to coordinate with the Coast Guard and his officers to keep the waterways safe.

Paul and Greg were close friends. They got to know each other through the campground and discussions of local politics and happenings around town. Their friendship was pretty well limited to the campground. They did not hang out socially, or travel or fish together, but they did have friendly conversations while Paul stopped in Big Daddy's Campground on his rounds.

Aaron and Greg were out driving around when Greg saw Paul's car pull into the lot.

"Eh, he can wait," Greg mumbled, while gesturing with his hand toward Paul.

Not sure who he was talking to, Aaron gave his uncle a puzzled look. "Huh?"

Greg pointed out the front window of the golf cart to the Sheriff's car and said, "That guy is a good friend of mine. He just came by to shoot the shit, but I … we have work to get done so that we can hang out with your pops before he leaves. If I go talk to that moron, I'll never get done," Greg laughed.

They pulled up to a trash bag and Aaron stopped the cart. Aaron sat there waiting for Greg to get out and get the bag. Greg was waiting for Aaron to get the bag. Finally, after a moment of sitting silently in the heat, Greg looked over at his nephew and said, "Uh, you gonna get your butt out and get that trash bag?"

Puzzled, Aaron glared at his uncle, and yanked himself out of the cart. He tossed the bag in the wagon and proceeded to drive through the grounds repeating the process. Greg had his nephew stop occasionally to introduce themselves to those walking or lounging at their campsite.

Once they were finished with their rounds, Greg directed Aaron to go up to the office. It was late afternoon and daylight was starting to hide behind the trees as the odor of warming grills and charcoal filled the air.

The two walked down the boardwalk to the floating office. Paul was talking to Tiffany, the desk clerk for the campground. Tiffany was just out of high school and ready to go to college when she became pregnant with her oldest son, Big Jim. He is now 17 years old, tall and built, with brown hair; his face always looks as if he hasn't shaved in a week. There is something mysterious about Big Jim, who looked like the type of guy everyone wants to get to know.

Aaron and Greg walked in on Tiffany and Paul mid-conversation. Greg joked with his friend, "Boy you must have a slow day today if you are out in these parts."

"Not quite, but I heard your nephew was arrivin' and thought I should stop by and say 'hi.'"

"We still have our understanding in place for tomorrow?" Greg asked Paul. Once a month, they had a big bonfire at the grounds. This was always on a Sunday night and it gave those who were staying for the week a chance to rest from traveling and the campground was not usually busy on Sunday nights.

All the employees and their families were invited. There was alcohol and under-aged drinking but as long as everyone was calm, cool and not belligerent, Paul looked the other way.

In the 10 years that the campground has been doing this, there had only been one minor incident. A couple of kids from out of town starting mouthing with the locals, and a small brawl had broken out. Paul and Greg were there and diffused the situation before any guests were injured. Most guests were oblivious to the whole thing.

"Good, I need to get going and get set up for tonight." Saturday night was Karaoke Night or open mic.

Greg formally introduced Aaron to all the employees at the office, showed him where to punch in and out, gave him his green uniform shirt and explained that Tiffany was in charge and whatever she ask him to do he needed to do without question.

At the end, Greg asked, "Any questions?"

"When do I get paid and how much?" Aaron thought his question was innocent but knew it would come across wrong. But, what was to be lost?

"All in due time my boy, all in due time."

"Yep, he is related to Greg all right," Big Jim laughed, spitting in a cup as Aaron and Greg walked out.

17

Jaime's driver pulled through the gates of the family's lake house estate. The sun was almost down and daylight could be seen through the tops of the trees but the winding gravel driveway was covered with darkness. The headlights of the Town Car went around the last turn and Joe, her driver, said, "Jaime, Betta, we're here."

She stretched and yawned, "Thanks for the ride. Are you staying in the guest house or going home?"

"Yes, I will be staying in the guest house." He got out and opened her door. "If you, or Betta, need anything, let me know."

Betta walked to the front door of the log home. The structure towered two stories and had a full, finished, walkout basement. The house had been remodeled after the inheritance. Mitch designed the basement and Jessie took care of the rest. The first floor was big and open. The kitchen, living room and dining room were all married into one space. The basement was filled with a wet bar, poker table, games and a home theater.

The second floor had a balcony that wrapped around the interior of the house with two bedrooms on either side. Eight bedrooms total with the bathrooms in the middle. The Andersons' master suite was on the northeast corner facing the lake and Jaime's was on the southeast.

Betta hugged Jaime tightly. "I have missed being here with you, little girl."

Jaime returned the hug. "I have missed it, too. Traveling on the road with Mom and Dad gets old after a while, especially all the fake smiles and phony people acting like they are our friends. The only reason they are nice to me is because they have to be."

"Wow!" Betta said to herself as she watched Jaime enter the house before following her. "Well, let's try not to worry about that right now. Let's consider ourselves on vacation!"

"Are you going to let me do whatever I want this summer?" She was smiling and laughing as she said this. She knew Betta would give her some freedom but she would not concede to her every wish.

"We'll see. You know we still have to worry about your studies. Your parents won't let me out of that one!"

Jaime sighed, "Yeah, I don't know what the big deal is."

"Well, they want you to be successful. Like them "

"I guess, but I want no part of that lifestyle," Jaime said as she hugged Betta again and walked into the house from the foyer. The night air was cool, so the windows were open. They walked through the house with their arms around each other. Jaime put her head on Betta's shoulder.

"I know Sweetie." She caressed Jaime as they walked to the deck. Jaime felt comfortable and at home, a feeling she loved but rarely had with her family's public life.

18

Larry pulled the junk-filled truck into the check-in spot at the campground. Dusk had begun and the sun's reflection off the lake was blinding. Tired bodies began to stretch and wake up as the truck stopped. He tossed the truck into park and told everyone to hang out in the truck while he checked in.

"Dad, I need to use the bathroom and Cosby needs to go out," Sis pleaded, "We all need to stretch!"

All of us chimed in with agreement. I could not wait to get out of that cramped back seat. It was big enough for three comfortably, but we each had gear and the dog. The way my legs felt, it might have been more fun being chained to a hubcap to get here.

My body fell out of the car and my knees gave way. Before I knew it, I was being pulled and my legs were asleep. Cosby, not used to being on a leash, took off running for a grassy area. I could not keep up with him. "Stop boy! Cosby, stop!!" I screamed.

Over at the truck, Mom, Sis and Staci were cracking up at me being dragged across the campground by a 40-pound dog. My face reddened with anger as the three continued to laugh. I got Cosby under control and my feet back on the ground. Catching my breath, I laughingly yelled back, "If the peanut gallery wants to laugh, they could at least try to help!"

Staci swiftly replied, "Nah! It was too funny watching you trip and tramp around the campground."

"Dang, he is a quick little guy, isn't he?" Aaron said, as he walked up and petted Cosby. It was my first time seeing Aaron and I must confess at first

glance, I did not really care for him. He looked and talked like a thug and seemed more interested in my dog than in me.

"Yeah, he sure is. When he wants to be," I said laughing.

Holding out his fist, he said, "Hey man, I'm Aaron."

Tapping his fist, I replied, "Bub."

"Bub?"

"Yeah, well I have kind of a gay name." I was laughing. "My real name is Conrad, my family calls me Connie, but my friends call me Bub."

"Ah, gotcha. How long you here for?"

"Man, like a week. We come here every year." I try to make people think I don't like coming here, but the truth is I always have fun. I guess it's just a cool attitude to have, like most kids my age. "How long you here for?"

"The entire summer. Workin' here with my uncle. I just got here and I hate it already. I'm hoping my dad will change his mind and take me home tomorrow." Aaron frowned and gazed at the grass beneath his feet. I felt sorry for the kid. I mean, it must be crummy being dumped here with no friends.

"You and your uncle close?"

Before I could finish my sentence, he said, "Nah, not really. I only met him once face-to-face before today, but he seems cool. He was telling me about this bonfire party they are having tomorrow night where the cops kind of turn their heads for one night. Sounds pretty cool. I am going to get smashed," he laughed. "You like to party?"

I did not want to come off as a dopey dweeb, so I lied. "Yeah, man. Good times!!"

"Is J.J. around here?"

Completely puzzled, I repeated, "J. J.?"

"Yeah, you know… DY-NO-MITE!"

"Huh?"

"Man you said 'good times.' Don't say that. People will think you are talking about a TV show or something … say killer, cool, dope, anything but 'good times.' Got it?"

"Yeah. I gotcha. So, you into games and stuff like that?"

"Yeah, sure am." Just as he said that, we heard his uncle yelling for him.

"Damn man, back to work," said Aaron. "You wanna hang later?"

"Sure. Got to help set this thing up, but after that I'm cool. It'll be good to get away from the girls for a while."

He held out his fist for me to bump and jogged over to the golf cart where his uncle waited. Cosby was lying in the grass at my feet, panting. I started walking over to the truck as I saw my pops come out of the office.

I wasn't halfway over to the camper when mom started. "Who was that boy? He looks like trouble."

My mother thought that every stranger looked like trouble, no matter what race they were. I was trying my hardest not to roll my eyes. If I had a dime for every time I heard, "Don't roll your eyes at me," my wealth would surpass some of the poorest nations in the world!

"I don't know mom, I just met him. I think he just got here today. He said his uncle worked here and he was here for the summer. He seems like a nice kid."

"We'll see."

Dad walked up on us and the subject changed. I was relieved. "Okay, we got our usual spot. Let's go set up!"

"I think me and Cos will just walk over," I told them. For a few blocks it wasn't worth being scrunched up again.

"Hey, wait up!" Staci yelled, "I'll walk with you guys." She ran toward me, wearing a T-shirt and shorts, with long tan arms and legs swinging, and blonde ponytail bouncing in the wind behind her.

Catching up to me, she asked, "Are you feeling better since your bathroom incident?"

"Don't. Don't call it that."

"Well, what would you like me to call it?"

"I don't know, but not that. That makes it sound like I crapped my pants or something worse."

"Worse?"

"Yeah, worse. It's a guy thing. Would you like me to go into detail?" I was hoping she would say no, I didn't know what else to say.

"Nah. I'll take your word," her face turned red as she faked a laugh.

My father really had no business driving a truck, much less a truck with a 40-foot trailer on it. I can't tell you how many times we have cheated death. He has hit stuff, backed into stuff and jackknifed it. When he jackknifed it, it was so bad he had to get a tire jack to get the trailer to uncouple from the truck. That day, traffic was stopped on our dead-end street for two hours. Oh, people were patient at first, but by the time it was over, I thought our house was going to be egged. It was shortly after that incident the neighborhood association passed a new ordinance banning campers to be even brought into the neighborhood, much less stored there. To this day, four years later, some neighbors still snarl at Dad.

So, now, here we are, watching him try to get this camper perfectly positioned and it is a race to beat the dark. Aaron and his uncle were already at the campsite when Staci and I walked up.

I was kind of embarrassed for my new friend to see me in this situation but as it turned out, Greg knew exactly how to navigate my father to the perfect parking position. I don't get impressed often, but that night I was.

"How did you learn to guide people in like that?" asked Dad.

Pipe Vision

"Oh, well, I guess I just learned over time."

My father introduced himself and our family to Aaron, and we all greeted Greg as a year had passed since we saw him last.

Our campsite was pretty simple but rugged. It sloped down toward the lake and a gravel area. There was enough space for the camper. The rest of the area was covered in dirt and tree roots, two big trees shaded the area and a metal picnic table with a wooden top and seats sat between them. It was one row away from the pool and bathhouse but lakefront. The site was far from the office and docks, but the boat traffic on the lake was incredible, even at this hour. There were boats going in all directions with their running lights on. As I watched the traffic, I thought, "This really is peaceful."

19

THREE DAYS EARLIER

"**M**an, we need to be careful. I can control this guy but not for long. You need to find a new location and soon. The traffic around here is infrequent and the locals will start to ask questions. This is a good gig and we don't want to blow our cover."

Zake looked around and tossed his half-smoked cigarette on the ground and crushed it with his worn boot. He stuck his fat dirty hands in his overalls and said, "Well, I wouldn't worry none too much."

Mollie, Zake's girlfriend, who was only around him for free drugs, was once a beautiful girl with a lot of potential. She was prom queen and valedictorian her senior year, but after finding drugs and alcohol her freshman year of college, she had turned into a thin, wiry, drug addict. She sat baking in the sun on a lawn chair, which was as old and worn as she. Matted brown hair covered her face and her clothes appeared to not have been washed for several days straight. She was 30 but could be easily mistaken for 50.

She pulled her hair behind her ears and exclaimed, "These people ain't that smart. We got nothing to worry about. As long as you keep Sherriff Paul happy, we're fine. He ain't smart enough to figure this gig out and, broke as he is, he can probably be bought. How come we never see your face when you come around here?"

The masked man responded, "You do not need to see my face. I get you the supplies and you pay me money. My name and face are unimportant to this. You got that?"

"Yes, sir. I got that. But, how do we know we can trust you?"

"Shut up, Mollie!"

"What? We don't know him … he could be one of them Feds. Look how he's dressed. Blue shirt, clean jeans, boots that ain't even scuffed. Shoot, he could be a Fed."

"Look, I am not a Fed or an officer of any sort. I told Zake when I staked him, no one but him would ever know my identity. Some drug fiendin' whore won't change that."

Mollie's face turned red and her legs quivered as she attempted to stand. It took her three tries to get out of the chair. When she did, the masked man pushed her back into the chair.

"Sit down! Zake, you better deal with this and get her under control. We can't afford some whacked-out bitch to screw this up for us."

"How dare you talk to me that way?"

"How dare YOU! Let's not forget who puts food you don't eat and, more importantly, drugs on your table. I can take all of that away."

Zake looked at Mollie, heaped over on the ground in a ball. "Look baby, just chill. Damn! Everything's cool. When's the next drop?"

"Tonight."

"The usual spot?"

"Yes."

The man in the mask turned to walk toward the woods, which surrounded them and the trailer. He looked at all the garbage around and said, "Get this place cleaned up!" He was angry Zake had let the place get so trashed up. "There is enough evidence here to put us all away."

"Nobody knows this stuff is here," Zake said, kind of cocky and waving his hands at the masked man.

"Man, you cannot be this stupid. You make drugs for a living, of course you are this stupid. You probably don't watch the news either. They look at images from space now to look for evidence of meth manufacturing."

Zake interrupted and looked to the sky. "There's people in space watching me?"

"Jesus Christ," the masked man exclaimed.

"What?"

"What do you mean 'what'?"

Mollie tightened up her frail body as she tried to get up, falling back in the chair a couple of times before mustering enough energy to get herself up. "He don't know what he is saying. There ain't no one in space watching us."

Bang! A single gunshot filled the wooded air.

20

Seth's plane landed in Metropolis, Illinois. After two layovers and numerous flight attendants treating him like he was a child, he was almost there. He hated being treated like a child. There was nothing he could do about it, so he rolled with it.

He was always nervous at this time in the flight. He had to meet a stranger. A stranger who was his father, but Seth could never relate to him. He was glad their meeting was delayed until the plane was emptied. The flight attendant signed him over to an airport representative who would be his custodian until meeting his father.

"Are you ready, Sweetie?" the attendant smiled at him. "This is Duane, he will take you to your party. Thank you for flying with us, you have been a joy to have on board." She reached out and hugged him. Seth thought, "Of all the good looking stewardesses in the world, I get hugged by the one ugly one.'

Seth wanted to say, "So, do you say that to every kid or just the ones who constantly make smart remarks and you are glad to get rid of?" But instead he replied, "Thank you. You have been most hospitable."

Her face flushed, but the only color on her round face was that of the caked-on makeup. "Um, well, um," she stammered.

Seth answered, "C'mon Duane, take me to hell."

"Aren't you going to be a fun kid to be around?" Duane said as they exited the plane. "I hope your dad tips well."

Seth stopped dead in his tracks and busted out laughing, "My father tip? Now that's funny."

They walked through the terminal, past the security checkpoint. Seth looked around for his father, who was nowhere to be found. "Great," he said to

himself as he pulled out his phone. He was so used to not having one he almost forgot about it. Turning to Duane, he said, "Let me call and see where my dad is." This was not unusual behavior for his dad. Sadly, Seth was used to it.

"No worries man. I'll hang with you until your dad gets here. It's no big deal. Would you like to sit over there? Can I get you a bottle of water?" Twisting his mouth and raising one eyebrow, Seth looked at Duane. "Airport rules won't allow me to get you anything but water. I know, it sucks."

The last thing on Seth's mind right now was a beverage. He wanted out of the airport; it was kid-control hell. He wanted to be free and on his way to see his friends in town. He looked up his father's number in his ever-present composition notebook. The notebook was his life.

"Ahh, here it is!" Seth said as he opened his phone and began to key in a number. "Ugh, this always happens."

"Dude, relax it's no big deal." Duane understood Seth's frustration as he had a similar situation with his own father. Reassuring Seth, he said, "He will get here when he gets here. Until then I am your buddy to hang out with."

"I guess. No answer," Seth responded absently.

Seth began pecking out a text to Bub: "Made it, Dad not here yet, who knows when I'll get there."

"Man, we just got here and are setting up camp. Text me when your dad gets there and on your way. Might be a killer party tonight. Met a new kid. Think he is cool. We'll see."

"Will do."

As the text session concluded, Seth's phone rang. It was his mom. In all of the confusion of his father not greeting him at the gate, he forgot to call her and tell her that he had landed safely. He had done this at every leg of the trip. Yet, he left out the most important call! "Hi Mama," he said. He wanted her to think that everything was alright.

"He isn't there, is he?"

"Not yet, but I'm sure it's just traffic or something. I'm not too worried."

Seth was reassuring his mother that everything was good. She was 3,000 miles away and feeling helpless. Seth liked being a smartass, it was in his nature. But, not to his mother or his close friends

"I'm sorry you have a louse for a father," she said, choking back her tears.

"Eh, Mom, don't start. He'll be here soon. I have already talked to Bub and there is some fun stuff going on tonight at his campground. So, I'll probably go over there and hang out."

"Try to spend some time with your father. He means well."

"Yeah, I will." Seth felt a tap on his shoulder. His dad looked completely different. His eyes seemed fuller and not sunk into his face. Jeff's weight was normal and his teeth were clean. "Oh, he's here now. Let me call you back when we get to his house and get settled. Mama, please don't worry if I don't answer or call you. I'm not sure how the signal on this phone will be and I'll be with Bub. You know how we tend to lose track of time."

"Yes, Sweetie. I know how you boys are, always forgetting about your mothers." She was laughing and Seth knew she was giving him a hard time. "I love you, sweet boy."

"Mom!" Seth hated being called sweet boy. "I love you, too." Closing the phone, Seth turned toward his father and said with a glare, "'Bout time you got here."

"Hi son, how are you? Ready to have fun the next few weeks? I have some time to make up for," Jeff said, as if they were best friends and he was completely clueless to Seth's tone and mannerisms.

"I'm good," Seth was astonished. His father was clean and well-groomed. Modern. There was no trashy girl with him. In fact, there was no girl with him at all. His dad had never picked him up alone. He always brought the flavor of the month. These strange women tried to make Seth feel welcome and tried to be his friend, but they always tried too hard and it just made the trip longer. "How far of a drive do we have? Bub is at the campsite and wants me to hang out tonight."

"You haven't seen your old man since Christmas and you want to know how far we have to drive so you can see your friends? It's about an hour or so, but I thought we could stop and get a bite to eat. Are you hungry?"

"Yeah, I am hungry and Duane is only allowed to give me water," Seth really wanted to say, "Probably because of some fat kid who was diabetic, lied about it, asked for a Coke and a doughnut, then went into some sort of shock or coma and now every other kid has to pay for it." But his better judgment overcame him.

"Yeah, man, I'm sorry. It's just airport policy and I could lose my job." Duane handed Jeff a pen and a slip of paper. "Please sign this. It releases him from the custody of the airline." Duane looked over at Seth, "You're pretty funny. Stay cool, dude, and enjoy your stay."

"Thanks. Have fun at your boring job shuffling kids all day."

Jeff handed Duane the paper and a twenty. "Thanks and sorry I was late. He's got a comment for everything, don't hold it against him."

"No problem, thanks." Duane turned to Seth and offered a closed-fist bump, "Have a safe trip, kid."

Seth and Jeff turned and walked to the exit. Duane had already retrieved Seth's bags.

21

"**F**uck!" Houston slammed his mask down on the ground. "I so don't need this."

"What the hell are you doing? Why did you kill her?" Zake asked, trembling and looking at Mollie's body, then back at Houston.

"Are you serious? Do I need to spell this out for you? What am I saying? Of course I do. Jesus, how do I get involved with such stupid people." Houston put both hands on his head and rubbed his eyes and slid his hands down his face. He continued talking to himself, repeating, "Smart people don't get into this. Maybe I am the stupid one." He looked over at Zake, who was standing there blankly, "All right, calm down, let me think here for a second."

Zake could not hide his stupidity. "Boy this is a problem."

"Ya think?"

"Yeah, we never *kilt* nobody before." Zake shook his pack of smokes and put one to his lips and lit it. He puffed away as he stared at the lifeless, bleeding body curled up beside his front porch.

Houston pulled out his cell phone, looked at it and returned it to his jeans front pocket. "What am I thinking? I can't make this call from a cell phone." He looked around at the mess surrounding him, knowing this had to go away fast. No one would really miss Mollie, but he had to clean this up. He turned to Zake. "Man, I need to go to town and make some calls from a line."

"What do you want me to do?"

"Ey, nothing just hang out and chill 'til I get back."

"Okay man, I can do that."

"I ought to kill you too." The man slapped Zake across his head. "Are you serious? Get this place cleaned up! Anything you need, you get it packed. You are moving to safe house number two. The drop is being pushed to the last-resort area. You are going to have to move the shit yourself."

"That's too close to town. We ain't got as much privacy there. Who am I going to get to help me? You *kilt* her! You do this yourself."

"Boy, don't you forget who you're talking to. I made you, I'll break you."

Houston walked toward the woods. "I'll be back in an hour. Get to work!" He really did not know when he would return but hoped by saying an hour it would motivate Zake.

"Yeah."

22

"So, how you been?" Jeff asked, as he they started walking to his State truck. The truck was off-limits unless he was working but, he had nothing else to drive.

Ugh, pointless conversation Seth thought, "Alright, man. Just going to school. I wanted to get a job this summer to help Mom out, since you don't. But, no one really wants to hire a kid who has to disappear for two weeks, right smack in the middle of the summer. Ya know?" Seth was unsure where to take the conversation and felt no real connection to the man. So, he decided to ask a cliché question, "How have you been? Still dating skanky, trashy women? I bet Mom was the nicest girl you ever dated. I'm sure she was the smartest. She proved that by throwing your ass away."

Jeff grabbed his boy's shoulder and spun him around almost knocking Seth's balance off. They were standing in the terminal, right inside the doors, and the sounds of cars and people flooded the space. After he was forcefully twisted, the sun was shining on Seth's face. He did not like this. He did not like to be forced to do anything. Seth had no regrets about what he had told his old man. None at all.

He looked at his father, "What? Can we do this somewhere without an audience or do you like the drama of an audience? I sure don't."

Jeff really did not want to cause a scene. However, this was important to him. "Look, I know I haven't been much of a dad. But, at least give me a chance these next two weeks." He stuck out his hand, "If at the end of this visit, you don't like me or want to come back or, hell, ever want to talk to me again, I'll understand. Deal?"

Seth was surprised at this little plea from his dad. This behavior was odd and unusual, almost freaky. What did he have to lose? Knowing he could never lose contact with his dad, the thought of having more flexibility was appealing. A card he would keep up his sleeve until the visit ended.

"Deal!" They shook hands. "Now, can we please go get some food and quit being mushy?" Seth hugged his dad. This was something that his anger had prevented him from doing at first sight. Seth knew the deal was empty for two reasons. First, his mother was a big proponent of Seth knowing and keeping in touch with his dad. Secondly, as much as Seth wasn't fond of his dad and was now confused by his behavior, Jeff was still his dad. Even though Jeff had turned his back on Seth and his mom, Seth's Papau taught him to never turn his back on family. No matter what!

"So, when do you think we'll be home?" Seth still wanted to see his friends tonight. The party Bub told him about sounded fun but, truthfully, he just wanted to catch up and hang out with Bub and Sis.

Jeff laughed. "I'd say couple of hours, by the time we eat and get on the road. Is that okay?" Pausing, as he looked over at Seth, "Or we can eat in the car and be there in about an hour, if it's important for you to rush home."

Seth wanted to eat in the car and fly to his dad's house but he also felt like his dad at least deserved some time with him. "No, I don't want to eat in the car. I just wanted to give Bub a timeframe. So, a couple hours, give or take, right?"

"Yes, sir!"

Seth texted Bub, "Be around there in a couple hours, wait for me to have fun!"

Bub's immediate response was, "Sweet!"

Half way through the drive, Jeff noticed a diner on the side of the road. The trip had been somewhat quiet with Seth texting his friends and Jeff not really sure how to relate to Seth. He poked Seth and then pointed to the diner, "Hungry?"

"Starving," Seth yawned and stretched as his dad whipped off the highway into the diner. "Can I get my charger out of the back so I can charge my phone while we're here?"

"Sure, you don't have to ask my permission. Just be yourself man."

"Alright," this was kind of a new side of his dad and he wasn't used to it. Usually his dad was moody and Seth never knew what to expect or what his reaction would be. For the first time in his life, he felt relaxed around his father.

The diner was rustic and aged. It looked as if the same family had operated it for the last fifty years. The menu was a homemade, laminated page, and emblazoned across the top was: HOME OF THE SPANKY-PANKY BURGER Seth knew right away that he wanted one of those, with a large soda. Jeff ordered the same while being seated.

Seth's curiosity could not be held anymore. "So, what's been going on with you? You're different. I didn't notice on our weekly phone calls, but I do now and I must say, so far, it's impressive." He could not help but wonder if Jeff had an ulterior motive. Was he trying to impress a new girl who is behind us, or following us, or, even better, stalking someone who is here, in the restaurant, giving the appearance of a loving dad?

"Thank you."

"What's your ulterior motive?"

"What do you mean, Son?"

"Well, in the past, the only times you have treated me nice is when you wanted something or were trying to impress a new girl. I'm trying to keep an open mind, Dad, but I must tell you I am wondering." Seth looked out the window to his right, "So, let's hear it," looking back at his father. "What do you want?"

Jeff sat there and couldn't believe his ears, "Damn, is that what you think? I am only nice when I need something?"

"It's what you've done in the past," Seth looked down at the brown, sticky table and sighed. "Whenever I visited before, it seemed that you wanted me to bless a new relationship, usually an empty relationship, or you needed me to help with a fight you and Mom where having." Seth tossed his hands in the air, "I don't know, can you see where I am coming from?"

Jeff was amazed at the astute observation by his son, "Yes," he said looking down and shaking his head. He reached up and wiped off his forehead, "Boy I am sorry, everything you said there was true.

"So what happened?" Seth asked, "Why the change?"

"Losing you and your mom was the worst thing that ever happened to me. I was a young dopey kid and I thought I could do whatever I wanted. When your mom and I got married, we were young, just out of school. We dated all through school and never dated anyone else after we met. Mom was good with that and I thought I was, too. We always went out to bars, traveled, and spent time together. But, once you came it was time to settle down and be adults. Mom was ready. I wasn't. I'd rather go out with the guys and play, than sit at home with a screaming kid. Your mom loved it. She never wanted to go out because you were her world. I just couldn't get there, and before I could control it, I started having affairs. Some of this I don't like telling you because I behaved poorly. Very poorly." He was staring at the wall behind Seth.

The waitress dropped off their drinks. Seth was distracted by her looks. She was his age, wearing a plain black tee, blue jeans and an apron. "Thank you," Seth said. He knew that she probably had a boyfriend, based on the class ring on her finger. But, hell, he thought, 'Nobody knows me here, why not?'

Seth looked at the waitress. He had heard an old, corny joke and figured he would try it, "Hey, do you know how much a polar bear weighs?"

The waitress smiled, "Enough to break the ice?"

Seth's smile evaporated from his face, "Dammit, you weren't supposed to know that one!" Laughing, "But since you do, what's your name?"

She smiled, "Samantha."

He returned the smile, "Seth."

"Nice to meet you Seth," she winked.

"Hey!"

"Yes?" Samantha was intrigued by the excitement in his voice.

"Can I ask a favor?" he didn't wait for an answer. "Could I get you to plug this in somewhere?" Seth held out his phone and his charger.

"Sure, Sweetie." Winking at him again as she took his phone and charger. Seth watched her as she walked off with his new toy.

"Player." Jeff said, smiling.

"Hey, why not? Seth shook his head to clear it, "Anyway, back to your story."

"Yeah, so, I missed having a family and I wanted another one so badly that I was dating easy women, trying to force something that wasn't there. The only ones I thought I could get, or would go after, were one's that had kids or didn't work and depended on, or wanted, a man to take care of them. I would get bled dry in the process. I finally decided, after you were home at Christmas, that I was going to quit looking, learn how to be single, and live life."

"I think I follow you."

"Well, this is another one of those you-will–understand-with-age topics. I really don't expect you to understand all of this right now."

"Are you trying to win mom and me back?" Seth's tone was direct.

"Just you. Your mom would never take me back. I cheated on her and I could not expect her to trust me again. I have to focus on you. I have let fifteen years of your life slip by and I don't want to lose anymore. I see these boys camping and shit with their dads and I am missing out. You are here for three weeks out of the year and when you're here you're not here. You're with friends."

"Jesus, Dad. What do you expect? Every time I come here, you spend more time using me to impress some girl you hardly know but already seems to be living with you. Would you want to stay home? I feel like Bub's family is more of a family here than you and they don't even live here!"

"I know, okay, I know." Jeff was hurt. He knew this was going to be a hard, unavoidable conversation. He had no idea how honest his son would be. In a way, he was relieved, in another, sad. "Boy, I have really let you down."

Before Seth could answer, Samantha showed up with plates of cheeseburgers and fries. Seth's eyebrows rose at how she looked more amazing with each new

glance and the incredible amount of food. They were the biggest burgers he had ever seen: three fat patties, Colby cheese between each, all the dressings and a thin bun.

Jeff couldn't believe his eyes either. In his forty-two years, he never saw such a meal. "Dang! We could have split one of these!"

"Nope, I'm starving. This is mine and I own it."

Samantha asked, "How does everything look? Need anything else?"

"Just ketchup and some extra napkins. This looks like it could get messy," Seth said while laughing. He wanted her to keep coming back to the table but without being obvious. This was an unusual feeling for Seth. No girls at his school really liked him. He was a dweeby, game playing, fat kid. The girls who were his friends, he had known since fifth grade and just never had this feeling about them. He wanted to hear and know everything about her. This was a new feeling for him and he liked it.

Jeff felt like the topic of conversation needed to change. At Seth's age, he did not need to know the real reasons for the illusion of his new, straight path. Jeff was completely out of money, spending his last dollars on the good plane ticket to impress Seth. He hoped that by acting as if he cared about Seth he would be invited to return to California. His biggest consequence for past behavior was a life filled with regret. Regret for the way he treated Seth's mother and his son. He missed too much of their lives and wanted the privilege of being allowed back in.

His past behavior just wasn't as important as getting to know his son and catching up on lost years was. Jeff leaned over his food with his forearms resting on the table's edge, "Well, I think we're done with that. I shouldn't have to work much this week, so I was hoping we could hang out and do some fun stuff. Maybe have Bub and his family over one night for dinner, go fishing or whatever you want. I did buy a game station and have a few games for us to play as well."

"I guess, Dad. I just want to see how the week goes."

Jeff had built higher hopes up in his head. He always did. He was examining the situation from Seth's angle as well and could understand why his boy was standoffish.

The conversation was minimal during the remainder of the meal, mostly because of the gobs of food piled on their plates. Toward the end of the meal Samantha dropped by again to hand off the check.

Seth's mouth could not be stopped. He had to find out more about this girl and knew he would regret it if he didn't. "Are you from around here?" he knew it was a stupid question to ask, but it was all he could think of to keep her at the table as Jeff fumbled around with his money.

"Born and raised, you?"

"Na, I'm from L.A.," Seth's chubby cheek bobbed as he winked at her and smiled.

"Wow! A big city boy!"

"Not really, I was born in eastern Kentucky but when my parents split, my mom moved us to Nashville to sing, then L. A. to act."

"Wow! That sounds interesting."

"It's," he paused, unsure what to say looking at his father, "been interesting," he laughed. "I'm here visiting my father the next two weeks."

"Cool, maybe I'll see you around."

Before he could stop the words from coming out of his mouth, he blurted, "I doubt it. We live, like, an hour from here." He shocked himself by being so blunt. 'A girl who looks like her actually talking to me and I say that? I'd drive an hour just to see her again, even better, to talk to her,' he thought.

She picked the money off the table, "I'll be right back with your change, sir."

Jeff nodded, "Thanks." He looked at his son, "Ladies man, eh?"

Laughing to hide his embarrassment, Seth said, "Not usually."

Samantha returned to the table, "Thank you, guys." She turned toward Seth, "Here's your phone and charger, Sweetie. Keep in touch and I hope you have a fun time with your dad!"

She was gone before he could get another word out. From nervousness to excitement, Seth was an emotional wreck. Frowning then smiling then frowning again, "Ugh I guess I blew that one, huh?" He said as he pulled his body out of the booth and headed with Jeff towards the door. Seth shoved his phone in his pocket, dangled the charger around his neck and they were back on the road again. "One more hour of travel. I'm exhausted."

Once settled in the car, he looked at his phone. He had two texts, one from Bub, asking if he was there yet, and the other was an unknown number. It read, "You're cute, it's Samantha, have fun and keep in touch. PS I live an hour away too and I really hope it is in the same direction!"

He did not know how to respond to her but smiled as he replied to Bub, "Be there soon!"

23

"**D**ammit, I didn't need this today," Houston grumbled to himself as he came out of the woods to the gravel road where his Jeep was waiting. "Of all the things I gotta deal with, now this. Well, I guess I'll have a bonfire tonight." Knowing he had to be careful and cover his tracks, he decided to go to the barn and get a couple of gas cans. This town was small. People notice stuff like buying lots of gas. He had to cover his tracks but needed help. The only people who could help him were hours away.

He returned to the parked Jeep and drove to the road where he sped down the flat, winding country roads. The top was off and the humid air was attempting to keep him cool. The midday sun prevented any shade from cooling the ride but he didn't care about being hot. He needed to figure the best plan. Before he knew it, he reached a gas station with a pay phone. He searched fruitlessly for change.

"Dammit!" He grabbed the gun out of his pants and tossed it under the seat.

"Good afternoon," the clerk said as he walked in the store.

He didn't respond or acknowledge the clerk. He focused on getting something to eat, something to drink and some change. The station had a diner, but he had no desire to go and sit and chew the fat with the geriatric crowd of regulars.

"Give me a chicken sandwich, wedges and I'll grab a drink. Need it to go. Also, I need one of your overpriced gas cans." He only had two in the barn and felt with all the trash they had to burn it would take three or more five-gallon cans. "I'm gonna go fill everything up while you get my food ready. Is that good? Or are these pumps pre-pay?"

The pimply-faced kid who worked behind the counter was a pothead, as most his age were in these parts. His daddy owned this gas station and three others in town. The kid had it made. All he had to do was be smart and straight and he'd be set for life. It was amazing how none of the young folks in these parts could see the big picture. Everything was about the here and now.

The clientele were mostly God-loving Christians. Yet, when you walked into the gas station, the music was loud and heavy metal, head banging bands such as Black Sabbath and Metallica. Every song that started you'd hear one of the old men yell, "Turn that crap off" or "turn that hollering down." It didn't faze the kid with the nose rings and the wide-gauge ear loops. He did what he wanted.

"Naw. Not pre-pay." The kid tossed his magazine up on the counter, let out a sigh and started digging wedges and chicken out from the heatlamp-lit case, Houston's meal.

"Thanks." Houston saw the cordless phone sitting on the counter. "Hey, can I borrow the phone to make a call?"

"Yeah, sure." The kid shrugged his shoulders and rolled his eyes.

"Thanks, I'll be right out here." He grabbed the phone, and the gas can and went out the glass door plastered with signs. He began dialing the phone with his thumb. His nervousness returned. The thoughts of the earlier events haunted him. He had never killed anyone before; so, why did he start now and was it worth it?

The phone rang. His hands were trembling as he pressed the phone between his neck and shoulder while he pumped gas, first into the can and then into his Jeep.

A muffled voice answered, "Hello."

"It's me. I need your help."

"What?"

"A clean up."

"You? Get real."

"Yeah me. I lost my head for a second and jumped the gun, pardon the pun." Houston gulped. "And it gets better."

"How?"

Houston started laughing. "This is, like, the busiest weekend down here because there's some festival going on and there'll be people everywhere starting tomorrow. I got to get this shit cleaned up, and fast."

"You down in the woods?"

"Yep."

"I'll leave in an hour and should be there by dark. Meet me at Shady Acres at 8."

"Don't tell the big guy yet."

Silence.

Houston hung up the phone and then the gas pump.

Inside the gas station, there was a group of old men sitting in the back. They were talking about the good ol' times and anything else they could think of to avoid going home to their empty houses or their wives. This store always seems to have about five midday coffee drinkers who met at the same time every day. They ranged in age from mid-50s to 90 and above. When one dies, another seems to pop up and they are back to their comfortable number.

Walking back in to the store, one of the old timers asked, "Hey aren't you a friend of Clifton's?"

"No sir, I think you're mistaken," Houston said, knowing that Clifton was the local sheriff.

"You sure? I think I seen a fellow that looked like you over at his house." The old man seemed very sure of himself.

"Sorry friend, I'm not from around here, just passing through." Damn, wrong thing to say he thought.

"Why the gas can if you're just passing through?"

"Dammit," Houston thought. A blank look over came his flushed face; he did not know how to answer. "Well sir, I need gas for my boat."

"I see," the old man looked puzzled and unsure of his answer. "Where abouts you from?"

"Erlanger. Up by Cincinnati."

Looking up at Houston, then said "$85.42."

Houston pulled his wad of money out and shielded it close to him. He handed the kid a hundred.

"We don't take those."

"What?" Houston snapped.

"We don't take anything over a twenty."

"What kind of policy is that?"

"Don't make it, don't break it," the clerk shrugged.

Houston was beginning to lose patience. It was all he had, except for a credit card and he couldn't use that. "Man, this is all I have."

"Sorry. Have a credit card?"

The clerk barely got the words out of his mouth before Houston snapped "No! Look kid, this is all I have." He jerked another hundred out of his wad and leaned in to the kid, "Here is another hundred. Keep the change and give me my food!" He slammed the bills down on the counter. Snatching the food and a citrus soda off the shelf, he swung the door open and left.

The old timer who had quizzed Houston walked to the window and said, "There's something about that feller I don't like. I am going to take down the plate and call it in to Sheriff Clifton."

Houston saw the old man through the window and cleverly pulled out of the parking lot so his plate could not be noticed. Or so he hoped.

24

After Greg and Aaron helped us get parked, they had to head back to Greg's house and meet Chief Davis for dinner. It was a much-needed dinner; they could hear the others' stomachs rumble.

As Aaron drove the wagon through the park, Greg said, "That Bub kid is pretty cool, huh? He and his family have been coming down here as long as I have been here and maybe before that. I have watched those kids grow up. It's been fun."

"I don't know, he seems like a goody-goody and a daddy's boy." Aaron was not really paying attention to what he was doing and almost ran off the road.

"Careful! Watch what you are doing! Why do you say that?"

"I don't know."

"Umm, don't you think he might deserve a fair chance? He could end up being your best friend."

Aaron hated being lectured and wanted to change the subject quickly. He pulled the cart into its dedicated spot in front of the house. His father was cleaned up and waiting for them on the porch. "Y'all have fun?" he hollered out as they walked up to the porch. He was clean in a fresh white golf shirt and shorts. Aaron and Greg were sweaty.

Even though Aaron did have fun touring the grounds and meeting new people, he would never admit it to his dad. "Eh, it was OK," he said, shrugging and walking past his dad and into the cool air of the trailer. "Uncle Greg, you got anything to drink?"

"Yeah, in the kitchen. Make yourself at home."

"So how did he do?" Dave inquired, crossing his arms as he waited for an answer.

"Fine." Greg shrugged his shoulders as if there was nothing more to discuss. He thought the day went better than expected and was looking forward to spending more time with Aaron. "Grab me a beer," he yelled in the house. "What's your plans, man?"

"Well, I thought we could go grab a bite and come back here and relax. I think I'm going to get up early in the morning and drive back. I wouldn't make it 50 miles feeling like I do now," he laughed.

Aaron walked out the door holding two beers and a soda. "I am starving."

The chief looked at Greg and said, "I hope you got enough food to feed this starving boy, he will eat you out of the house."

"Ain't nothing wrong with that! Tell you what, let's you and me get cleaned up and we will head down to Mom's and get us some country cookin'."

"That sounds good."

They quickly cleaned up, taking sink baths and putting on fresh clothes, headed out.

Mom's was a dive. It looked like something straight off Food Network. The smell of grease and fried food filled the air. The waitresses wore baby blue dresses and white aprons, the waiters and bus boys wore white shirts and baby blue pants.

As the trio walked in, the Chief said, "This reminds me of that milkshake place when we were kids."

"I know," Greg agreed.

As they were seated, the Chief continued, "When we were lads," a term he always used when he talked about his childhood. Aaron never knew why or cared enough to ask.

Apparently, Greg did, "Lads?"

"Yeah, would you rather me say dopey kids?"

"It'd be true!"

"Can I continue?"

"Sure, use crazy words like that though and I'll probably interrupt."

Aaron's dad laughed. "Ok, you never were one to cut me slack."

"Hey guys. My name is Rose and I will be your server tonight." She handed out menus and adjusted their silverware. "What can I get you to drink?"

Aaron ordered a chocolate shake and Greg a water, while Dave proceeded with his story. "When we were kids, there was a milkshake and ice cream stand around the corner from our house. We didn't have anything. So, we would ride our bikes all over the place looking for pop bottles to turn in."

Greg looked over at Aaron. "Yeah, when we were kids, they had these long, narrow glass pop bottles that you would turn in and get two cents for."

"Like the bums do now for the five-cent cans."

"Yeah, but it wasn't stereotyped like that. It was an innovative and a creative way for kids to get money."

"Anyways, your uncle and I would spend the summer days doing chores and looking for bottles, just to get a chocolate shake. I think for three bottles you could get enough for a shake and the dang thing was big enough for three people!"

"Mom would always know when we got one because we couldn't finish our dinner."

"Sounds corny."

"We didn't have all the Gameboys, mp3 players, cell phones and neat shit that you kids have now. We didn't stay home. If we did, we were put to work and that was no fun. To our parents, we were free labor. There was no such thing as an allowance at our house. Ask your grandpa for money and he'd say 'I don't get my money for free. Why should you two?' Looking back, there was a lot of truth to that."

Aaron thought, "Oh my God, here we go with this speech again about something for nothing. Really?" He picked up the menu and asked his uncle, "How's the fried chicken?"

"Aaron, relax. I am not going to rant about that tonight. I want us to have fun before I leave."

"Okay." Aaron rolled his eyes, trying to change the subject. "Umm, how's the chicken?"

Rose appeared from nowhere with their drinks, "Are you guys ready to order?"

"I think we are all going to get the fried chicken and taters."

"We'll get that right out." She walked away from the table toward the kitchen.

"So, you going to be able to handle my boy?"

"Ahm, well if I can't, ain't nothing a pine box can't cure," Greg laughed.

Aaron did not see the humor in this. He knew the be-on-your-best-behavior lecture was next. He was racking his brain on how to prevent the lecture. Nothing. He was stumped.

Aaron had wondered how well his uncle knew the Chief. They knew one another too well. Greg was running offense for him.

A greasy haired kid showed up with their meals and carelessly tossed them on the table. However, he did give Greg a nod, which was returned as he walked away.

"Mmmm mmmmmm, this looks dandy!" Greg said leaning over his plate and inhaling the steam.

The three ate their meals and there was very little talking. The day's travels made them famished and no time was wasted with talk.

Aaron got a text from Bub as he was leaving: "Man, you need to get back here soon. This party is starting."

He sent a reply as he asked, "Are we going straight back? Bub wants to know when I'll be back."

"Bub?" asked the Chief.

Greg was paying the tab and counting out his money. "He's a regular, comes every year with his family, good kid, they met today."

"See, you're already making friends."

Aaron did not acknowledge the comment as the three walked out of the restaurant.

"Hey, I need to make a stop real quick. I forgot I got to check on something. It's not too far out of the way," Greg said, as he unlocked his little Corolla. It was a 1975 brown station wagon with close to 400,000 miles.

"All right. We are at your mercy." The Chief winked at Aaron across the roof as they got in.

Greg continued: "There is a public official who has a lake house down here. He called me today and said his daughter and her nanny were coming down to spend the summer." Aaron's ears perked up. "I just want to go by and make sure she knows who I am and has my number, in case of emergencies. Mitch also asked me to drop by unannounced every now and then to see what's going on."

"Smart man."

The two brothers continued catching up as Aaron sat in the back and darkness set in on the two-lane tree-lined road. His only knowledge of Kentucky was basketball and stuff he read in books or from TV, so his curiosity took over.

"Greg where are the mountains?" Aaron asked.

"Mountains?" Greg glanced at Aaron through the rear-view mirror.

Aaron now wondered if his question was stupid. "Yeah, whenever I see a show about Kentucky, it looks like it's covered in mountains."

"Well, that's eastern Kentucky and about six hours drive from Cadiz. This side of Kentucky is flat with wetlands and has two major lakes, Lake Barkley and Kentucky Lake, with a recreation area in the middle called Land Between the Lakes."

"Oh."

Greg continued, "It is a pretty popular fishing destination around these parts and nearby states."

Aaron was losing interest in the conversation and replied with a simple, "I see."

"You lost him, man," Dave said while looking at his son mindlessly staring out the window.

They pulled up the winding driveway to a huge house. Aaron had never seen such a place and was amazed that people had vacation homes this size. The driveway was gravel and ended at a circle. On the right appeared to be an old carriage house turned into a garage and on the left the biggest, and the only, log cabin Aaron had ever seen, except for the little ones on his dad's western movies. He could tell the house had an open plan by glancing through the illuminated windows.

"Wait in the car. I won't be long," Greg said, making sure the car was in neutral and the emergency brake was on before getting out and walking toward the house.

Aaron and his dad both agreed to wait in the car. Aaron texted Bub: "We are at some lake house, my uncle has to check on some girl, then we will be back."

"Where?" Bub responded, forgetting he was unfamiliar with the area.

"I don't know, some rich guy's house, it's huge."

"That narrows it down," Bub followed with a smiley face to indicate he was teasing. The shoreline was filled with big houses.

Aaron responded with, "I'll text you when I get back," ending the text session.

Bub was really curious as to where Aaron was. In years past, there was a big house on the cove with the prettiest girl Bub had ever seen. He knew he would never meet her. She was out of his league, but he would always slow the boat down and drool and gawk like a moron when passing.

Greg walked up to the door. Betta was there waiting for him.

"I was hoping that was your car pulling up the drive," she said.

"Oh yeah, why's that?" Greg said, smiling and reaching his hand for hers.

"It's always nice to see you. You don't come around much when they ain't here."

"Well, I do but it's sneaky, so you'd never know," Greg winked at Betta.

Betta always flirted with Greg. She always wanted to go out with him but he never asked. She had never really had a man in her life, just other people's kids, never had any of her own. The thought of love and a spouse was always intriguing to her, having someone to call you for no reason or greet you at the door with a kiss. A fairytale like what she sees in the movies. The reality is the children and families she stayed with gave her love and attention. It was not the attention she dreamed of, though.

In the car, David pulled out his cell phone. "I think I'll try to give Mom a call." He tapped her number into the phone and listened as it rang. "That's odd?"

"What?"

"Mom is not answering her phone."

"She's probably out with Aunt Jane. You know how those two are when they get together. She'll call back."

David was concerned, but he did not show it.

Betta was flirting with Greg. "Well you don't have to be so sneaky. You might scare this old lady."

"Ey, we don't want that now, and besides, you ain't an old lady. Did Ms. Jaime make it? Her daddy called me. He told me she would be down and to drop by."

"Yes. She made it. She's fine. "

"Well good. Would you give her this?" He handed Betta his business card. "Tell her, if she has any problems — call me day or night." He turned and headed down the stairs. Betta stood in the doorway, hugging the door, holding the knob.

As she began to close the door, he turned toward her. "Hey, young lady… what are you doing tomorrow night?"

"Well, I don't know. Nothing, I suppose." She was hoping that he was going to ask her to dinner. Her attention was on every word he spoke.

"We're having a big bonfire and cookout tomorrow at Big Daddy's Campground. You guys should come over and hang out."

It wasn't quite the invitation she was looking for, but she was excited to get to hang out with him, nonetheless. "Sounds fun, I will talk to Jaime and maybe we'll try to make it."

She thought to herself, "I'll be there no matter what."

25

Houston drove to his safe house to get the supplies he needed. He was trying to figure out how to get this mess cleaned up with minimal, noticeable damage. It was usually hot and dry this time of year, but a storm hit the night before and the ground was saturated. He knew he had to be careful driving and walking around Zake's place. No evidence could be left.

There was a lot of equipment and unsold meth inventory that needed to be moved. Bart would help with the property and the body but the rest of it was up to the two of them. He felt guilty of his actions but knew that he had no choice. Not only his income but his life was riding on this venture. It wasn't worth the chance. He warned Zake when he brought Mollie to his place that it could turn out bad.

Zake was calling, but it was too risky to answer on a cell phone. The call was ignored.

He had a few hours before Bart, the cleanup guy, would be in town. Once the jeep was stuffed with everything he might need — shovels, plastic, gas, weights and chains — he was ready to go. Houston was exhausted and knew there was a long night ahead of him cleaning up the mess Zake started and he had to finish. Over in the corner next to the door and the Jeep was a folded army cot. He decided to lie down until it was time to meet Bart.

Zake called again. The phone calls would be non-stop unless Houston took it.

"Hey man, I know I said I would be back down in an hour, but the guy who is going to help me is driving down and won't be here for a few hours," said Houston, without giving Zake a chance to answer. "I'll be back down there after dark. Chill 'til then. The other thing is canceled until this is solved."

He spoke quickly while setting up the cot. "Don't freak out and don't call this number any more." He hung up and tossed the phone in his shoes, the only article of clothing he had removed.

Houston jumped up out of a deep sleep, a quiet voice startled him, a shameful whisper: "Why did you let this happen? How could you be so foolish? You knew Zake was stupid and Mollie was nothing but trouble."

There was no one else there. "What's going on? Who said that?" He reached for his gun, which was no longer tucked under his leg. Finding it on his left, while rolling to get out of bed, he yelled, "Hello! Is anyone out there? I have a weapon. Show yourself!"

It was dusk and he was paranoid and had never felt this way before and did not like it. He was raised better than this but did not like living paycheck to paycheck. No one knew of the self-designed hideout he was in. When an uncle died several years prior and left him land in Kentucky, he thought, "What am I going to do with scrub land in western Kentucky?" Then, when he needed to hide some money to start saving for his exit, the idea came to him.

He built a simple little pole barn, but in the middle dug a bunker for storage of weapons and money. The entrance looked like a floor drain but when the drain cap was removed, he could reach in and lift a section of the floor, exposing a staircase. The area wasn't lit, only by flashlight and lantern. To the left, there was a closet for weapons and a floor safe. To the right, there was a passageway leading to the forest. The forest exit looked like the cap on a septic system, with a slotted cap instead of a solid one. There was a lock on both sides so he could easily enter or exit.

When the guys came down from up north and asked him to run the operation, he knew it was wrong, illegal, and dangerous. The opportunity for wealth and power trumped all of that. It wasn't him the guys wanted, it was his connections and reputation that they needed. No one would ever suspect Houston. His plan was simple: Save a million dollars, get out, relocate and retire. Everything was working out great. He was at the halfway point and there were no wrinkles, until today. He hoped that this was going to work out and if it didn't ... well, there would be a fight.

Stretching and looking around as if trying to recall where he was, he popped up. "Oh shit, what time is it?" Rubbing his head and his eyes, trying to focus on finding his shoes, which were right in front of him, he cried, "Ow, dammit! What the ..." he pulled his socked foot out of the shoe, reached in and pulled out his phone. "Guess it would help to take my phone out of my shoe before putting it on," he laughed. Finishing putting on his shoes, he hopped in the Jeep and headed to the meet.

The barn was metal with a dirt floor. It had a sliding manual door that locked only with a padlock. It could fit four cars, two by two. In the middle of the barn floor was a round drainage grate. It looked like it weighed a ton but it didn't. It was his safe for money and weapons. He was the only one who knew about it.

He was certain Bart was waiting for him, but he needed to grab a few items from the stash. "I can never get this damn thing open on the first try. Let's see if today is my lucky day," he said to himself, grabbing the dial with his nose in the air and his eyeballs peering down at the dial. "Right twice to 36, then spin left to 17, right back to six, here we go, let's see what happens." He latched on to the lock and pulled down. "Dammit!" On the fourth try and 21 "motherfuckers," later, the lock popped open.

Houston had spent a year designing the grate and could open it in a flash when he was calm. He lifted the handle inside the drain and went down the stairs. There was another door with no knob, only a deadbolt. There were two keys, one on him at all times. The backup was in a safety deposit box a day's trip from here, in Harlan County.

In his will, there is a letter to his son, with whom he has lost contact over the years. It includes directions to the barn and instructions on how to get the safe open.

Houston opened the door and grabbed a flashlight that was mounted to the inside of the outward swinging door. Inside, green, red, and blue rubber boxes were neatly stacked. Green for cash, blue for clothes, and red for guns, color-coded in case of emergency. If he was in a hurry, he knew which box to grab for his needs. Each box held $50,000 in cash, 10 Ziploc bags holding 50 one-hundred-dollar bills. He grabbed two green boxes and a couple of handguns out of the only red box stored in the closet. He locked the door and went up the steep, narrow stairs, hoping the money he grabbed would buy off Zake, pay Bart for his services and allow him some time away to strategize his retirement.

Placing the boxes in the floorboard of the passenger side of the Jeep, he closed the door and looked around the pole barn to see if he had forgotten anything. There were two other cars in the barn that ran but were never used. They were emergency escape cars that were replaced every couple of years and usually bought in Ohio, Tennessee, Missouri or Michigan.

"Let's get this over with," he said while backing the car out of the barn and hopping out of the Jeep to slide the barn door shut. Rain started to drizzle down. "Great, just what I need," he said to himself.

The hotel where he was meeting Bart was about 15 minutes away. It was a flea bag, a third generation hotel that was run down. Houston twisted down the dark roads in the misty rain to the main stretch of highway. The Jeep rocked as he maneuvered over the potholes of the crumbling parking lot and into a space behind the hotel. Shaking his head, Houston could remember

how pristine the hotel was before the previous owners fell on hard times. The sight of this place now left a bad taste in his mouth. When the hotel sold to the foreigners, all hope was lost.

As he made his way around to the front of the building, he dodged the lonely Greyhound bus that was slowly lumbering across the lot. Once inside the lobby, he walked past the abandoned check-in counter and into the windowless bar area. Even here, Houston could smell the mildew in the rooms. He wondered if bedbugs would live in barstools and scanned the area. Houston truly hated the thought of driving by the fleabag, much less setting foot into it.

Bart and he usually met at the bar when he came down. All of the other times he was here to pick up a bag of money. Not this time. This was a mess.

Scanning the bar he saw him right away. This guy stuck out like a sore thumb in these parts. He did not even try to fit in. It didn't matter because everyone in these parts was nice to you until proved otherwise.

Houston pulled out the bar stool next to Bart. He looked at the bartender and mumbled, "Beer." Taking a seat on the stool, Houston said to Bart, "Safe trip I see." They were close but not too close. It was purely business. They did not know about each other's families and did not care.

"Yup, I had to, kind of, lie. The big guy wanted to know why I left town so quickly without reason."

No one knew really who the big guy was or where he lived. All that they knew was that he could make or break them. It was their job to keep him happy. Money was all that worked.

"Don't worry. I have something to take care of you," Houston said. "We need to get out there, my guy is probably about to go ape shit by now."

"You trust him?"

"Yep. Just not the girl, which is why you're here."

"Gotcha."

26

Campgrounds on a Saturday night are chaos and this night was no exception. I was used to it. Aaron was in shock or awe, not sure which. There were kids everywhere, on bikes and skateboards, playing Frisbee and other games. Dogs walking and running, big dogs, little dogs, some leashed, others not. There were campfires burning with parents sitting around having a beer, watching their kids play and others getting to know the people next to them. It was usually a festival of activities with unknown friends. There are no strangers at a campground.

Staci, Sissy and I were sitting on the benches outside the pool fence, close to the shower house. It was a high-traffic area and we could see almost the entire campground.

Seth was on his way down from his dad's house. It was about a half mile up the road from camp, a 15-minute bike ride, twice as long by foot. He and I had made the journey many times.

I wondered to myself if he was as excited to see me as I was to see him. He was probably one of my closest friends. In the four years we had known each other, I do not think we have ever fought, even when Sissy was being, well, Sissy.

As we sat there talking about nothing and watching the people in the moonlight combined with the white lights of the street lamps, I heard the quick crunch of gravel approaching me. "Hey doofus!" It was Seth!

"Hey man!" Wow, he had changed over the last year. He was now taller than me. His hair was down to his shoulders and he appeared to be into skateboards or just wanting to dress like a skateboarder. Did I look different? "What's going on, brother?" I asked as he jumped the fence behind us.

"Not much. Been a long, strange day."

"Tell me about it. I am glad we are here now so we can hang out. So what's your dad got planned for you this week? You gonna be able to hang out?"

"I hope so, we will see. It's different this time."

I had been around Jeff, Seth's dad, several times over the years and the one thing he has always been is predictable. The only time he changes is to keep the flavor of the month happy.

Curiously, I said, "How so?"

There is one thing I have learned over my 15 years. Adults change when it is to their advantage.

Sissy and Staci were not interested in our conversation and walked down to the shore in front of us. The sun had just set and there was a yellow reflection on the water. Seth was staring at Sissy while she walked down to the shore. "Sissy is looking fine in her white T-shirt and short jean shorts."

"Dude, that is my sister!"

"Yeah, I know but she still looks good. Anyways, it doesn't matter. I met a cool girl on the way down here. She took my number off my phone while it was charging."

He shook the hair from his eyes, which seemed to be a new habit.

"I don't know. We've texted a few times but . . . " he paused and looked toward the water bouncing off the shore from a group of twentysomethings riding jet skis. "Girls just freak the shit out of me. They make me nervous."

I wanted to know more about the girl thing, but needed to change the focus back to his dad. "Okay," I said, spitting in the dirt between my legs as if on a bench in a dugout. "Tell me about your dad, what is going on there?"

"Oh yeah, seeing your sister got me off subject."

I punched him in the shoulder. "Talk to me man."

"Jeff, has cleaned up," he said. I always thought it was interesting that he called his dad by name, not Dad. "Cut his hair, 'in' style, non-Wal-Mart clothes, clean shaven." He paused to copy my spit. "More importantly, he says he feels guilty and wants to take this summer to get to know me better." Turning towards me, he said, "To make up for lost time."

"Wow." Jeff always acted as if we were a bother. "What do you think about that?"

"I think I want to know what he wants," Seth laughed, with a snort. "I am confused."

"Man, don't worry about it. It's your first night here. Let's see how everything goes. You have always complained that your dad was a shit. Give him a chance not to be without reading something into it."

"Bub," he said. He turned, put his hand on my shoulder and looked me in the eye. "You are so full of shit!"

We both started laughing so hard we fell into each other to keep from tumbling on the ground. Once I gained my composure and got the air bubble out of my throat, I asked, "Why don't you bring your dad fishing in the mornings with us. A couple of days around us and he will probably get back to normal."

"I hope you're right." He pulled out his cell phone, showed it to me and smiled, "I am cool now! I have my own phone. My Papua surprised me before I left and I love it! I know it's a generic, crappy phone but it's mine and I don't have to share with Mom."

As we were sitting there catching up, Greg's red Buick stopped in front of us. "You guys getting into trouble?" he yelled, as the back door opened and Aaron popped out.

"Always!" I yelled. "I know you got my back if I get into some shit." We were all laughing.

"Yeah, well I don't need any mothers banging on my door in the middle of the night looking for their teenage daughters," he laughed. "By the way, this is Chief David Davis, Aaron's dad. Keep his boy out of trouble. You get me? I know your daddy wouldn't mind me bending you over my knee if you got into something. Tell him he has the same right with that one," he said, pointing at Aaron, "if he gets outta line."

The Chief leaned forward and waved at us, saying to Aaron, "You get home by midnight. I want to see you before I leave in the morning."

"Yes sir," Aaron yelled back as he walked toward us. "Hey man." he reached out his fist for a bump, doing the same for Seth.

Sissy and Staci walked over to us as we watched the car drive off. We all stood there for the longest time, all silently trying to think of something to say. Finally, Staci picked up a broken stick lying on the ground and approached Aaron and talked into the stick as if it were a microphone. "So, since none of us know you, why don't you tell us about yourself."

"Stop it, Staci," I interrupted. "What are you doing?"

"I am acting like a reporter. If I don't break the ice, you lame-o's never will!" She had a point.

Aaron stood there looking at us, then at Staci standing there with the stick in his face. He shrugged, "Yeah, I'll play. I got into trouble at home and my punishment was a trip to Hillbilly Land to spend the summer with my uncle." He paused and smiled, "I also get to work for my uncle for free, cleaning up after campers and doing whatever else he tells me … like cleaning up after you all!" He grabbed the stick out of her hand. "Your turn," he said, and shoved it in front of Staci.

She pointed straight at me. "He is a psycho and dragged me down here because we heard voices."

"What are you talking about?" I couldn't believe she broke our pact. They all stood there looking at me. All I could do was fake laugh but I knew with my reddening face my laugh was not believable.

Staci giggled, "I am playing. I've always wanted to come with Bub and Sis here on vacation and this year they let me."

"I'm here from Cali visiting my dad and met Bub down here, like, five years ago and we keep in touch all year, then play video games and fish the whole time we're here."

We continued drinking sodas and telling stories about friends, activities and events of the past year. It seemed like we had just met up, but before we knew it, the midnight curfew had arrived.

27

Annissa, Dave's wife, rolled over and stroked Gabe's chest, while leaning on her hand supported by her elbow. "I want him gone and you have the power to make that happen."

Gabe rose and reached for a robe, "For Christ's sake! Are you serious? We are talking about the Chief of Police!"

"In a nothing, shithole town."

"That's even worse."

"Yeah, but you have untraceable out-of-town contacts. They would never know it was us."

"Shit, you get a rookie detective who wants to be someone one day, they'll do whatever it takes. Why can't you divorce him?"

"We have too much debt. If I leave him, the debt gets split. If he dies, I get the life insurance, the debt goes away and I have enough for my son and me to live on. It ain't that hard to figure out."

"What is going on here? We just met, and now you are asking me too off your husband?"

Annissa had done her homework. In her heart, she was not a cheater, but she knew that Gabe would be discreet. He was a playboy. He had a secret few people knew about: he was a gangster with his own secret crew. Every cop knew he was dirty but no one could catch him.

A few weeks prior, Chief Davis had come home frustrated about a botched drug bust where an informant was going to set Gabe up for the Chief to bust. Gabe paid the informant off and there was no bust. In the midst of venting to his wife, Dave also let it slip that Gabe was a ladies' man. Soon after, she met Gabe at a political fund-raiser and exchanged numbers.

When Dave decided to take Aaron to Kentucky, she devised a plan. A plan to get to know Gabe and attempt to blackmail him.

"I have read about you and I know you can make this happen and if you don't I will get my husband to make your life very difficult. I used to love him, but things change and now I can't stand the sight of him. I know that sounds horrible but I can't wait for him to leave. I can't wait for him to go to work and I dread when he comes home. Look, we are talking about a lot of money here. It won't be hard either because my son will be gone for the summer. Do you know how many people that man has pissed off? The list of possible suspects would be a mile long … maybe longer." ·

"All they have to do is tie us together."

Annissa interrupted: "We are talking about a lot of money here."

"How much?"

"$750,000, maybe more, but I have to pay my debt out of that. Retirement and pension savings are not included in that. Who knows how much that is?"

"I hate to tell you, but not much money these days."

"Seriously?"

"Yeah, a good clean hit and you're looking at $250K minimum. No one will go for a percentage of your take."

"I have got to figure out what to do. He is going to be home tomorrow." She tensed her tall, slender body, gritted her teeth and pointed her finger at Gabe. "If I have to spend the whole summer alone with him I will go insane. Postal."

Gabe was pretty smart. He was used to being tricked and could see ulterior motives a mile away. "So you think you can use me and blackmail me into getting what you want?"

"Yes, and you will or I will tell him about us and you will become his personal mission. You have no idea how vindictive that sorry fucker can be."

Gabe grabbed her throat mid sentence and threw her on the bed. "Look, don't make me kill you. You know I will. Don't you ever try to blackmail me."

His phone rang. He fumbled with his pants, digging it out, trying to answer it before it went to voice mail. "What?!" he snapped. "No. I don't know where Bart is. He was supposed to go to the docks and take care of that job."

His body began to shake. He began screaming into the phone. "A NO SHOW? WHAT DO YOU MEAN, A NO SHOW?" Walking around the room in his boxers, he said, "You find him, and I mean NOW! He is your cousin and I swear if you don't get me some answers, I will kill you both myself, you understand me?" He snapped the phone shut, yanking his pants around the cheap, smoke-smelling hotel room. "Has everyone in my life lost it? It's not that hard! You do what I tell you and you have a sweet life. Don't do what I tell you and your life becomes difficult, as does mine."

Annissa lay there, afraid to breath. He looked at her. "Get up!" he commanded.

She lay motionless.

"Get up before I get you up."

She slowly raised her head. Her neck had handprints on it.

"Don't fuck with me! If I find out that you told that dumb cop husband of yours about us and about me, so help me, you won't have a family." He threw on his shirt, grabbed his suit coat and stormed out the door, making a statement by slamming the door behind him.

Crying to herself, Annissa pleaded, "What am I going to do? What have I done? Please God, guide me." She reached in her purse for her phone. She pushed the home button. "Oh my God." She noticed the two missed calls. She never missed his calls. Was she really that unhappy in her marriage? Yes. Did she want to kill him? No. There was no other way, or so she thought.

28

Bart followed Houston as they drove down the gravel road. Bart was driving his grey Lincoln, which was not made for anything other than paved roads and was keeping several car lengths behind. He did not want to give the appearance of a late-night caravan through the woods. These roads were not highly traveled, especially at this late hour.

Bart called Houston on his cell phone. "I am going to park down here. I don't want my tracks on the scene, come back and pick me up."

Houston turned the Jeep around to pick Bart up. He had no idea where Bart was going to sit, since the Jeep was filled with the necessities for the evening clean-up: shovels, tarps, gas, rope, and tools. Bart was the guru, a clean-up man, making accidents and mistakes go away as if they never happened. Houston knew Bart was not to be challenged or questioned.

He pulled in behind an abandoned barn that looked like Swiss cheese and could topple any second. This was a good place to hide the Lincoln, because it was right off the road, with a gravel drive behind it. Bart was already waiting by the road when Houston pulled up. Not waiting for him to stop, he jumped on the side rail and held onto the roll bar.

"You okay riding like that?" Houston asked as he whipped the Jeep in a U-turn, running off into the grass. "We ain't got that far to go, it's a few miles down this road."

Straining to hear over the wind, Houston leaned over to the passenger side to catch what Bart was saying, "What's the road up to the house like?"

Houston yelled, "Gravel, dirt and mud. My tracks have never been on it."

"Okay, does this boy have a truck, or something he can drive and meet us?"

"Yeah."

"Call him. Tell him to meet us where you usually park. So no unusual tracks show."

Houston did as he asked. They pulled in to his spot in the woods and waited on Zake.

The two men were standing in front of the Jeep as they heard the rumbling motor followed by the headlights flickering through the high grass. As Zake made the turn, he blinded the two men with direct headlights. Zake's truck was a beat-up blue Ford about 20 years old, and the driver's and passenger windows were smashed out. The glass was still in the floorboards. The front and rear windows remained intact. It was a single cab and had a short bed. Houston bought it for him to get supplies; he figured no one would suspect anything with this truck. It was what the locals called a farm truck and most households had one.

"Kill the headlights!" Bart yelled as Zake pulled up to them.

"Hey man, what took you so long? I can't keep her around like that."

"Man, shut up. I did the best I could."

"Gentlemen," Bart interrupted, "we have a lot to do, so, let's get the shit from the Jeep into the truck. We do not have much dark left."

While Zake was helping carry gear from the Jeep to the truck, he said, "Hey Houston, I want to thank you for buying me this truck. It has really been helpful." The tailgate slammed down as Zake fought the rust to open it.

Walking to the passenger side and pushing the button several times to get the door to release, Houston said, "Yes I can see your appreciation by the excellent care you have taken of it." He slammed the creaking door shut.

"Go ahead and get in the truck, Houston. Zake and I got this," Bart yelled as he tossed shovels in the bed and followed Zake back for the final two gas cans. He hopped in the bed of the truck as Zake turned around and headed up his dirt and gravel road.

Pulling up to Zake's trailer, Bart could not believe his eyes. "Sweet Jesus, what have you gotten me into." Trash was everywhere, empty milk and drain-cleaner jugs, pill boxes, empty beer cans and fifths of alcohol. The area looked like a dumping ground.

"Here's the plan," Bart said, jumping out of the bed of the truck, "we need to deal with the body first, and then we will take care of the site." He looked at Houston, "What all did you bring?"

"I didn't know what to bring. So, I thought of those gangster movies and brought shovels, plastic, chains, a weight and some gas. I had no idea what your plan was and it was not like I could ask you from a filling station phone what I should bring to hide a body." Houston was more nervous now than ever. He knew if he did the wrong thing here, he and Zake would join Mollie. "Jesus, please let Zake be smart here," he thought.

Bart nodded at Houston, pointed and said, "Break out the plastic. Wrap her up and put her in the back of the truck. There's got to be a lake around here somewhere, right?"

"Yeah, a couple big ones," Houston laughed. "And it won't be that hard to find a boat either."

"Great. We will need to find the deepest area of the lake. That way she will never be found, if we do it right. Can you get the boat in the next half hour?"

"Yeah."

"Zake, we are going to need to borrow your truck. You need to stay here and keep getting all this trash piled up. We are also going to need," he added, looking around, raising his eyebrows, and sighing, "a lot of wood to keep the fire hot enough to burn all this trash. Also, you need to find dirt and gravel to cover up the blood by your porch. You are going to have to dig up the bloody dirt and put it in the fire pit and replace it with new and blend it in. Can you handle that?"

"I guess."

"You guess?"

"That's his answer for everything," Houston said.

"How about you say, 'Done, no worries. I got it covered man!'"

"Yeah," Zake said with a smartass, half laugh and instantly was staring down the barrel of Bart's Glock. "Whoops, wait, wait, you have no worries. I'll do it! I'll do it!"

The gun was put up as fast as it was drawn. The situation went from being relaxed, to tense, to relaxed, in one breath.

Houston and Bart loaded the wrapped, chained body into the bed of the truck and headed toward the lake.

As they approached the docks, Bart killed the lights and stopped the truck.

"There is a road down on the left with lake access. It's an old abandoned state access road that no one uses. Park at the end, I'll be there as soon as I can. I will get as close as I can. Hopefully, I won't beach the damn boat," Houston said, laughing nervously as he got out of the truck. He wasn't about to share his limited boating skills with Bart.

It was after midnight and the marina was dark and empty except for the streetlights and the occasional resident taking a midnight stroll. Houston walked quietly down the boat ramp to the rental boats and untied the boat while boarding.

He did not want to draw attention by starting the main engine. Houston used the trawling motor until he was out of the no-wake zone. Looking around in the darkness for midnight fisherman, Coast Guard or police, he started the main motor and pushed the throttle to full power. Houston knew where Bart was located. He had been there once before on a fishing trip. It was the only condemned property on the lake. Local residents were used to high school and college kids hanging around the property. Headlights and campfires were a common occurrence on the property.

It was a basic aluminum pontoon boat with an upper deck and waterslide. Houston steered it at a safe, unnoticeable speed, until the alcove was in sight. The water was murky and there were branches and trees poking out. Seeing Bart's reflection in the moonlight, Houston killed the motor as he floated close to shore. The water was still. Houston thought about dropping the anchor, but he knew the boat would be fine as he hopped into the knee-deep water, wading ashore to meet Bart.

"Why didn't you just leave the boat at the marina? It is about as far as the boat," Bart shouted in a sarcastic voice. "I think we need to carry this heavy shit another 10 yards or so," he added, tempering his voice as Houston walked up the beach.

"Well, I could have driven closer and gotten stuck so that we can explain the package we have on board to the Coast Guard."

The two lugged the body to the boat, returned to shore for weight and chains, then headed to the drop point.

"Do you know a good spot? I would think right in the middle would be the deepest?"

"Yeah, I know a good spot and nope, it's not right in the middle. There's an inlet over here which doesn't get much traffic and should work great. The problem with the middle is there is a lot of traffic there and the water gets stirred up." Houston stopped. "And think about what you just said."

"What?"

"Dropping the body in the middle of the lake."

Bart was a city guy and did not have a clue what Houston was referring to. He just stopped, looked blank and shook his head.

"It's the middle of the lake, moron. It isn't like the lake is closed with no traffic. There are fisherman and police out there, we need to be discreet. Now let's get the rest of the shit before anybody sees us."

Once the two were on the boat, with Houston aiming toward his favorite fishing spot, Bart was still confused about not dropping the body in the middle of the lake. He could not resist asking. "I guess that's bad, even with the chains and weights?"

"What?" Houston glanced over puzzled.

"The middle of the lake is not a good spot even with chains and weights?"

"Chains and weights rust over time and frequent water movement could snap the chains. We are almost there. Make sure the chains are wrapped securely and attached to the weight. We don't want her to float up. Who knows how that hillbilly did it but I want to make sure she never floats up. Also, not much slack on the chains."

Bart quickly reminded him who was in charge. "Yeah, I think I know how to wrap a body. Remember, you hired me to help do this. If you know more, I can go home."

Houston didn't respond. The location was close; he did not want the owners of the boat noticing there was fuel missing. He idled the motor. They looked out to see if they saw any boat lights. When they saw that all was dark, they dragged Mollie to the side of the boat and rolled her in. Watching the whirlpool over her head as she sank to the bottom, they both breathed a sigh of relief.

They motored off and returned to the shore and parked the boat. Neither one of them spoke. Houston started to feel guilty about his actions. As he pulled into the channel after dropping Bart off, he noticed some kids sitting down by the dock. He sat where they could not see him until they left. Slipping and tying it off, he headed for Zake's truck.

The ride back to Zake's was as silent as the boat ride to shore. It was all business now. Zake was sitting on the front deck looking almost lifeless and the yard was still a mess. Houston looked over at Bart: "He hasn't done a damn thing."

"Nope and we got to burn this shit and kill the smoke by daybreak, three hours' time. I hope he took care of the blood."

"Doubt it."

Bart was exhausted. He had traveled all day. He had started mid-afternoon in St. Louis, headed home to Detroit, but since people knew he was in the area he was asked to travel two hours out of his way. Adding eight more hours to a nine-hour trip. He was in even bigger trouble because the boss had not granted him permission to leave the area. He needed to get back, and fast. Every time his phone rang, he feared that it was Frank wanting help, or asking where he was. Frank gets very upset if Bart can't jump when he says to.

Surveying Zake's farm as the two got out of the truck, Bart said, "What the hell, man? What the hell have you been doing?"

Zake looked up blankly. "I did what you told me. I got the blood cleaned up and dug out. That was hard work, man. Took me awhile."

Bart was frustrated and was trying to keep cool, "We can't screw around, and we need to torch this." He started pointing and kicking trash toward the fire pit, "Now let's start piling all this shit up." Bart really wanted to get on the road and the moon was getting lower. Daylight was coming and they had to get rid of evidence,

Houston looked puzzled. "Do you think we should burn the trailer? Vacate it?"

"No, that would be too obvious. We just need to make it look like we had a big bonfire. There's no way we can make the trailer disappear this fast. You don't want to. If anyone comes around asking about the girl your response is, 'She disappeared,' you don't know why. Got it?" He looked at Zake,

"Yeah, I got it."

"Make no more drugs here, either. Now pour that gas on the pile and let's get this thing lit." He pointed to Zake. "Go get all the dry wood you can find!"

Zake rolled his eyes, got up off the porch and walked to the trees in the back of the house. Bart and Houston were busy dousing the fire pit with gasoline.

"Are you sure this guy is ok? He seems a little shaky."

"That's putting it nicely. I really don't know, never been in this position with him before. Don't worry, I have it covered."

"You sure?"

"Sure about what?"

Zake walked up behind them carrying wood.

Bart spoke his mind. "I am worried about you, how you'll handle pressure. Whether you will crack under heat."

"Heat?"

"Cops, shit like that. When they come to question you about the crack whore."

"Don't call her that!" Zake's forehead wrinkled as he put his toothless face to Bart's.

Bart laughed and walked away, "Okay, the outstanding citizen who was staying here doing free drugs."

Zake was scared and you could tell in his tone. "No man, I won't crack under the heat." He pulled a Kentucky's Best smoke out of the pocket of his overalls and lit it. "Need a light?"

"You moron, I am standing right by a wood pile soaked with gas and you light a friggin' smoke? Do you have meat sauce in that head of yours?"

Zake looked at him blankly.

"Just light this damn pile of shit so we can get this over." Houston was exhausted. This was not how he had planned his day and he was ready for it to end.

Bart snatched the lighter out of Zake's hand and walked over to the bed of the truck. He grabbed a broomstick and wrapped a rag lying beside it around the handle.

"Well, boys, you're about to see some fun shit here." He soaked the rag in gas and lit it with the lighter. "Let's back up a little." He speared the stick in the pile and turned his back as a gush of a fireball erupted.

"Holy shit," Zake said as a fireball went up into the night sky.

They spent the next two hours in the heat of the summer night piling trash into the fire before the sun rose. Once the fire died down, Houston went to the truck and pulled out the bags.

He tossed one to Zake and said, "This is for you. By taking this cash, you understand and agree that today never happened and that Bart was never here. Got it?"

"Yep."

Handing the second bag to Bart, "Here, I think this is your usual, plus extra," he looked at Zake. "Now, take us to the Jeep."

29

Walking into the dark house, Aaron found his dad sitting motionless at the kitchen table. "What's up?" he asked.

"In all of the years that I've been married to your mom, she has always returned my calls. She never goes hours without calling me, until today. I haven't heard from her since this afternoon, have you?"

"No?"

"Hmm, now I am worried. I have called everyone and no one knows where she is. I hope she is okay." He reached for the phone, "I am going to try one more time and if there's no answer then I am going to send a patrol car to the house."

"Dad, I am sure she is fine. Maybe she fell asleep on the couch watching TV. I wouldn't worry," he said as his father listened to the ringing phone.

She answered on the second ring. "Hello."

"Where have you been?"

"I...I...I forgot my phone at the house. I went to see a movie after work. No one could go so I went by myself. It was a waste." Annissa was nervous. Being a liar was not her nature.

"I have been worried about you. I was about to call and have a squad car sent to the house." The Chief's voice was trembling

Her tone was different. Was she hiding something? He couldn't place what was wrong and asked, "What's going on?"

"Nothing,"

"Don't lie," he said calmly, although he wanted to scream.

"I'm not lying. Why would I lie? I have nothing to hide. Why did you call? Did you need something?"

He lied. "I think I am going to stay here a few days while Aaron adjusts."

"I'm fine," Aaron interrupted.

His dad held up his finger to quiet him.

"I have enjoyed spending time with Greg and I want to take my boy fishing. We've never done that."

"Baby, whatever you want is fine with me."

She was scared. He had never changed plans before and had never taken off from work unannounced. Ever. She rolled with it, speaking calmly and without fear.

He was a policeman and trained to listen to gut instincts and his said Annissa was nervous and scared. He was determined to find out why. Aaron was too young to be involved, but he already knew his parents were either in an argument or about to be. Kids always have this strange sense of knowing when their parents are having difficulties and the tensions in Dave's voice and mannerisms clued Aaron in.

Greg walked into the room. "What's going on?" He could see the blank look on Dave's face as he watched him slowly close his phone and toss it on the magazine-covered coffee table.

"I don't know, but I am going to find out. She is either in trouble, or she has done something wrong. The last time I heard her sound like that was when she thought she was pregnant."

"Dad, what are you saying?"

"She is in trouble and we need to find out why."

He knew a good private eye and that was his next call. He reached for his phone. "Greg, can you get us a boat and fishing gear for in the morning?"

"Yes."

"We going fishing, dad?"

"Yes son, we are. I have never taken you fishing, a rite of passage between a boy and his father and I feel I have failed you as a father."

Aaron had no desire to go fishing. However, he could tell his dad needed a friend, a buddy. Aaron would be his buddy, no questions asked. "Fishing? Really?" he thought. Dad hates outdoor stuff. He began to worry that something might really be wrong.

Aaron sent Bub a text: "I think Dad and I are going fishing tomorrow. Are you all?"

"Yes, at daybreak," Bub replied.

"Damn that's early."

"Yup. See you there?"

"I'll let you know," Aaron replied.

"Cool," Bub texted.

30

When Staci, Sissy and I walked into the trailer, Mom, Dad and Cosby were sitting on the couch watching a movie.

"Hey guys," Dad said, sitting there half asleep. "Whatcha kids been up too?"

"Nothin'."

"Did you see Seth? How is he?"

"Yep, sure did. But, I don't know if we will see him much this week. I guess his dad is feeling guilty and wants to spend more time with him. Seth is not sure about it all."

"Well, I think it's great!" Mom chimed in. "That boy has been without a father for too long. It's time that man stepped up to be a father." Mom was always one to lecture us about family values and a family staying together. My mom and dad were both products of divorce and were determined to give Sis and me a loving nuclear family.

"Yeah, I know Mom, but it is new to him. He is scared, but hopeful. Are we going out on the boat in the morning or bank fishing?"

"Bank. I couldn't get a pontoon until Monday. I thought we would fish around here in the morning and take it easy. Then, we can enjoy the party tomorrow night." Dad always wanted to take it slow after a day of lugging the camper and traveling.

"Cool. Think I am going to bed." I looked at the girls. "What are you all going to do?"

"Go back to the room and watch TV," Sissy said.

I walked back as they followed like two lost puppy dogs. It was tight quarters. The camper was about 30 feet long and divided into three areas: master bedroom, to the right, when you entered; the living room, kitchen and

our bedroom on the opposite end. There was a small bathroom by the kitchen, which was only used for midnight pee breaks. Dad had removed the closet cabinets in our bedroom to add a bed, and he turned the shower into storage. Our room was tiny. The door swung out, and there were bunk beds to the right when you entered, a single bed to the left and a cabinet with a small TV and space for storage in the rear. I took the top, so the girls could lie beside each other and talk without disturbing me. Even though we were all family, we were still modest, refusing to change clothes in front of each other. Sis and Staci did, but I was too embarrassed; I think it was teenage years more than anything. After all, I am a boy!

Sissy went into the bathroom to change. "Have you had any more incidents?" I asked, trying to be covert and hoping she would know what I was referring to. We were both sitting on our beds with our feet dangling, facing each other.

"No. You had any more?" She asked.

"Nope. Do you think it was just your house?"

"I don't know, it has never happened before, that I know of. I ain't never asked Mom about it."

"Anyone or anything ever died in your house? Do you think it's haunted?"

"Not that I know of, this has really got me on edge, though. I'm glad I'm with you, Bub. Before you got there today and told me, I was so scared. I never had anything like that happen to me. Thought I was going crazy." She leaned over and gave me a hug. I don't know why but I felt safer in her arms, maybe it was the teenage hormones or the fact we were going through the same issues.

"I know. I ain't scared," I lied. "We'll figure it out I'm sure." Sissy walked in and we quickly changed the subject. "You ever been fishing?" I asked Staci.

"Yeah, all the time. It's about the only thing to do where I live that don't cost no money." She looked at the linoleum-covered floor as if she was embarrassed, reached to the back of her head and pulled her ponytail out, wrapping the band around her wrist. I grabbed the remote, looking for something to watch. "That and creek swimming with the dogs."

"That sounds fun," Sissy said, crawling under her covers.

"It is." Staci said as she walked out of the tiny room to change clothes.

"You know, she is our cousin and that's illegal, what you are thinking," Sissy said.

I was shocked, "What? What are you talking about?"

"You have the hots for her."

I could feel my face flush. I tried to hide it but the damn lights were so bright there wasn't any hiding it. "That's gross!" It was all I could come up with.

"But it's true."

"Don't worry about it."

"You can't wait to see her in a bikini, can you?"

"Stop it, Sis. I mean it. Don't say a word. The last thing I need right now is one of Mom or Dad's lectures." I sat on top of her. "Got it?" I did not have the hots for my cousin. The truth was that I was intrigued by the fact that she was suffering from the same voice episodes as I had. Knowing I could not tell Sissy the truth killed me. We told each other everything, and if she knew the truth then she would go straight to Mom and Dad, then doctors would get involved. Which I had no desire for. The truth was that I wanted to see where the visions took us.

"Yeah, I got it. Now get your bony ass off of me!"

Staci reappeared. "What are you two doing?"

"She's a goober. I had to put her in her place." I left the room to change.

Staci asked Sissy, "What happened to him since last year?"

"What do you mean?"

"He is actually nice. It's weird."

"No, no he isn't. He is faking it." Sissy smiled. "Bub's only nice when he wants something. Then, when he gets it, he goes back to being a jerk again."

"OH."

"Yeah, don't let him fool you."

We heard my dad and mom returning from their nightly walk with Cosby. Mom stuck her head in the room, "You kids get some rest. You have an early morning tomorrow." She kissed each of us and tucked us in like babies.

I know we talked for a while before falling asleep. But we were so tired that I can't even remember what we talked about.

31

Mitch was sitting at his desk in their hotel room while dawn was breaking outside. Jessie was sleeping on the bed, across the room, wrapped in the sheet and curled in the fetal position. He was reviewing pages of bills, some already passed, others he was helping to write.

His phone rang, "Mitch Anderson."

"We have a problem." It was his assistant. Mitch had been in talks with the Governor of Michigan about being a possible running mate. He was a young guy and seemed to be liked by all age groups. After being in office for only two years, he had boosted the economy of Michigan and replaced the lost jobs in the car factories with new technology and oil refineries, lowering the income and sales tax.

"What?" Mitch hated hearing those words.

Alex Schaffer had worked as his assistant the majority of his career, and besides his family, Alex was his closest friend. They had grown up together, were roommates in college and godparents to each other's children. Mitch had the charisma and personality for public life, while Alex had no desire for public life and was content being a behind-the-scenes lawyer.

"There is a police chief in a town near Detroit whose wife is accusing Gabe of being involved in organized crime and meeting girls of all ages off the Internet. The press doesn't know about this yet and I think we have time to investigate. However, for now I think we need to distance ourselves from him. He has donated to all of your campaigns but, again, let's not jump to any conclusions."

"Dammit!" Mitch slammed his fist down on the table, waking his wife. "I told you I wanted good vetting before we even hinted at who we were considering. Who did the research?"

Alex did not want to answer this question, but he had no choice, "I did, I looked everywhere. Jesus, and on paper I'd nominate this guy for sainthood. There is no trace, yet. I can email you the papers."

"No. How long do we have before this gets out to the press."

"I'm not worried. A few days, maybe three? I am headed out to talk with her now."

"Okay, keep me up to date."

Mitch slammed his phone down on the desk, "Dammit."

"What's wrong, Sweetie?"

"Gabe Maddox might be dirty."

32

Jaime and Betta did not do much but talk before they went to bed. They were both exhausted from the day's travel.

Jaime slept well the first night. She was comfy, cozy and in familiar surroundings. Most kids think it is cool to live out of a suitcase and travel. This was true at first, but she did not have any girlfriends or friends besides the staff. She was lonely.

She lay in her warm bed, not wanting to get up. The sun was bright and she could hear the boats full of families and fisherman already out on the lake enjoying the Sunday. Unable to delay the day, she decided to get up, shower and dress. Her plan was to start breakfast, but Betta beat her to it. The smell of bacon and pancakes met her halfway to the kitchen.

"Good morning," Jaime said as she hugged Betta. "I wanted to make you breakfast."

"That's funny. I didn't want cold toast this morning!"

"Cold toast?"

"Yeah, white bread." Betta smiled and winked at her so she knew she was teasing.

"Ha-ha, very funny. I took Home-Ec. Well, kinda."

"Kinda?"

"Yeah, Mom and Dad have been home-schooling me, which really sucks, but Dad thought I needed some type of cooking class. So, while we were campaigning, he made me shadow a chef."

"Learn much?"

"Well, I learned how to cook gourmet food in a gourmet kitchen. But, that's not practical. The good news is that I already knew how to do the basic stuff," Jaime laughed.

"Well, that's good!"

"Yeah. So, what are we going to do today?" Jaime always asked this. It drove her parents crazy because they wanted her to learn how to entertain herself and not be reliant on other people.

"Well, there's a party tonight at the campground. It might be fun. I think there'll be kids around your age. Greg stopped by last night to make sure we got home and he invited us." Betta stood straighter as she mentioned his name. Everyone in the house knew she had a crush on him. "I think we will get Joe to take us."

"I can drive us," Jaime said proudly.

"I know you can, but I want to drink and, with you only having your permit, that's probably not a great idea."

"Can we go driving at some point?"

"Yes. Now, as far as today goes, I was thinking we could relax and have a pool day. You also need to do some homework at some point. Your dad sent me your assignments."

"Man!" Jaime rolled her eyes and sighed.

Betta laughed. She hated being put in this position, but she knew it was part of the job. Although she gave Jaime freedom with it, she still made sure the work got done. Betta put the bacon and pancakes on the table for Jaime and called Joe to see if he would drive them and invited him to come to the main house for breakfast.

Arriving a few minutes later, Joe poured himself a cup of coffee and joined them at the breakfast bar. He was retired F.B.I. who worked for the Andersons as security. Part of that gig was driving Jaime around. Jaime and he were close but not like Betta. Joe lost his wife to cancer a few years ago and was not the same afterward. He went from being loud, outgoing and outspoken to being quiet and reserved. His wife had two children from a previous marriage and he never had any children of his own. His contact with her children disappeared with the wife, leaving him to stroll the path of life alone.

"We are going to hang out here today by the pool and relax. You can join us if you are looking for something fun to do or a good excuse to get out of the house for a while. The party starts at seven-ish, so I want to leave around six, to help Greg."

"Ahh, I see. This is Greg's party," he winked at her. "Well, I think I am going to go down to the state park and play golf. I will be back around five and take you gals wherever you want."

Betta's face turned red when he made the Greg comment. She hoped it wasn't too noticeable. But, apparently it was. The two girls thanked him, finished their breakfast and started their day.

33

Thankfully, our camper had air-conditioning. Otherwise, I know Staci, Sis and Mom would not be with us. Truthfully, I don't know whether I would be here either. When Dad woke me up to go fishing, the camper felt great. However, the second we hit the outside, steam, humidity, and stickiness hit our bodies.

We gave each other questioning glances and seemed to be thinking, "Are we sure we wanted to do this?" I was doubtful about going in this weather. The thought of my cool bed was too tempting but we didn't get to fish much at home so I gladly suffered. Fishing is a special bonding time with my dad and nature. Even though our conversation is limited, there is just something about the spinning sound the reel makes when you toss a line and hear the "plop" when the bait meets the smooth water. When you hook a fish and reel it to shore, what a great feeling! It is self-gratification at its finest. For those few minutes, your fishing buddies stop what they are doing to see your catch. Early morning is the best time to fish, the lake is calm, it is a little cooler and only truly serious fisherman get up before the sun!

"Your friends coming today?"

"Seriously, I don't know." While putting rods and reels together, I could tell that Dad didn't want anyone coming with us. He never did. Dad was a man of few words and all he needed in life was us, his family.

Our gear was together and we were heading down to the bank to start fishing when I heard, "Hey man, what's going on? You gonna catch anything today?" Seth said, as he appeared from behind the camper.

"Man, I only get skunked when I fish with you. So, no, probably not," I laughed.

"Hey, Seth, how have you been pal?" Dad asked as he reached out to shake his hand.

"I'm Larry. I think we met a long time ago." He went from Seth's hand immediately to Jeff's. "Do you guys have any gear?"

"No, man. My son here didn't give me enough notice to go pick any up. This was all kinda thrown on me last minute. We don't want to intrude on your time with your son," Jeff said.

"Nah," I quickly said.

My father chimed in, "Nonsense, I don't...well, I know." Dad bobbed and cocked his head. "The girls aren't going with us. My, once-tomboy daughter has turned into a girly-girl and now thinks fishing is gross." He laughed as he walked to the spare picnic table and grabbed two extra poles. "We'll get you guys set up here. What kind of work are you doing these days?"

"Ey, still a park ranger. Five more years and I can retire." Jeff joined the park service right out of high school. It was a good stable job; the retirement and benefits were great but the pay sucked, which is why he had to sell boats at night and on his days off.

They continued on with their endless and boring adult conversation, acting as if they were really interested in each other's life.

"Dad, do we have time for me to fix some sausages?" I yelled.

"Sure, we are on vacation. There's no schedule."

Seth walked over and sat by me as I fired up our campsite stove. The camper had a stove and oven but every time we used it, smoke filled the camper, setting off the smoke detector. It just wasn't worth the effort.

"How was last night?" I asked while walking over to grab the sausages out of the camper.

"Man, I had a great night." He was smiling ear to ear.

"Went that well with your pops, huh? Hang on, I got to run inside and get the food!" I opened the door, "Hey boy," I called to Cosby, "you want to come outside with us?" I put him on his leash, grabbed the links and quickly returned to the stove. My sunglasses fogged up as I walked back outside. "This weather sucks."

"Yep."

I started cooking and watching all the other campsites get moving, "So man, what happened last night?"

Seth paused, looking at the lake as if unsure what to say. "Well, remember the girl at the diner I told you about?"

"Yeah, what was her name?"

"Samatha. We texted each other all night. She seems really sweet, nice and is the first person I have talked to that listens to me."

"Thanks man, that means a lot."

Seth cluelessly asked, "What?"

"You just implied that I don't listen to you."

"Oh," he said, laughing, "I guess I did. Sorry, Bub."

"No worries. So do you like her?"

"Yeah man, I think I do and I really didn't think I would ever hear from her again but she texted me when she got home last night and we texted all night. I'm not sure, but I think she actually lives somewhere around here."

"Really?"

"Yeah."

I shrugged my shoulders, "Why don't you invite her to the party tonight?"

"Huh?"

"The bonfire!"

"Yea, I know, the bonfire! I just, I just never asked a girl out before."

"Like I have? Look at me, girls run at the sight of me." This wasn't altogether true but it wasn't a lie. I wanted Seth to feel good about himself and boost his self-esteem.

"Man, I'm an ugly, fat kid who lives 3,000 miles away."

"Dude, if that's all she sees, you don't need her. Got it?" I was a little frustrated. He was a good kid with a big heart and, like me, wore his heart on his sleeve.

"Naw. Not like that. But, what if she says no?"

"Then she says no. You'll know sooner than later. But, dude she's not going to say no. She'd be nuts to say no." The sausages were done. "How many of these you want?"

"Ten."

"Seriously? That's all I have."

"Oh, okay, five."

I yelled, "Hey dad, how many links do you want?"

"Whatever is left after you animals get done."

"Jeff?"

"Whatever, doesn't matter," almost parroting what Dad said. "Oh, I will eat whatever is left over."

We ate quickly. Dad finished baiting all of us and we were off.

Fishing lasted only about an hour. It was hot and sticky and not fun for Dad or me. Jeff and Seth knew very little about fishing, lures, baiting hooks or really even casting, for that matter. Jeff was completely worthless. He couldn't filter hot butter through a strainer, much less bait a hook. We ended up being babysitters and yes, I did get skunked again, meaning I didn't catch a thing! One thing I did accomplish was talking Seth into asking Samantha out. I must admit I was envious. Little did I know what was about to happen.

34

Aaron and David were still sleeping when Greg left to go do his morning errands. It was an hour before sunrise and he wanted to be sure Big Jim and Tiffany opened The Lodge up. The bait shop, restaurant and general store were all housed in one building on Big Daddy's Campground. They called this building The Lodge. Greg was responsible for everything on the property. He had to be sure the office, store, restaurant and the shower houses were clean and operational, in addition to going around and picking up any trash guests may have set out. Even though he wanted to show Aaron these chores, because they will be his responsibility, David was still there so he decided father-and-son time was more important and did not wake him.

Tiffany and Big Jim had already opened The Lodge when Greg arrived. Except for an occasional day off or oversleep, they always beat Greg to The Lodge in the mornings.

"Good morning," Tiffany said, looking up from counting out her drawer.

"How are ya?" Greg smiled and waved as he headed toward the restaurant for a cup of coffee. "Hey, do we have any John boats available for this morning?" he asked as he walked out of the kitchen and over to the register. " I know all the pontoons are booked." The wall behind the register was covered in pegboard and cork, covered with clipboards, rules and regulations, state and federal posters, plus any other solicitations or flyers they did not know where to put. Big Jim grabbed the rental clipboard off its hook, "Yeah, looks like we have one left."

"Hold it for me. My brother wants to take his kid fishing."

"Your nephew, right?"

"Yeah. You ready for tonight? What do we need to get? I think the weather is going to be perfect, little humidity and cooler by sundown."

"I don't know off the top of my head, but I will look. I think we already ordered most of the food. Just might need some odds and ends. The vendors should be coming soon to set up."

They used to handle the food prep themselves but the event had grown from a simple bonfire over the years to a music festival and art show for the locals. There were even some campers who scheduled their vacation around this occasion. The goal of the event was not to make money for the campground, but to allow artists an opportunity to share their crafts in a low-cost venue. They welcomed all types of art, having a schedule for musicians and an area for crafters to set up booths.

"Okay, I need to go set up the stage. Big Jim, can you help me? I think we can knock it out pretty quickly. The sound guy will be here this afternoon. I think the kiddo karaoke starts around noon-ish. Did you pick the stage up yesterday?"

"Yes, it's in the truck. I was gonna set it up but didn't know where you wanted it."

"I think right in the middle of the pavilion." The Pavilion had green legs that supported a rusting grey metal roof and was in the middle of the camping area, surrounded by the pool and tennis courts and it was the highest point. "I don't think there are any campers in the way. If there is, we'll push them out!" he said with a big grin on his face.

He knew there was no one in the way. He had made a point before the weekend to block off the needed campsites for the festivities. Plus, the interior sites were the last to go. Every camper wanted beachfront sites, even if they cost more.

"I'll grab the truck and meet you there." Big Jim grabbed his trucker hat hanging on a nail and headed out the rear glass stormdoor, which was closest to the lake.

35

Bart had driven all night and pulled into his apartment building craving sleep. He had been thinking the entire way home from Kentucky whether he wanted to continue this life of crime. He had started right out of high school because his parents did not have enough money for him to go to college and the thought of being a working stiff for low wages was unappealing to him. Watching his parents use drugs and too much alcohol as a kid, he knew to stay away from that lifestyle. He had no means of getting a college education and his only chance at lucrative income was to sell habits to drug users. Hating to deal with the people directly and becoming closer to the suppliers, he became the invisible man. Not long after joining the game, competition and suppliers started to notice how well he was moving the product. It was really simple to sell stuff at half the market price, making less on each transaction but selling more overall. He also cut the local supplier out by traveling to Kentucky for half the price of Detroit. Everyone wanted in. He did not want to be a part of a gang or crew. He wanted to be a boss but the Detroit crime crews were too powerful. The other factions selling meth in the area saw Bart as stealing their money and believed that he had to be stopped.

There were two major dealers in Detroit and they fought for a year for his employment, neither realizing he was playing them both. He denied any knowledge of what they were talking about. After a bad deal at a bar, Bart had to kill a doped-out crackhead who pulled a knife on him and he had no choice but self-defense. It was late and in an empty parking lot, beneath the sodium lights, and he tried too quickly get the body hidden before anyone saw, but it was too late. Two of Gabe's guys saw it happen. They told him they would help him with his situation and all he had to do was meet with their boss and hear his offer.

Conceding and giving up his lifelong quest to never have leverage against him, he accepted the offer and met with them. He moved up the ranks more quickly than usual for one reason. Money. He fed the bosses money as much and as fast as he could by using his Kentucky contacts and undercutting everyone else in the market. Since he was turning such a high profit for the bosses, anything he needed, wanted, or asked for he got, with no questions asked.

Frank was Gabe's number two guy. Gabe was a popular public official who had aspirations of one day being President. There was just one problem. He was the leader of an organized family hiding behind Frank, who ran the show. The only time Gabe was involved was when someone tried to go over Frank's head. Which only happened once.

Bart had stashed money away his whole career and wanted out as soon as possible but he had to be sure he had enough to survive on because when you leave an organization you have to leave in the middle of the night with no trace. You pack your bag and money. House stays. Car stays. Everything stays but you and your money.

Frank was sitting on Bart's steps with his elbows on his knees, his hands folded and his tie dangling between his thighs. "So, where ya been? You haven't checked in lately." Frank was a slender, bald guy, with a short rim of hair that went around his head and gold glasses with brown tint. "People been looking for you."

"Oh yeah, who?"

"Doesn't matter. Where ya been?"

"On a business trip."

"Who authorized it?" Frank stood up and brushed dust off the shoulders of Bart's leather jacket. "I know I didn't. Did you, Timmy?"

"No." Timmy walked around from the side of the house.

"So who said you could leave town?"

"Since when do I need permission to leave town?" He knew to check in with the boss before heading out of town, but this time was different, he didn't care. "Who do you think you are?" He turned sideways and tried to force himself up his stairs and between Frank and his overgrown shrubs. "Damn, I should have cut these back," he thought.

Bart looked at him blankly. The insects of the summer were as loud as a chainsaw. His gun was tucked in his back waistband, hidden by his coat. The only way to access it was a noticeable, obvious reach. Leaving Frank and Timmy a shoot-first-and-ask-questions-later scenario. He was ready to make the bold move of shooting them if necessary.

"No worries. You are back now." Frank was squeezing Bart's shoulder hard. "The boss needs you. Let's go for a ride."

Frank snapped his fingers, took the keys from Bart and tossed them to Timmy. "You drive."

36

Aaron was slowly starting to wake up as he heard his dad rummaging around the kitchen and talking on the phone. Stretching his long, narrow body and looking at his surroundings, he was unable to remember where he was. He could hear the emotion in his father's voice going from sad to angry. He did not know who the conversation was with but he knew it wasn't his mother. It sounded too business-like, too official.

"Look, get your best men on this. I might be able to stall coming back one or two days, but after that I gotta get back to work. I will have my phone on me all the time. You need anything, you call. You got me?"

Dave stood there silently listening to the phone. Aaron tossed the covers off and raised up off the couch, pulling down his bunched up shorts and stood there with his arms crossed, watching his father.

"Yeah, yeah, that's covered. Just send the bill to my office." Aaron's dad hung up the phone and turned around, "How long have you been standing there?"

"I just walked in," he lied.

"Okay, you ready for a big day of fishing? I think Uncle Greg has a boat for us. I was gonna go find him and scope it out."

"I guess."

He really did not want to go.

"We don't have to go if there is something else going on that I need to know about," he paused and looked his father in the eye. "With Mom?"

David did not want to lie to his boy but he didn't know the truth himself, "Son, I don't know yet and when I do, I will tell you." He knew unless it was good news, he would not share it. However, putting Aaron's mind at ease was important.

Aaron did not want to push his dad, he did not want to be lied to and, most important, he did not want to go fishing. "Dad, I think Uncle Greg could use my help today. Do you care if I hang around here and try to make some money? I promise we will hang out tonight at the party."

"Okay, can we have breakfast together at least?"

"Sure," he smiled at his dad. "Why don't you help us? You haven't forgotten how to do manual labor, have you?"

"No, I haven't. But, I avoid it like the plague," he smiled. It was true, David didn't even like to cut the grass, and until Aaron was old enough to do it, he had always paid a neighborhood kid. Spending time with his boy and brother was important to him. So, he was glad to help.

The two were sitting in the kitchen when Greg walked in: "Hey, good. Glad you're awake. Two things: got you a boat and I need some help for a spell."

"I think we are going to pass on the fishing and just help you, if that's alright."

"Yeah, that's great. I am going to call and cancel the boat reservation."

"Sit down here, man. Eat some grub and we'll go work." Dave stood and offered Greg his chair. "What should we start on?"

"Let me eat really quick and we will all go together." He radioed Big Jim and told him he would be out there in a little bit with some help.

37

There is nothing like a long cast of a fishing pole and hearing the spin of line going out towards the water. There are two types of fisherman — those who cast and wait and those who cast non-stop. I am the latter and enjoy throwing the line out and reeling back in. Seth could probably care less about fishing. He is afraid of the hooks and does not like peeling a slimy fish off of a hook. That part is unappealing for me as well, but throwing a line and watching it sail long and far is awesome. I learned over the years to add extra weight on my line so it will carry as far as possible.

I remember that day vividly, the lake was clear with reflections of trees in the water. Bank fishing was not as much fun as boat fishing because there is too much driftwood, seaweed and people for a hook to get caught on.

Thinking is a big part of fishing. I use the time to think about my life, my family, and my friends. Seth was 10 paces away and talking. It appeared he was talking to himself because I could not hear a word he was saying. For me, this was practice until we picked up the boat tomorrow, when the real fishing began.

"So, how long you been coming up here with your family?" Jeff asked my dad, as he almost dropped his pole in the water. He was failing to hide his frustration.

"You need help with that?" Dad asked while casting another line out. "Damn, I missed my spot." He looked over at Jeff as his untucked, unbuttoned, flannel shirt flapped in the wind revealing his T-shirt. "Me and the wife have been coming here since before we were married. We always come this time of year and try to come once a year without the kiddos. This place has been good to us." Dad was smiling as he reeled in another empty line.

"Really? That's pretty cool. I like living here in the fall and spring, but the summer and winter are just miserable. The people are great though, nicest people I've ever been around."

Dad grunted as he tossed another line out "You know, you got a good boy there. Bub really likes hanging out with him."

"Seth speaks highly of Bub." Jeff leaned his rod against a tree and pulled a red bandana out of his pocket. He sighed as he wiped the sweat from his brow. "I hate the humidity."

The two men were laughing. I whistled over at Seth, "Looks like they are getting along!" I stopped walking along the shore and looked back toward him. He kept playing with his phone and I was thinking that I was the only one he texted with. I shouted, "Hey, who are you texting?" stopping and casting a line out, while waiting for Seth to catch up.

"No one," Seth said walking up and stopping. He put the phone in his pocket and fumbled with baiting the hook,

"Stop! Here, give me that," I said after watching him almost hook himself. I handed him my reel, baited and cast and took his unbaited rod and reel. "So, come on man, who are you texting with? You been doing it nonstop since you got here last night," I started laughing. "I thought I was the only person you texted with," I said, slapping him on the back of his shoulder.

He started laughing. "Hey look," he said, pointing at his bobber bouncing in the lake water.

"Man, I gave you that reel."

"It's the guy who reels it in is the guy who gets the credit," he confidently stated, laughing as he spun the reel of the bending rod. "Looks like a big one, I'm having trouble reeling it in." The line was wiggling and shaking as the pole bent toward the water.

"Yeah, yeah, but the guy who reels it in has to take it off the hook."

Seth's smile went away instantly as he pulled the mid-sized, large-mouth bass out of the water. "What?" The fish was spinning on the line as it dangled, while Seth looked at me with his mouth hanging open.

"I gotcha covered brother, I just wanted to see your reaction," I set my pole down and grabbed the spinning fish. "Do you want to keep it?"

"No."

Laughing as I released the slimy bass back into the lake, I asked, "So did you hear anymore from that Samantha chick you were telling us about last night?"

Red-faced, he said, "Yeah man, actually she don't live too far."

I interrupted. "Is she coming tonight?"

"I think so, man. She had to talk to her dad. She doesn't have to work at the diner, but she says her dad is kinda weird about her hanging around people from out of town."

"Huh, well, she'll be able to come. It'll all work out brother."

"I was hoping Aaron could join us today. But, I am sure with his dad going back home today, he will stick close and try to go home with him," Seth said, attempting to change the subject.

"He seems like he will fit in," I said, falling for the subject change.

"So, why is Staci with you?"

"Why, you got the hots for her, too?" I was giving him a hard way to go.

"Nah dude, ain't like that." His chubby cheeks turned red again.

As we continued to fish, I told him of the visions that occurred at my aunt's house and how my vision became tunneled and I saw other people and future events. "Yeah man, it was weird, my body got all tingly and I felt like I was floating."

"Really?" I don't know if he knew what else to say.

"Yep."

"So what else happened?"

Unsure how much to divulge, I said, "Man I will tell you more, but you have to promise you will not tell my Mom or Dad. I don't want to end up at a doctor or some goofy shit like that."

"Man, you know I won't tell a soul."

"I knew who Aaron was before we got here. When he walked up to me, as we were setting up camp, I recognized him immediately from a dream I had the other night."

"Dang!"

"When it happened the other night, we were at home and I didn't think much of it, but the more I think about it, my body was tingly."

Seth interrupted, "What do you mean by tingly?"

A good question and I had to think for a minute. I was puzzled and unsure how to respond. I picked up the fishing pole, baited and cast it and handed it to him. "I am thinking," I said, looking at him. "Ahh, I got it. You know how your leg feels when it goes to sleep?"

"Yeah?"

"Imagine your whole body feeling that way, your vision becoming tubular and your hearing muffled as if someone was yelling at you through a toilet paper tube."

"Wow dude, that's freaky!"

"You should be on this side. Man, your phone has gone off like the whole time we have been talking." It was my turn to change the subject.

Seth laughed, face turning red again.

"Must be Samantha if your face is turning red."

"Shut up! Has it happened again?"

"No," I lied.

Cosby started barking in the background. He went running into the lake with Dad running behind and trying to stop him.

I put my pole down and ran over to Dad and Jeff.

"Cosby, get back here!" we yelled.

"What's he see?" I inquired. Cosby was a very focused hound. When he started on scent, his nose and feet go a thousand miles an hour until he is satisfied.

"I don't know, Bub."

Cosby grabbed something, turned and headed toward shore. He scrambled up the bank and sat up tall to present his find to us. A wet sneaker dangled from his mouth.

"Hmmm, that's odd," said Dad, reaching down as Cosby released the shoe. "This is a brand new shoe. Ey, it probably fell off someone's pontoon boat."

We were all bored with bank fishing and decided to head back to camp and see what was going on. The bonfire celebration was about to start and we wanted to stick close to the camp. I was really hoping to see Jaime there. I had seen her from afar so many times before and I was determined to meet the face I dreamed about. Like it or not, Aaron and his uncle were my ticket to meeting her, I thought.

38

Before his investigation started, Chief Davis knew what his wife was up to. He had seen it too many times before. It made him sick to his stomach to think the woman he had built his life with was a cheater. The love of her husband and child meant nothing to her, Dave believed. He could see this, not in her words, but in her actions.

Aaron came out to the sticky air on the front porch. Sitting next to his dad, he could tell that Dave, deep in thought, was unaware of his presence. "Dad, are you good?"

"Yeah, Son. I'm fine. I want you to go hang with your friends today. I need to spend some time with your uncle." He patted and then rubbed his boy on the shoulder, hoping the physical contact would hold back his tears.

"Dad it's okay. I know I was wrong in the past. I want to spend time with you."

Before Aaron could finish his sentence, his dad interrupted him. "I'm not mad at you any more. I want to spend time with you too. But, today I need to spend some time with my brother. I was too hard on you on the way down here. I'm giving you the week off to hang out with the kids you met. They seem nice and, right now, I think you could help each other. Tomorrow, I am renting a pontoon boat and I am going to take all of you out for the day. Sound like a plan?"

"Yeah."

"Look at me." He pulled his son's chin to him. "I am fine. Don't worry until it is time to worry, okay?"

"Okay." Aaron wasn't stupid. He knew something was wrong but he had no clue what it was. He knew his father well enough not to challenge him. "Dad, I will be around the grounds. If you need anything, please call me."

Pipe Vision

"I will." The Chief reached in his pocket and pulled a twenty out of his wad, "Here, have fun. I love you, Boy."

"I love you too, Dad."

39

Her fear of facing Dave had kept Annissa awake most of the night. He knew that something was amiss and she could not predict what was coming next. She and Dave had always joked about her boyfriend leaving just before Dave got home from a trip, but it had always been a joke. She knew that she was losing control over the situation and panic was washing over her in waves. She loved her husband more than life. How could she have let herself hurt him this way? She regretted the conversation she had with Gabe. She did not want him killed. She wanted the man she married and to figure out how to return their relationship to its original, romantic and loving state.

As much as she loved Dave, she still could not get Gabe out of her mind. There was something about him. Maybe it was his authoritative and controlling presence. She wanted the best of both worlds and knew that Dave would never agree to her having a male friend, especially not Gabe.

She reached for the phone and dialed. Every ring seemed like an eternity, but he finally answered.

"What do you want?"

"Good morning to you too, Baby."

He interrupted her in a cold, callous voice. "Don't call me 'Baby.' We are done. You tried to blackmail me and no one blackmails me and . . . " He cleared his voice and started talking slow and clear. "I do not respond well to that. End of story."

"No, please Gabe. I am sorry."

"Too late, bitch. You made your bed, lie in it."

Pipe
Vision

"Gabe, you talk to me like that I will go to the authorities and have you served with an Emergency Protective Order. I don't want to take out an E.P.O., but…"

"You wouldn't," his voice trembled as he interrupted her. "You listen to me carefully. If you even think about getting an Emergency Protective Order or going to the cops or telling anyone, " he said, raising his voice, "anything ever again, I will put you and that little family of yours in a place you never dreamed of. You hear me, bitch?"

No one had ever spoken to her this way and she was scared. Losing control of her faculties, she hung up the phone and fell to her knees in tears and screamed, "Oh God! What have I done?" She had no choice but to confess her sin to Dave — there was no way out.

40

We passed Greg's house as we took the shoe to the campground office. Aaron yelled, "Hey, what are you guys up to?" He and his dad walked off the porch toward us.

"Look what Cosby found in the lake," I said proudly.

"It's a shoe?"

"Yeah, we are taking it to the lost and found. Dad seems to think it fell off a pontoon boat and someone might want it back."

The Chief grabbed it out of my hand, looked it over thoroughly. "I'd be surprised if anyone claims this. It has traces of blood."

"What?"

Rotating it to an upright position, the Chief pointed to the stitching near the arch of the shoe. "Right here. Probably nothing to worry about, blood in shoes is not as uncommon as you think. Take it on to the office."

Greg pulled up in the golf cart. "Hey, what are you guys up to?"

"The boys are getting ready to go goof off and I was headed out to find you."

"Hop in. I got a lot to do today."

The Chief pointed at his son. "Be good. I'm watching you!" He winked and smiled as he got in the cart.

As they pulled out, Greg asked, "How are you today?"

"Honestly, my mind is racing, I don't know what to do. My police instincts are telling me not to jump to conclusions until the evidence directs me but my human nature is taking over and pointing to the worst."

"Chill man, chill. Let's not worry until it's time to worry."

"Yeah man, easier said than done." Dave started to laugh. "The funny thing is, I gave Aaron the same advice," he said, looking at the lake over his brother's

head as they sped through the campground. "I guess I should practice what I preach, huh?"

Greg laughed with his brother. "I know, believe me, I know."

"I know that you don't like to talk about it… but, can I ask you something about your divorce?"

Greg stopped the cart. The tires squeaked. "Look man, you are my brother, right?"

"Yeah."

"You can ask me anything, but I will warn you that my case was unusual and screwed up so I don't know if it will help."

Silence overcame them. The wind was blowing off the lake, but not enough to help the stagnating heat.

Dave was pensive. He did not know where to start or what to ask first. The silence was finally broken by his nervous voice. "How, how did you know she was cheating on you?"

"In my gut. I think I always knew but wanted to fool myself into thinking that I didn't pick a cheating whore as a wife. But, that is what I did."

"How so?"

"I ignored all of the signs."

"What signs?"

"About a year before our marriage, I was out of town for work. I was selling cars at the time and had to go pick up a car for a client. This was right when cell phones came out and we were calling each other all of the time. You know how you are when you first get together… we were all googly-eyed for each other and wanted to talk on the phone all of the time."

"Yep, know all about that."

"Well, one day I was on the road and I was passing through a big city where I knew we could talk for a while without cell coverage dropping but there was no answer. I tried and tried."

"How long was it before you got a hold of her?"

"Three hours."

"Three hours?"

"Yeah, when I finally did get a hold of her she had…." Greg paused. His eyes stared into empty space as he sat there.

"Are you okay?"

"Yeah, sorry. When I did talk to her, her voice was different."

"Different?"

"Yeah." Greg turned to his brother. "You know how you talk to someone who has just had sex and his or her voice is different? Relaxed?"

"Yeah, I know what you're talking about."

"It was a three-day fight. Her side was that I invaded her privacy because I asked her friends where she was and talked to them about how I didn't trust her, blah, blah, blah."

"Obviously, you ended up believing her."

"It took some convincing. I didn't tell you about this when it was happening because I knew you'd tell me that I didn't have to marry her. We got along great and had so much fun together. When I got home from that trip, I sat her down and pretty much laid down the law. I told her that if she wanted an open relationship then she had to find someone else; I wasn't the man for her. She swore to me that she was not that type of person and she knew how it felt to be cheated on and would never do that to anyone. I fell for it hook, line and sinker."

"I think anyone would have. So, you went ahead and got married?"

"Yeah, and God only knows who I forfeited for that bitch."

"You were only married for five years, right?" said Dave, verifying his thoughts.

"Yes."

The Chief sat there silently digesting the conversation and really had only one question: "If you had doubts before you married, why did you?"

Folding his hands on the steering wheel and using it as a support for his chin as he leaned forward, he sat there in deep thought, mustering up the right words.

Reading his brother's body language, Dave offered, "Man, it's cool if you don't want to talk about this."

"No, no, it isn't that. The truth is, I never really thought about it. We were in love, got along great and had the same interests. We cared about each other and were living together so it made sense."

"Would you have done it again?"

"In a heartbeat man, in a heartbeat. We just hit a lull and instead of talking to me about it, she went looking and I couldn't live with the doubt for the rest of my life."

"Doubt?"

"The trust issues, was she really going to see her parents overnight or was she going to have a fling in a hotel room."

"That is the hardest thing, I am told, about recovering from infidelity," Dave said, patting his brother on the back as he leaned back up.

"Yeah, so I hear." Greg started the cart again. They headed toward the office. "They say love is blind but, the truth is, love causes stupidity...dame bramage."

"What the hell is dame bramage?"

Greg laughed. "It's when you know the right decision to make, but since there's a girl involved, you completely disregard your common sense."

"I wouldn't go that far, but you're close. The marriage overall was good though, right?"

"For years, until one day." They pulled up to the office and Greg got out and walked around to the front of the golf cart. "One day we had an extra ticket to see a Broadway show... '42nd Street' I think it was. She and I loved going to the travelling shows that would take Broadway shows to other cities. We had season tickets to the series in Paducah. Anyway . . . " He paused. Dave hopped out of the cart and walked over to him. "We had an extra ticket and she had a friend who was in town and going through a divorce. The story was that they had run into each other at the store that afternoon. She offered the ticket to him. I am a trusting person. Why would my wife, the woman I loved, hurt me? Boy, I was wrong."

"She took him on a date with you?" Dave asked in a puzzled voice.

"Yeah, and I believed her until the end of the night. Then, I knew something was screwy."

"How so?"

"You know when you run into someone from your past there are always stories about the past? I call them, 'Hey, remember when,' stories. Well, there were none of those."

"Okay, that makes sense. What did you do?"

The two walked into the back of The Lodge. Greg started pulling stuff together for the events of the day. He started throwing boxes around. His hidden rage was starting to escape through his actions. He did not like talking about this to anyone but he knew his brother needed help.

"I learned a long time ago that you never show your cards. So, for the next week or so I went on like there was nothing wrong, but I hired a friend of mine to follow her around. My suspicions were right. She was having an affair and, no, they did not go to high school together. He was a silk-suit thug named Bart something."

"Holy shit, what did you do?"

"Protected myself. The day after I found out about it, I approached her. I asked her if she was having an affair. One of my cards was, if she was honest and told me that she was having an affair, I was prepared to fight for my marriage. I was ready to go to counseling, or whatever it took. Instead, she denied it and started a fight. She told me she was going to her mother's. I knew she was lying. I followed her and she went to his place and left me alone."

"What did you do?" The Chief took a box from his brother, grabbed his shoulder and motioned over to a chair. "C'mon, let's sit down for a minute."

"This is useless. I've never told anyone this before."

"No, it's helpful for both of us. Please continue."

"I.....I don't know." Greg sat there. "The days after that were a blur of fighting and yelling. It was over."

Again, silence overcame them. They were both gripped by sadness, Greg from his past, Dave for his future. Dave knew what his future was...there was no denying it. Once the suspicion of cheating enters a relationship, the damage is done.

"His name was Bart and I can still see his face as clear as day. I tried not to let it bother me too much. But, once I found out he was living in the house I was paying for and sleeping in my bed, my hatred toward him swelled. What was more painful about it was when we were talking about maybe reconciling, he would not back off. A gentleman he is not. He broke up my family."

"Man, I am sorry. I didn't mean to go into your divorce this deep. I now understand why you kept it to yourself so long."

"All of this is important because once trust is gone, it's gone. Gone. You tell her nothing about your life. If there is anything in that house you need, have someone get it out today."

"Well, I am still not sure what's going on."

Greg looked at his brother, "Plan for the worst, hope for the best. You're taken care of and right now I'm the only friend you've got. So let's call a private detective and prove your suspicions wrong."

"Okay, you're right. I know there is more to your story and I would like to hear it if that's okay?" The Chief did not want to pry too much, but at the same time, he knew it would help his brother to talk about it. While the two men finished getting supplies needed for the bonfire and walking back to the office, he could not help but ask himself why he had let time get between him and his brother. There had been no falling out. They just grew apart.

They would never get that time back.

41

Sis and Staci were at the pool hanging out, when Dad, Seth and I returned from the office. Cosby bolted through the door as it opened and jumped up on the couch, panting.

We saw the look on Mom's face and tried to get back outside before she could speak, but Dad was the only one who made it out. "You know, I am not going to spend the rest of this week cleaning up after you guys."

I looked at Seth and raised my eyebrows, silently saying, "Come on! Help a brother out!"

It was my mess and I did not want Dad to take the heat, "I know, Mom. I'm sorry we took off. I planned on cleaning it up. I'll take care of the dishes tonight." I knew we would be eating dinner at the bonfire tonight and Sis and Staci would be stuck having to do tomorrow's dishes.

Mom ignored my comment and asked, "How was fishing?"

Knowing he was off the hook for leaving a mess after breakfast, because Mom blamed me, Dad came back into the camper followed by Sis and Staci. The girls were dripping wet and shaking from the chill of the air-conditioner. Dad told Mom about our day. Sis and Seth were sitting on the couch and were facing Mom and Dad, who were standing in the kitchen, being nosey.

I decided to take the opportunity to talk to Staci and see if she had heard any more voices. When she popped out of the bathroom after changing from her swimsuit to jean shorts and a white T-shirt, I followed her into the bedroom. She was lying on the bed flipping through channels with nothing sparking her interest. "Have you seen or heard any more?" I asked, looking at the speeding channels on the TV.

"Nope, I sure haven't," she rolled over on her stomach and rested on her elbows with her fingers crossed. "You?"

"No, but Cosby found a shoe in the lake while we were fishing and Aaron's dad said it looked like there was blood on it. I don't know if he was being serious or if he was playing around trying to scare us."

"He was probably just trying to scare you."

Sis came into the room as I left to head back outside to see if I could find any more of our crew. The sun was beating down. Fishing was over for the day and that meant we could do what ever we want. Feeling like I was melting, I wanted to swim. Seth was right behind me, looking for anything to do other than go sit at Jeff's house alone. His dad left for work right after fishing, so the house was empty.

Seth was shy and a follower. Fortunately, he always followed the right people and did not get into too much trouble.

"What do you think, man?"

"What do you mean?"

"Do you think there's a body out there?"

"Huh?" I really didn't need to say the "huh," but I wanted him to think I wasn't thinking the same as him. Truth is, I had been thinking about nothing else and had already imagined what it would be like to find the body. I had never seen a dead body outside a funeral home, much less a drowned or murdered body. I thought about how neat it would be, forgetting that if it was a real body, it was a member of someone's family.

"Don't be stupid." He grabbed my arm and flipped me toward him. "Do you think there's a body out there? Should we go look?"

"Man, you can if you want to, but I'm going swimming." Yes, I was playing it cool. I did want to go look for the body, hell yes. But, I also have seen enough cop shows to know the ones who find the body go through the ringer first and, to be honest, a dip in the pool sounded a lot better than searching for something that probably existed only in our imagination.

"Come on man, think about it," Seth said, grabbing my shoulder. "If we found that body, we would be famous! They might even put us on TV and shit like that." He looked at me and when I did not respond right away said, "C'mon Bub, think about it."

I shook my head. "No dude, that's just a bad idea, man. It's the second day of our vacation and all I need to do is piss Mom and Dad off and ruin this vacation."

"How would they find out?"

Before I could answer Aaron walked up, "Hey, what's up?"

I looked at Aaron, "Genius here wants to go look for the body. What do you think?"

"There ain't no body out there. That shoe fell off a boat. We'd do better looking for the other shoe because that's all we're gonna find."

"Hey…" Seth had a gleam in his eye as he looked at Aaron.

"No, Seth. Don't say it." I knew exactly what he was thinking.

Aaron looked at me puzzled, "What?" He looked at me and pointed his finger at Seth. "Umm, what's this guy thinking?"

"Don't Seth."

"Your uncle has keys to all of the boat rentals, doesn't he?"

"Dammit, Seth."

Aaron looked dumbfounded. "Yeah, so?"

"Why don't you go steal us some keys and we'll go look for ourselves."

"Man, I came down here to stay out of trouble not get into more." Aaron couldn't fool me. He wanted to steal a boat as badly as Seth. I, for that matter, wasn't about to be a co-conspirator to theft. I saw Sissy and Staci walking towards us from the trailer. If there were a sure way for us to get caught, it was to let Sissy know. She loved to squeal to Mom and Dad about these things just to witness Dad going ballistic on me!

The girls caught up to us and before I could stop Seth, I heard, "Hey we are going to look for the body that goes with the shoe. You all in?"

"Yeah!" they said together.

Before I knew what happened, Aaron took over the conversation. "So guys, here's the plan." He seemed to like being a leader of mischief. We walked toward the pool and Aaron continued, nervously looking around. "I have to help my uncle until after lunch. While I'm in the office, I'll get keys to a boat. When everyone is at the bonfire, we will go out and look, okay? Tell no one of our plan. It is a pact between the five of us. You got that, girls? If any adult hears about this, we are doomed." He looked at all of us and put his hand out. "Deal?"

Seth was second on the pile. "Deal!"

The girls followed and I, reluctantly, was on the top of the pile.

"Deal."

42

Dave and Greg were doing the mundane task of setting up speakers and lights for the afternoon karaoke session. Dave had just positioned a 50-pound speaker for Greg to mount when his phone rang. There was no way he could answer it. Out of the corner of his eye, he saw Aaron with his friends and hollered for his assistance: "Son, grab my phone and answer it for me."

Aaron reached into his pocket and grabbed the ringing, vibrating phone and flipped it open, "Hello?" He paused as he waited for a voice on the other end to take over, "Hey, Mama!"

"Hi Baby!" Annissa quickly switched to mommy tone. "Are you having fun?"

"Yes, Mama. Dad and I had some rough patches on the way down here but, well, umm . . . "

"What Sweetie?"

"Everyone down here is so nice that it is hard to have the same attitude that I had there, if that makes any sense... I mean, I tried to not like Uncle Greg and give him an attitude but he just gave one right back. I know I haven't been here long, but it seems like it's easier to be nice here than to be tough."

This was more than Aaron had talked to her since she could remember and she loved it. This new Aaron made her almost forget about her behavior but she quickly remembered the heartache that she was about to cause. "I see. It's amazing how Dad and I have been telling you this all along, huh?

"Yeah, Mama. I know and I'm sorry. I see those kids at school and it's two choices: thug or geek. Down here, people are just people and I want to be an individual. I have met a good group of friends and we get along good but they are only here for a week. So, I don't know what I'll do the rest of the summer. Probably just hang out with Uncle Greg and work."

Her voice started to crack with sadness as she spoke. "I am sure you'll find something to do. I just want you to stay out of trouble and listen to your uncle. Your dad and I are very proud of you, but at the same time we worry about you. We want nothing but the best for you. However, you have to want it too. Okay?"

She could sense him rolling his eyes through the phone. "Yes Mama, I will try. I promise."

"Okay Baby, is your dad around?"

"Yeah. He's helping Uncle Greg," he walked over to where Dave was standing. "Dad, it is Mom. Let me take over for you."

Dave's brow was dripping with sweat and his shirt was soaked. "We're almost done here. See if I can call her back in a few minutes."

"Mama, can he call you back?"

"Yes, tell him it's important and not to forget about me."

"Okay, love you." Aaron snapped the phone shut before she could answer.

"Well, I guess we still need to work on phone etiquette. Now the waiting begins." she exited the kitchen and went into the family room and sat in a meditative silence. The room was warm. They had spent many nights as a family in this room and her words to Gabe the night before had stung her until she wept. How could she say such things about the man she loved? The silence was too much for her to handle and she prayed the phone would ring soon.

Dave finished helping his brother. "How did Mom sound?" He really did not care what the answer was, but wanted to seem interested. He was not sure if Aaron knew the situation, but he knew kids were not dumb or immune to adult conversation code.

"She was good. I guess she sounded fine."

From his past interviews of wives who cheated, he knew how to find guilt, and he could smell it. He was not sure how to forgive her but knew he wanted what was best for his family. He had come close to cheating on Annissa once, but when it came time, he chickened out.

He knew he did not want to be around his son or brother when he called her, "Hey Greg, is your house open?"

Greg was fumbling around with the D.J. "Yeah, it is."

Dave looked at his son. "Okay, I am going to run out for a while. You stay here, I'll be back."

Nervous shakes overcame him. By the time he left Aaron, he was almost in tears. He wondered, what did he do wrong? Why was this happening to him? He tried to keep himself from speculation, but in his heart he knew. He couldn't help but think, "Oh my God what if she leaves me? But, if she did do it, do I want to be married to a cheater?" All were valid questions and all needed answers. For years, they had shared this life together. Maybe they had not paid as much attention to each other as they were supposed to, but right now that did not matter. What mattered was seeking the truth.

His feelings had changed overnight. Last night, he wanted to be a sleuth and find out what was going on by using a private detective. Now, he just wanted to talk to his wife and get her story. Any good cop knows you get a story first, then you try to find holes. Right now, all he had was hours without a phone call and a different-sounding voice. Guilt at this time was possible and probable but not founded.

His phone was ringing as he walked through Greg's door. "Hello?"

She could not wait for his call any longer. He longed to talk to her, but was unprepared.

"It's me," her voice had a whimper behind it. "Can you talk to me?"

"Yeah, can you give me a few minutes? I want to get out of here away from Aaron and Greg. I am sweaty right now and want to take a quick shower. When I get done, I will leave and go someplace where I can talk without ears around."

"Okay, Babe, I understand but please call me."

"I will," his voice was cold and direct.

"I… I love you," she said, unseen tears streaming down her face.

Dave wasn't sure how to answer other than in the same way. "I love you, too." He closed the phone and as he turned on the shower he called his office and talked to his deputy.

"Hey, it's Chief Davis. Do we have any extra cars?"

"Yeah."

"Put one on my house. She goes anywhere or has any visitors I want to know about it. You understand? Unmarked and plain clothes."

The Deputy's voice tightened. "Yes sir, what's this about? Are you okay?"

"I am fine. Oh, how hard is it to pull GPS locations on a cell phone?"

"Not hard but it takes a warrant."

"Texts the same way?"

"Yes."

"You have any friends at the phone company?"

"Yes, what's this about?"

"Right now, the less you know the better, okay?"

"Okay. I will work on this for you."

"No emails or texts. You call me directly. Anyone asks you anything, you play stupid. If they ask you why my house is being watched, you say Aaron

Pipe Vision

has had some trouble and with me being away, YOU wanted to be sure my wife was safe."

"Yes sir, I just need some phone numbers."

"Okay, 456-555-0099."

"Got it. I will let you know."

"Thanks. I'll be in touch, the code word for this is 'golf cart.' Got it?"

"Yes, sir."

The chief snapped his phone shut, hopped in the shower and deliberated on questions to ask his wife. He dressed quickly and grabbed his gun, police department shield, phone and keys. He was puzzled about what his future held.

43

Big Jim recognized the shoe in the lost and found and his face flushed immediately. He knew Zake and Mollie from town. Zake and he were close at one time but once Zake moved to the woods and starting polluting the bodies of Trigg County with drugs, Jim wanted no part. He had talked to Paul about it occasionally, but Paul would blow him off saying that unless they caught them in the act, there was nothing he could do. Saying, "They are just too smart, man. I can't catch them in the act." Jim always wondered when he heard this answer. It sounded too rehearsed.

Returning to the store from the private office, Big Jim held up the shoe to Tiffany. "Where did this come from?"

His mom looked away from her customer briefly to see what he was talking about. "Oh, that. One of the camper's dogs found that in the lake."

He did not let her finish. "Who and where?"

"I don't know. I think Greg found it. Why? What's the big deal?"

"I am going to see Greg. Call me on the radio if you need me." He put the shoe in a Ziploc bag and grabbed a radio. He looked at his mom as he threw the glass door open. "I hope my gut is wrong about this." He ran up the landing and yelled Greg's name on the radio to find him.

"Who found this?" he asked Greg, after tracking him down at the pool. "I need to know."

"Why? What's the big deal?" Greg was puzzled at Jim's inquiries about a dumb shoe.

"Yeah, yeah. Just tell me who. It's important."

"Bub's dad, umm, Larry. He found it. My brother said it looked like it had blood on it. I didn't think it was a big deal. We find shit like that all the time in the lake."

"Look at the shoe."

"I don't get it," Greg pulled the shoe out of the bag. "Okay, it's a left shoe," he examined the shoe carefully, turned it over and looked at the sole, "Oh shit, c'mon."

"Yeah, you get it now?"

He look over at Big Jim, "C'mon, we need to find Larry and see exactly where they found this."

Dad and Mom were sitting under the awning, talking and thumbing through magazines when Jim and Greg walked up. Dad rose when they approached and reached out his hand, "Hey Greg, how are you doing?"

"Good. I'm sorry to bother you, but I need to know more about this shoe. Where did you find it?"

"Well, we were over in the cove," he pointed to the left side of the camper, facing the lake. "The damn dog took off running into the lake. I couldn't stop him. He swam out into the middle of the cove, grabbed it and swam back. I didn't think the dog had it in him. I hadn't seen him move like that since he was a pup."

"Can you walk us over there?" He looked over at Mom. "Do you mind if we steal your husband for a while, ma'am?"

"Mind? No, please do, I could use the quiet time." She was smiling as Dad bent down to kiss her goodbye.

The three of them started to walk toward where we were fishing and Dad asked, "What the hell is this about?"

"We don't know, but I think that shoe belongs to the girlfriend of a known, local drug dealer, but I'm not one hundred percent sure."

"Huh?" Dad was puzzled.

"Meth is big down here."

"It's big everywhere," Dad replied.

"Yeah, but down here we have a big manufacturer of it and no one can prove how he gets his stuff or what he does with the product. That shoe, based on the wear of the sole, looks like it belonged to his girlfriend. I could be wrong, but I wanted to investigate before we went further."

Dad stopped walking, looked at Greg and Big Jim, puzzled, "The sole?"

"Yep." Greg flipped the shoe bottom up and pointed at the top left. "See this wear pattern on the center where the big toe is?"

"Yes, it looks like someone who drags their foot."

"Yep and there is only one person who does that in these parts and she is the girlfriend of a known drug dealer."

Dad was bewildered, "Sounds like a job for the police."

Dad was cut short by Big Jim's laughter. "Boy, down here the police are poor. They look for other ways to get paid. We can't go to them until we are sure, and even then it will be hard 'cause everyone knows everyone and is related some way or another. See, Greg and my family aren't locals by birth. So we are always the first ones they suspect. When I saw the shoe, I knew we needed to try to dig up the story. If a body showed up on these grounds, we would be tried, convicted and in jail before we knew what hit us."

"I knew it was a good ol' boy club, but I had no idea it was this bad."

Greg looked at Dad, "Yeah, it's like a bad cop movie on steroids. So, you were about here and the dog went in? How far did he swim out?"

Dad was trying to think of a good frame of reference, to give them an idea where Cosby found the shoe. He pointed to our camper, which was visible from where they were standing. "Okay, if you were to walk out the front door of my camper, walk straight and swim, and Jim were to start swimming from here, where you would meet is about where the shoe was. Does that make sense?"

Greg followed his finger from the trailer to straight out. "Okay, I got it." He looked over at Big Jim, "What do you think? Should we tell Paul about this?"

"Hell, no. I think we should ride out to the clubhouse and have a look-see."

"I agree," Greg said as they started walking back to the trailer. "I think we should go check out Zake's place."

"Yeah, sooner than later," Big Jim said.

"I'm coming with you," Dad stated. "We can take my truck. No one around these parts knows it."

Greg stopped walking, and turned to Dad. "Larry, I don't think I can let you do this. I don't want you to get into trouble. You have a family and these guys could make you a scapegoat. I don't want that."

"The way I see it, you have no choice. I can corroborate your story if they try anything. Honestly, I do not think this is a big deal. I think you two are paranoid about nothing. It's just a shoe."

They continued walking. "I hope you're correct, but there's a lot of folks around here that want us shut down. They feel cheated that an outsider is buying Big Daddy's Campground. Yeah, it sounds stupid I know but it's the reality of it all."

"Not really, that gives them motive."

"What are you boys up to?" Mom asked, as we all met back at the trailer. Seth had sent me a text saying he was on his way over from his dad's to hang out. Aaron and I left the girls at the pool when we saw Dad, Greg and Big Jim walking back to the camper.

Me, being the meddlesome person I am, asked, "Dad, what are you all up to?"

"Greg and Big Jim need me to take them somewhere. I have to get my keys. I'll be right back."

Dad went inside and grabbed his keys and his pistol, just in case, although he never really went anywhere without it.

As he came down the steps of the trailer, he looked at Mom. "We shouldn't be gone too long. If you need me, I will have my cell. Do you need anything while I am out, Babe?"

"No Baby, just hurry back." She stood and kissed him.

We all started walking to the truck, "Just where do you think you are going?"

Greg asked Aaron the same.

"Stay here," Dad commanded.

I wasn't used to my dad not letting me go with him. I tried to argue but got nowhere. They were in the truck and gone before I could persuade him to let us go.

"Mom, what's that about?" I pointed toward the truck.

"I don't know, Baby. Your dad will tell us all about it when he gets back. Now, go play."

"Yes, ma'am." There was no point in arguing.

44

"C'mon, girl! We need to go!" Betta was excited about her day with Greg. It was not a formal date but, for her, it was close enough.

"Okay! Okay!" Jaime yelled down from her room. "I will be right down." She hoped there would be kids her age to hang with. She missed having girls her own age to talk to. She did not know anyone who lived around here. Usually, she spent her time alone or with her family. The few friends she had envied her. Most of them had siblings and never had any time to themselves. Having her solitude time was a dream to them. "Here I come," she announced as she skipped down the stairs.

Betta was in the foyer. "Aww! Don't you look cute?" Jaime was wearing jeans and a simple white T-shirt. She did not feel cute, but took Betta's word for it.

As they were talking, Joe popped in. "You gals ready?"

Even Joe was dressed casually. He usually wore suits and ties when he drove them, but today he was wearing shorts. Betta was impressed with his casual wear.

"Did you play golf this morning, Joe?" Betta asked.

"No, that was my plan, but after that wonderful breakfast this morning, I plopped in front of my TV and fell asleep. I decided to rest up for tonight. I think it's going to be fun."

"I agree, but we are depending on you to get us home safely." Betta laughed, knowing Joe never drank. "Have you spoken to your parents today, Sweetie?" She asked, running her fingers through Jaime's silky blonde hair.

"No, not yet. Maybe I better give them a call before we go."

"Yeah, that might be a good idea. Careful what you tell them about where you are going tonight. You know how they are about you being in public."

"Yep, I know," Jaime said as she pulled out her phone, dialed her mom and waited for an answer.

"Hi Sweeties," her mom bubbled on the phone. "How are you today?"

"I am great, Mama. Thanks for letting me come. Betta and I are having so much fun. We are going to cook out tonight and enjoy the lake."

She thought that by saying they were cooking out, then she wasn't lying to her mother, but she knew she wasn't being completely honest. It wasn't a good practice, but she wanted to have one day in her life when she felt like a normal kid, whatever that was.

"That sounds like fun! You need to relax, but don't forget about your studies. I want you to get into a good school."

"Yeah Mom, I know." It was always the same conversation with her mom and it got old. Jaime made the best of it. It was easier to agree with her and end the conversation than it was to fight it. She quickly tried to change the subject. "Where are you guys?"

"Dad has to go see a guy up by Detroit. So, we are headed to the airport in Chicago. Would you like to talk to him?"

"Yes."

Jessie handed the phone to her husband. He was on his cell phone but immediately ended his call to talk to his daughter. "Hi, Babe." His voice was tight, his stressful voice.

"Hi Daddy, what's wrong?"

"Oh, nothing, Baby. Same old stuff that you don't need to worry about. What's on your agenda for today?"

She told her father the same story as she had told her mom and her dad didn't give her any jazz about school. They spoke briefly about their day, and then he had to cut the conversation short because they were pulling into the airport. He told his daughter he loved her, to be safe, and that they would talk tomorrow.

She ended the call, and looked at Joe and Betta who were patiently waiting, "Let's go!" She raced out the door and to the car. They followed.

Jaime got to the front walk and looked at the vehicle. It wasn't their usual car, but a green Chevy SUV instead. They would be taking Joe's car. "What's this?" Jaime inquired.

"Well, I figured since you wanted to blend in, it probably wasn't a good idea to take the Town Car."

"Yeah, good point, Joe," Jaime laughed.

They were off to have a fun day with no reality. The public life was on hold, temporarily and they were getting to be regular folks, or so they thought.

45

It was already 1 P.M. and Annissa was no closer to clearing up her problem, the person she loathed the night before she couldn't wait to hear from. There was a path worn through the house from her pacing and her stomach was empty. The thought of eating made her ill. "Why won't he call me?" she kept saying to herself. She had sinned and wanted to correct her error.

Dave Davis knew he had to call her, but his body shook with anxious nerves. He was sickened by the thought of another man caressing his wife. Knowing he couldn't put off the inevitable, he pulled into the welcome center at the Land Between the Lakes state park. He was parked cockeyed in the lot closest to the road.

He dug into his pocket and pulled out his cell phone. Flipping it open, he saw a text waiting for him: "please call me." It was from his wife. His body trembled as he dialed the number and waited for an answer.

The phone rang half a ring and "H…hello," came through the earpiece.

"Annissa, what the hell is going on?"

"David, please don't be mad at me. I've made a mistake and had an affair."

His voice tightened with anger, "A mistake? A mistake? A mistake is accidently buying two percent instead of skim milk."

There was a tearful silence.

"How could you do this to our family?"

"I don't know, I guess I was missing something, or so I thought, but I was wrong and I am sorry. I hope you will find it in your heart to forgive me."

Dave was silent as tears filled his eyes and then they began streaming down his cheek. He was experiencing pain that he had never dreamed. He wanted to

scream, yell and curse at his wife but he could not get his lips to move or voice to speak. He just wanted to hang up on her.

Lost in his thoughts, he heard, "Hon, are you there?"

All he could muster was, "Yes."

After several minutes of thought and meditation to calm down, all Dave could ask was, "Who?"

He knew, whoever it was, the first thing he was going to do was pull his sheet. One of the benefits of being a cop was that, no matter who you met, you could do a quick background check and have the upper hand. He never dreamed it would be the name that he was about to hear.

"It's Gabe Maddox."

"The Governor?"

"Yes."

Talk about Governor Maddox's true profession remained unspoken. Thanks to the press, he was portrayed as a squeaky-clean businessman who served blue-collar workers and was a self-made millionaire. The reality was that he was a crook. He was a slick crook with New York mafia ties. Chief Davis had secretly tried to blow the whistle on the Governor but could never find enough evidence to go public. A scandal like this was what he had been waiting for so that he could turn his guys loose, but he did not want his family involved.

He sat there thinking.

"Babe?"

"What?" His voice was sharp and shrill.

"Your silence is more than I can take right now. Please talk to me. I am scared. Gabe has turned nasty and threatened our lives. He told me that if I went public, you could kiss your job goodbye and he would appoint a special prosecutor to investigate your office. I do not know what to do."

"How did this happen? Where did you meet him?"

"Why? What does that matter?" She was confused.

He knew Gabe did not like him and was wondering if his wife was used as a pawn to get him gone. Dave, over the years as chief, had started many initiatives to clean up his office. He had weeded out the local politicians and even some state ones. He made several enemies and avoided threats. This concerned him.

"It matters. Gabe hates me and I am wondering if he seduced you to get to you to try to blackmail me. I have done nothing wrong."

"That's right, you have done nothing wrong and you are reading too much into this. I can't believe you are more worried about your damn career than our marriage right now. I have been up all night worried about our marriage. I haven't slept. I haven't eaten. Yeah, I know I did this to myself, but dammit show me that you care about us. Everything that we have right now is meaningless without your love."

He heard her. He still loved her, but some things in life are unforgivable. Right now, he wanted to forget all of this. He wanted the life they had before learning about this affair. Would that ever happen? Could it? He didn't know, time would tell.

Not realizing how long it had been since he spoke, he heard her say, "Are you there?"

"Yes, I am. I was thinking."

"About?"

"Whether or not we can overcome this."

"That's the second question. The first question is do we want to overcome this?"

"Is he the only one? Ever?"

"Yes, I swear."

"How long and how many times?"

"Dave, baby, don't put yourself through this. I will tell you if it's that important to you, but I don't think it matters at this point in time."

He disagreed but did not want to push the issue right now, knowing this couldn't be solved today. He decided to change the subject: "Aaron cannot, and will not, know about this. When I get back I want to go to therapy and get help."

"That's fine." Her voice was filled with sad joy. All she could do was pray.

"When's the last time you spoke to him?"

"This morning. I told him I was going to tell you and he wasn't very happy."

"Did he threaten you?"

"No, just called me a bitch. It didn't bother me. I want nothing more to do with him."

"He will be back, I promise you. What are his numbers?"

"Dave, no."

"No?"

"Baby, what good is it going to do for you to call him?"

"Call him? That's the last motherfucking thing I want to do. I'm not going to call that no good, piece of shit."

In so many years of marriage, she had only heard him curse a few times. He just didn't practice it in everyday language. "Why do you need his numbers then?"

"So I can block him from calling, Annissa. You could not have picked a worse man to have an affair with. He has lots of affairs and the women tend to disappear when he is finished. Now, I wasn't going to tell you this. However, you were honest with me. I have assigned a car to follow and attempt to catch you but since you

told me the truth and I know who it is, protecting your safety is more important."
He had mixed feelings, but he knew Gabe. He knew his behavior well.

"Am I in danger?"

"I don't think so, but we are going to take precautions."

She agreed and gave him the numbers.

"I will be in contact," he said. "Don't tell anyone, and I mean no one, about this."

"Yes Baby, I won't. David, I am so sorry and I love you so much. I hope one day you will forgive me."

"Have you? It's important?"

"Have I what?"

He felt like he was in a sitcom. She was never this ditzy, so he knew her pain was not an act. "Told anyone?"

"Oh, no. I swear."

"I don't care, I just need to protect any and everyone who might know."

"I love you," she broke down.

He did not respond to her. He slowly closed his phone and drove out of the lot.

"Son of a bitch." This was a feeling he never wanted. He remembered a friend, one time, who told him to embrace any problem that came his way, because God would steer him with wisdom. If he disregarded the problem, it would fester and grow. It was hard, he knew, but it was the right path.

He grabbed his phone off the console and dialed Don Becker, it rang several times before a bubbly voice said, "Hello."

"Don, please."

"May I ask who is calling?"

"Chief Davis."

She did not respond and the phone started ringing. "Hello," Don answered on the third ring.

"Don, Dave Davis here, we spoke last night."

"Yeah, I'm sorry. I haven't started on your case, yet. I am waiting on some background paperwork to come through."

"Don, don't worry about it. Something has come up and I had to bring in the authorities. I'm sorry I troubled you."

"No trouble, if I can be of help then call me back."

"I will." Not in the mood for small talk, he snapped his phone shut and called his office. His only reason for hiring a private detective was to know whom his wife was banging and to get dirt. Since it was the Governor, he now had all the dirt he needed and was going to use it to his advantage.

"Deputy Samuels, please. It's the Chief."

"Yes sir, putting you through now," the desk sergeant was a quiet guy and went out of his way to avoid a conversation.

"Samuels," said the desk sergeant, but before he could say any more he heard numerous pops under his seat. "What the hell?"

All of the uniforms were around his desk laughing and pointing at his reddened face. Someone had pranked him and put a bag of Christmas ornaments on his seat, covering them with his cushion. They shattered when he plopped his fat ass in the chair. They were always playing tricks on each other and the Chief was just as bad. He was laughing, as Samuels was riding out the guys for the prank. "Great! Now I am going to be picking glass out of my ass. Yeah, yeah, Samuels here."

"They get you again?"

He recognized the voice, "Damn, you had to hear that didn't you, sir." Chief and Samuels were close and gave each other a hard time off the clock, but during work, Samuels was all business.

"Yep, sure did. Go into my office and shut the door." Samuels agreed and put the Chief on hold.

"You there?"

A minute had not passed. "Yeah." Dave spilled his guts to Samuels, telling him everything his wife had said while holding back emotion. "Now, I need you to keep doing what we talked about this morning plus a couple more things. Oh yeah, I left out a critical detail. The guy, guess who?"

"Yeah, I was wondering if you were going to give me a name so I could pull a sheet and see what kind of warrants he had. I'd love to pop the guy and rough him a little before putting him in the pen."

"Slow down, we will get there, just guess."

"Fuck man, I got no clue. Um…um…Gabe Maddox."

"How the hell do you know that?"

"What the fuck? I was right?"

"Yes."

"Jesus." He took a sip of coffee that had been there since before the Chief had left. "Oh God." His face shriveled in distaste.

"What?"

"Nothing, what are you going to do?"

"Protect her. Nail him."

46

The three men drove the rest of the night, arriving in Detroit around daybreak. Bart had been traveling for close to 24 hours and he needed a shower and a hot meal.

"Where are we going?"

"The boss wants you to take care of something?"

Bart knew what this meant, which is why he wanted out. This life, although lucrative, was dangerous. Two roads lay before him, death and prison. Neither was appealing to him.

"I told you, I am going clean. I want out. You take care of it."

Frank smacked him across the back of his head. "You have no options. I own you. What are you going to do, run? You run, we find you. We find you, we kill you. It's that simple."

Bart never wanted this life. When he flunked out of college, broke and homeless, he borrowed money on the street and gambled. He wasn't a good bettor and before he knew it, he had racked up a hundred grand in debt and no more bets were allowed. The hoods gave him a simple choice, do what they said or be killed, his plan was to pay the debt and move away. The debt was paid fast and cash was rolling in. He was young and the future was so far off. He decided to stay in the game, but before he knew it, 20 years had come and gone. "Twenty years wasted," he murmured.

"What did you just say?" Frank asked.

"Nothing." Bart did not know he spoken aloud. "So, what's the job?"

"A hit. He did it again, slept around with a problem and now the problem has to go bye-bye. Got it?"

Bart really was done killing, but he thought "Eh, what's one more? I will whack this broad and when I leave to hide the body I won't come back. All that is waiting for me is money and freedom."

"Yeah," he said. "Usual price?"

He was usually paid fifty for a hit like this and these jobs were quite frequent. He had become good at distorting evidence and cleaning up without a trace. It was as if his victims just faded into the background.

"This one is pro bono."

"What?" Bart snapped, looking at Frank. "No sir, if I take all the risk, then I get a reward."

"Who do you think you are talking to?" Frank smacked him with an open hand across the brow, palm to forehead. "You will do this my way and how I say." He grabbed Bart's hair and brought his face to his. "You get me? You nobody motherfucker, you."

The temptation to spit in Frank's face was there. But he wanted to get out of this position, so he submitted to Frank's request. Timmy sat there motionless in the driver's seat. He knew the drill and wasn't going to defy his boss.

"Yeah," said Bart.

"Yeah, what?"

"I'm with you. What's the plan?" Frank freed him.

"There you go, boy. You got the idea now." Frank smoothed Bart's hair and jacket as he sat up in the seat and looked out of the tinted windows. "Here's the plan: Before daylight, some housewife, wife of a cop, she needs to take a swim. Usual deeds, toss the house, look for any evidence connecting her and Gabe, no blood in the house, extract her and we're out and the rest will be up to you."

"Got me a good ride?"

Frank nodded.

Bart sighed, "You got me." The car sped down the street.

47

"**T**wenty-nine to base."

"Base."

"Got a green T.C. plate, Michigan, five-one-four victor romeo tango."

"Stand by, 29."

"How long do you think we will have to do this?" Greta asked Sean, her partner. Both were rookies and usually at a desk putting in their time until making street duty.

"As long as we have to." The radio interrupted Sean.

"Base to 29?"

Sean gave the okay.

"Follow the car. Repeat. Follow the car. Update as transit occurs; backup en route. Copy."

"Copy, base," Sean announced over the radio while looking over to his partner.

"Interesting. Thankfully, they gave us weapons," he laughed. "Unfortunately, we didn't get much of a car."

They were in an Olds Eighty-Eight. The department was crime-quiet, with a few undercover units. So supplies were limited but all were available for use on the Chief's case.

"I wonder what this is about," Greta said as she reached for the radio, watching the Town Car make a quick exit down the street. "Twenty-nine to base, in transit."

Samuels was listening to them. He decided to take a ride. "Keep me updated," he told the desk sergeant and walked out the door.

The desk sergeant yelled, "Hey, what's this all about?" Samuels didn't answer.

Not wanting to be seen, Samuels bypassed his squad car and hopped into his truck. He dialed the Chief and patiently waited for an answer.

"Yeah." Dave recognized the number.

"We got a Town Car with a plate for a stolen Dodge on your street. Annissa is in the house. She is safe and is being watched. I don't know any more, but we are trailing the car. What's the next move?"

"Any idea how many are in the car?

"Based on radio traffic, two, maybe three."

Dave's adrenaline began to pump, thinking about how he had left town once without his wife in the last 10 years and now was a time when she needed him most. "Okay, tail them. If they go to a public place, call."

"Shit," he clapped his phone closed, then reopened it and dialed Greg.

"Hey bro!"

"Where are you?"

"I had to run out and check on something. I will be back at the grounds in about an hour. Everything okay?"

"Not sure, will tell you when you get back. Aaron with you?"

"No, he is on property."

"Fuck," the Chief mashed down on the accelerator, "I got to get back to him. Hurry back."

"What's going on man?"

"Never mind, I just need to hurry back." Again, Dave hung up and immediately started dialing.

He did not wait for a hello. "Where are you?"

"At the pool," said Aaron. "Why Dad, what's up?"

"Get to the house. I'll be there in a minute. Lock the door."

He knew the tone and did not argue. He just started walking towards the house. "Yes sir, what's going on?"

"Just get to the house."

48

After driving on flat, never-ending country roads for 45 minutes, Greg finally told Larry to pull off to the right. The road was tree-lined and no houses, or anything else for that matter, were visible.

"It's up here," Big Jim said, pointing off to the left. "See that mailbox up yonder?"

Larry squinted his eyes in the sunlight. "Yep, gotcha." He was at a complete loss. "Why are we parking back here?"

Greg laughed and cleared his throat. "We aren't. I just wanted to pull over and give you a chance not to go any farther. This cat is about as hillbilly as it gets. You not being from around here, I don't know if you want to step into a mess like this."

"Yeah, I really don't. I also don't want you guys to get hurt. I meant what I said about helping you. What's the plan?"

Greg cocked his .38, hoping he would not need to use it but checked to make sure it was loaded and ready. "Right now, the plan is to see if the crack-whore is there. If she is, then we go home and it's someone else's shoe. If she isn't there, then," he paused and looked out the window to the right, "we wing it."

Big Jim looked at Greg, confused, "What are you doing with the piece? This guy has never been violent, he is just a stoner. I'm not going to provoke him into a gunfight. That's what Clifton gets paid for."

Greg laughed, "Clifton, that's funny."

"What?"

"Man, Clifton is as dirty as it gets. Zake probably has Clifton in his pocket."

"Zake?" Larry asked.

"The guy we are going to see."

"That's his real name? Boy, that sounds like a name from a bad horror novel." Images of being chased through a cornfield by a one-armed man in overalls popped into Larry's head. He shut his eyes and shook his head to try to make them disappear. "Are we ready?" He looked at Greg sitting in the back seat.

"Yeah. Ready Jim?"

"Yeah."

The truck shook as Larry put it into gear and traveled the few feet. Slowly turning on to the gravel lane, Larry asked, "This guy doesn't have land mines on the drive or anything like that, does he?"

"No, worse. He has broken mason jars." Jim was laughing. "There's nothing that would kill us."

"Wonderful." Larry proceeded up the worn and rutted gravel road. It had not been graded or graveled in a long time. It was flat and the trailer, even though a quarter mile away, was visible through the overgrown hay field. "Does this guy have a car or leave here much?"

"Not that I am aware of."

As they drove closer, the door to the trailer opened. The men pulled up about 20 feet from the trailer. Larry's blood was pumping. "Now I start to get cold feet!" he thought. "Couldn't this have happened before I got to this point?"

Zake walked out the door and spit, cigarette in one hand, holding a sawed-off shotgun against his dirty overalls-tank top combo.

"Jesus," Larry was speechless. "Where's the camera crew? We have to be on reality TV."

"You are partially correct. This is reality but it ain't no TV show," Big Jim said, looking at Larry. "You wanna wait here?"

"No, but I am leaving the truck running and sticking close to it." He pointed to the pile of ashes still smoldering from the night before. "Look." He nodded toward the pile. "They had a big cooker last night. It's a miracle, as close as the pile is to, well . . . " he said, pointing to a brush pile with grass, leaves and sticks less than four feet to the left of the bonfire pile, "I'm surprised that didn't ignite off the bonfire heat and that it didn't flame up."

"Yeah, lucky us," Greg said, as he slid out of the truck. "Top of the morning, Zake."

A cold stare was the only response given to Greg.

Big Jim cleared his throat, "Sir, the man spoke to you, I believe he said, 'top of the morning.'"

"I heard him," Zake said in his twangy voice, "I don't talk to people like him."

Pipe Vision

Larry couldn't believe his ears. He had never heard such comments. He was not used to the backward culture of the country. He stood silently observing the conversation, never taking his hand off the gun on his belt.

Big Jim observed Greg, as the groundsman said, "That's okay, Jim. He don't have to talk to me, just listen." Jim threw the bag containing the shoe to Greg, who caught it without looking, "See sir, we found something at the lake we think belongs to Mollie and we'd like to talk to her."

"She ain't here. I don't know when she'll be back," Zake said, the un-ashed cigarette sticking to his lips. "I'll let her know you's looking for her, though."

Zake was looking at Big Jim, refusing to make eye contact with Greg as he reluctantly answered. Zake knew Big Jim and was scared of him since their high school days when Big Jim sacked him in a football game. Damn near broke his neck. Zake was scared at the sight of Jim.

Greg looked back at Jim for a second and was trying to be as cool as Zake was acting, "Yeah? When's she coming back?"

"I don't know. She was gone when I woke this morning. You writing a book?"

Greg chuckled, "No, no, I can't say that I am. See we found this shoe over in the lake, and it looks pretty close to hers. If I am not mistaken she only has one pair."

"I wouldn't know."

"I doubt that."

The two men's eyes were locked, neither blinking, both focused. Greg heard Jim fumble with the gun. Jim raised the gun, and Larry felt his shorts get wet.

Greg gulped, "Now put that away, Jim." He started walking backwards. "If you see her, tell her I have her other shoe."

"Leave it here and I'll give it to her."

Without moving his lips, Greg said, "Get in the truck. Get in the truck." He smiled at Zake. "No, Zake. I'll take good care of it," he knew it was needed as evidence. "You know where to find me."

They scooted into the truck. "What was that?" Greg asked.

"I don't know, but he sure don't like you, does he?" Big Jim said.

"Doesn't matter. She's dead, though. He killed her. I just hope some kid doesn't reel the body in."

The truck was idling. Larry was sitting there speechless and had no clue what to do. He wasn't about to turn around with Zake still standing on the porch watching them. In his mind, Zake had nothing to lose. What's three more bodies? Time was at a standstill, frozen along with his muscles. Larry felt safer in the truck and wanted to get the hell off the property.

"What are you waiting for?" Greg asked.

"Him to go inside. I don't much like the idea of turning my back to him."

"Back down the road a ways. He is probably too drunk to get a good shot."

Larry did as he was instructed. They found their way to the main road. After a while, they let out a simultaneous sigh of relief and the rush was over.

"What the hell? I've never been in that position before. Damn I should've been a cop or an agent. Damn, that shit was fun."

"Yeah, tons. That's why you pissed on yourself," Big Jim snapped his dip can and threw one in, a habit in which he only participated under extreme pressure.

"Let's go get a beer. God knows we deserve it," Larry laughed.

"Can't. Something is going on with my brother. I need to get back to the grounds. I hope he's okay. He's having trouble with his wife."

The trio raced back to the campground where a line was already forming to get in for the festivities.

"Thanks, you guys," Greg said. He was out of the truck and running to find his brother before Larry could pull into his campsite.

49

The phone rang as they were keeping a safe distance behind the Town Car and the only noise was the cold summer rain pinging off the windshield.

"Hello," Greta answered.

"Where are they?" It was Samuels.

"Travelling south on Brookside. Wait, they are turning into a diner."

"Stay in the lot. I'm five minutes away."

Greta gave the directions to Sean as they pulled into the lot. "I wonder if this guy has a plan," he asked.

"I don't know, but based on the looks of these guys, they are up to no good and they are probably not from around here. I am really hoping to keep tailing them without being noticed."

They were sitting in the car, watching the three men about to walk into the diner, when there was a metallic tap on the window from a flashlight. The tap startled Greta. She jumped in her seat, spilling her coffee on Sean.

"Jesus Christ, I'm glad you weren't pointing a gun at me!"

"At least I wouldn't have to hear you complain anymore."

"Are you two done?" asked Samuels.

Their silence proved that they agreed.

"So, what's the plan, boss?"

"I am going to try to turn one of them. There are three of them and one has to be alone at some point. Come on. Let's grab a table and see if we can save a life and catch some bad guys."

The chilly night air, coupled with the warmth inside the diner, created a fog on the plate glass window that veiled them from the patrons inside as they walked toward the entrance. The façade was faded from not being shown any love in several years. As they walked into the diner, they saw that there were stainless steel booths with blue worn vinyl and matching barstools at the counter.

Samuels stopped. "You know, I have an idea here. There was a TV show or movie I saw where they needed to stop a crime before it happened and the cops waited in the bathroom for one of the bad guys and flipped him to get the plan. I wonder if it will work. There is a door back there, Greta. Go wait by that door, and I'll let you in."

She agreed. The two men proceeded toward the diner. "Get a table," Samuels directed Sean. "I need to go use the restroom."

"You the manager?" Samuels asked a silver-haired, chubby guy sitting behind the register reading a folded sports page.

"Yeah."

Samuels lifted up his shirt, revealing his badge tucked into his jeans with the shield out, "Come with me."

"How do I know you're a cop?"

Samuels reached into his back pocket and fumbled though his wallet for a business card. "Because the next time you get arrested, you have a 'get out of jail free card.'" He handed the chubby guy the card. "Now come with me," he said softly.

Taking the card and following Samuels toward the back, he mumbled, "How do you know I get arrested?"

Samuels ignored the question as the two men walked to the back door. "Here's the deal, there are three suspicious characters in your restaurant. We need to use your restroom to try to isolate one and get him to talk to me. I am sorry to do this here, but we are out of options.

The chubby man's face paled. "Whatever you need, man. "

"Unlock this door, then go back up front and act normal."

"Yes, sir." The man did as directed.

Greta was waiting outside. "About time, I am freezing out here. What's the deal with this cold rain during summertime."

Samuels ignored the weather question. "Go into the men's room. I will text you when one goes in." She did as directed while Samuels rolled his eyes, walking off and pulling out his phone. "Time to update the Chief."

"Need to reassure him, eh?" Greta asked while closing the door.

"Hello," said Chief Davis, answering Samuels' call.

"Well, you were right. There were visitors scoping out your house."

"Who?"

"Don't know. Three men. We have them pinned at a diner. The goal is to isolate one of them and get the plan out of him. We have another car at your house, front and back are covered."

50

"**K**eep me up to date." The Chief closed his phone as he walked through the front door. Greg and Aaron were standing in the living room, waiting for the Chief to finish his phone conversation. "Go play with your friends but do not talk to anyone you don't know," the Chief told Aaron. "If you feel weird, you call me."

"What's going on, Dad?" Aaron inquired as he walked toward the door.

"Just do as I say." Dave had no emotion in his voice.

"I can't believe this is happening to me," he said, looking at Greg as he dialed his home.

"What?" Greg asked as he sat on the couch.

Dave held up one finger as Annissa answered the phone. Her voice cracked as if she had been weeping. "Hello?"

"We had visitors watching the house. They are gone now, but I want you to get dressed, pack a bag and be ready to leave."

"All right, baby. I am so sorry for this."

"Has he contacted you?"

"No."

"He will. I want you to promise me that you won't answer. I am working on a plan. I can't go into detail, but need you to follow my direction. I have to go."

"I am sorry about all of this," she repeated, hoping he would respond to the second plea.

"Yeah," he closed the phone, leaving her to cry alone.

He stood there, silently still. Neither he nor Greg spoke. Only the sounds from the party penetrated the walls. After the emotions settled: "What a day!"

"Tell me about it," said Greg, as he stood and went to the window. "But mine's not near as bad or personal as yours. Do you want to talk about it?"

"Not really. Let's just say this, I know who he is and I know he is a bad guy. Her life and my livelihood are being threatened."

"Who?"

"Gabe Maddox."

Greg shook his head while looking at his brother, "No clue."

"The governor."

"Oh, I've never heard of him."

"Well, I have. He is dirty and I have tried to bust him a couple of times but he always comes out looking squeaky clean. He is known for making mistresses disappear. I'm using department funds on this, which could get me fired because I am here and not there."

"Look man, you're doing all you can do. Let's enjoy the day and try to forget all of this for a while. There are some good-looking sweeties out there. Maybe you can get your revenge," Greg laughed.

"I don't think so."

"**I** got to take a whiz."

Frank reached in his coat while saying in a monotone voice, "Don't you think about disappearing. I will find you, got me?"

"Yeah," Bart said as he left the table. His mind was racing. He knew there was no way out of this. He was done and he did not want to kill any more people, except for the two he had to have breakfast with. He opened the door to the men's room, pushing on the first stall. Locked.

Greta was about to puke from the odor that was permeating the confining stall. "I hope this is him," she thought. Her phone vibrated in her pocket. She stood on the toilet and peered over the stall at Bart who was relieving himself at the urinal in front of the stall where Greta was hiding. Slowly, she stepped down and opened the stall door, pulled out her gun and whispered in his ear with the gun pressed against his back, "Merry Christmas. Put it away and turn around!"

She put her gun down. "I was hoping it would be you. How are you, Baby?" They kissed.

"I am good. I wanted to call you when I got home last night but I had visitors. I was ready to get out of this and move away with you. I think they know what's up, but the boss wants me to do a job. These goons won't leave me alone until it is done."

"What's the job?"

"C'mon, you know I can't tell you that. You are on the wrong side."

"Yeah, well we think your target is the Chief of Police's wife and they are out in full force to protect her. If I help you, they will know about us."

"Does that matter? I mean, if we are going to disappear after today?"

"Yeah, you kill her, it'd be like killing a cop. Everyone would be looking for you."

His head sagged in frustration. "Look, I got to get back out there."

"I need details. Tell me Baby."

"Tonight at dusk I am supposed to cap her. Help me get out of it."

"I'll be there. Now go, before they get suspicious." They kissed goodbye.

Timmy was walking up the dark, narrow, paneled hallway to the bathroom, "Thought you fell in. Frank is getting nervous."

Bart slapped Timmy on the shoulder. "Well, let's go calm him down."

The two men walked back to the table. "Oh yeah, Frank told me to give you this." Timmy handed Bart the check and smiled. "I gotta make a pit."

Bart felt like he should try to talk Timmy out of going into the men's room because of Greta, but they were already suspicious. He did not want to cause any more trouble. His nerves had calmed down since seeing Greta and he knew she would protect him.

"I got this," he said, raising the check.

After he paid the check and returned to the table, Frank said, "Feel better dipshit? You were in there long enough, weren't you?"

"Yeah, well you know how it is when you haven't peed all night." It was the best thing he could come up with, spur of the moment. "What's on tap for the rest of the day?"

Frank looked at him, confused, "We have to go stay with the target. You know how this works."

"Yeah." Unfortunately, he knew all too well how this worked and he hated it. In his mind, the other killings were okay because the victims were bad like him, but this was different. When Greta disclosed the target, he couldn't believe it. He wanted to know more, but could not ask too many questions.

"Man, how could you stay in there that long," Timmy asked as he walked up to the table. "God, that room stunk."

"Didn't have a choice."

The three asked for coffee to go and returned to the car. Samuels went to pay the tab and asked Sean to trail the men. He and Greta would catch up.

As he walked up to pay the chubby man, he asked, "What do I owe ya?"

"It's on the house. Come back and see us when off duty."

"Thanks." Samuels scurried up the hall and found Greta. "How did it go?"

"They are going to whack her at dusk. He wanted immunity."

"Damn."

"We'll get the other two."

"Yeah. C'mon, let's go."

52

"**F**ive bucks to park."

Joe handed the teenage girl a bill. "Is there any way I can get closer to drop these two off? I'll return and park."

"No, Joe. I'll walk. No special treatment today." Jaime was sitting proudly in the backseat with her sunglasses on looking at the people in the pavilion. They were sitting in chairs, standing and talking. It was a warm and humid night and the dress of the folks fitted a campground. Most were in shorts, T-shirts, swimming trunks or tops. From a distance, everyone appeared to be relaxed. Booths with crafts, homemade snacks, pottery and other works of art surrounded the pavilion.

"I guess we'll park and walk up." Joe grabbed the ticket from the girl. "Thanks." He moved the SUV to the nearest parking space. "Are you sure about this?" he asked Betta as he exited the vehicle and opened Jaime's door.

"Yes, I'm sure. She needs this. No one here even knows who she is. Without the Secret Service detail, we will blend in as a local family." Jaime had not been used to the Secret Service being around; they were new to the family since Mitch decided to run for President. She felt like she didn't have any freedom and it was getting worse as the election neared. The opposition against her father was full of hatred and threats against the family were a daily occurrence. The only reason they were not with her now is because Mitch assured them Joe would keep her safe at the lake house. The press pretty well left Jaime alone, as she was not old enough to create scandals.

"Yeah, 'til you run off with your man," Jaime joked with Betta as they left Joe fumbling with lawn chairs and a cooler bag.

"Oh, come on now!"

"It is okay, Betta. I know you like him."

"And has for a while," Joe cracked from a distance.

They all laughed together as they walked up the shallow hill to the pavilion.

I noticed her immediately. Guys like me dream of girls like her. Getting up and leaving the conversation to verify whether my suspicions were true, I wondered whether it was the girl from the lake house we watched from the boat last year. It could not be the girl that I had thought about for a year. Was I that lucky?

"Hey Bub, where are you going?" Although I could hear Seth yelling, I chose to act as if I could not hear.

I was halfway to the beginning of the pavilion when I felt Seth's hand turning me around. "Hey man, where are you going?"

"Look," I said, pointing discreetly at Jaime.

"Yeah, a hot chick you have no chance with, so?"

"No, look at her. Remind you of anyone?"

"No. Should it?"

"Last year, over there," I said, pointing to the middle of the lake. "On the pontoon. She was on the dock, lying out while we were all trying not to be obvious while we were gawking at her."

Seth squinted his eyes. "Yeah, I remember now."

Aaron walked up. "What's going on?"

Seth quickly popped off, "Oh, nothing. Bub is just getting his jollies with the girl in white. He doesn't have a prayer of meeting her." He was laughing as he nodded her way.

"Her?" Aaron asked, "You want to meet her?"

"Yeah," I said, probably a little too quickly. "What, you know her?"

"YEAH! I met her the other night with my dad and uncle. Truthfully, I thought she seemed a little stuck up. You want to meet her?"

"Nah."

"You don't?" Aaron looked confused.

"Hell, yes, I do, but I am sure, no. I can almost guarantee she wants nothing to do with me." I hid behind my two friends as she walked past.

"C'mon man. You are going to meet her."

"No, no, I . . . I wouldn't know what to say."

Aaron grabbed my hand, "Dude, you are a chicken shit. You'll never have a girlfriend if you keep this up."

"Yeah, here you were, lecturing me about Samantha and you are just as chicken shit as me," Seth snapped.

"Yeah, well it is easier to watch someone else make a fool of himself than take a chance."

"But Bub," Seth said in a whiney voice.

"If you never take a chance, you will never know, now, will you?" Staci asked.

"Um, how long have you been behind me?"

"Long enough to know what's up." She smiled. "Go and meet her."

I looked at Staci and pointed up, "Did . . . ?" hoping she knew that I was talking about having a vision the night before, where I met a girl in a white shirt.

"Yes," she said, meaning she had the same vision. Disguising our conversation, she said, "I heard everything, Bub. There's nothing wrong with liking and wanting to meet someone. Now Aaron, go and take this shy kid to meet that girl."

"Did what?" Seth inquired.

Staci and I looked at each other, then looked at Seth and said in unison, "Nothing."

Wanting to change the subject as quickly as I could, I asked Seth, "So, where is Samantha?"

Seth quietly backed off and went to find Sissy. "Come on man, let me introduce you. So I can take care of that thing," Aaron said as we walked off.

"What thing?" Staci asked.

I yelled back, "Don't worry about it."

I could hardly walk I was so nervous. I wanted to do this, but I didn't want to at the same time. I always went out of my way to avoid situations like this. Unfortunately, there was no way out of this one.

Joe, Betta and Jaime were sitting around, people watching and deciding what to do. Aaron, politely tapped Jaime on the shoulder. "Pardon me miss, we met the other night."

Joe rose from his seat. "No Joe, it's okay. This is Greg's nephew, right?" Betta said.

"Yes ma'am," he smiled and reached out his hand. "I was waiting in the car when my uncle stopped by. I guess we were not formally introduced," he smiled, "but, my uncle told me who you were, I'm Aaron and this is Bub."

We both extended our hands. I made sure to wipe the sweat off my palm before offering it to them. "It's nice to meet you," I said.

Betta said, "Likewise. My name is Betta and this is Jaime and Joe."

I must admit I was so excited to meet her that I did not know what to do or say. I just stood there.

Aaron leaned over and whispered in my ear, "Dude, you are acting creepy, say something."

"My real name is Conrad or Connie. My friends call me Bub." It was probably not the best thing to say.

"Is that a family name?" Jaime asked.

I could feel my face turning red. "No. I don't know where it came from, maybe my parents had a death wish for me or something. I don't know," I laughed, staring at the ground, too nervous to make eye contact. "So are you from around here?"

Jaime smiled at me as if she thought the question was cute but she stood there silently looking at me. After standing there speechless for a minute, she said, "No, I'm not from around here. I live in Indiana."

"Well, that is a pretty big area, any particular part?" I said while winking in a poor attempt to flirt with Jaime.

"I kinda need to leave it there for now," her face turned red.

Mysterious. I had never met a girl, or person for that matter, who did not want to share where they lived. "Well, I know you have a home over there," I pointed across the water.

"How . . . how did you know that?" She became nervous and frightened as if I were a stalker. I knew I had to calm her down.

"Relax. I saw you on the dock last year when my family was out on the pontoon. I didn't mean to freak you out."

"Oh," she giggled, "you didn't freak me out."

Sissy came walking up behind me. "Hey Bub, whatcha doing?"

Instead of rolling my eyes, acting like my usual jerk self, I was polite and introduced my Sis to Jaime. It actually helped the keep the conversation going. We discussed nothing important. It was a typical, pointless, kid conversation.

After about 15 minutes, silence fell over the three of us. I didn't want to leave, but I had nothing else to say.

"Hey Bub," Aaron yelled across the picnic area. "We're ready." He was holding up keys. They were boat keys, with a plastic buoy as a keychain. "C'mon, let's go."

"Way to be discreet," I thought. I wanted to ask Jaime to go with us but before I could, I heard Sissy ask, "You want to go on a pontoon boat with us?"

Staci was now running up beside us and Seth soon followed, all saying, "Come on, we need to hurry."

"So much for being discreet guys," I snapped.

"What are you guys getting into?" Jaime asked.

"Oh, just a little boat ride," I answered.

"A boat ride, huh?" She snickered. "Sounds like a bit more than that."

I felt my face rush with heat. I was blushing, again, and I did not know why, nor could I help it. We were going to look for a body, not on a dirty adventure. Although we were teens and our hormones were raging, the thought never crossed my mind.

"I better not. I think I'll stay here. I'll be waiting for you when you get back," Jaime said giving me a smile and a wink that almost caused me to tell the guys to go without me.

My face was starting to cool. "Sounds great!"

I turned, and as I did, I tripped on the ledge to the pavilion, falling and landing square on my face. Leave it to me finally to meet the girl of my dreams and I shatter the moment with a fall. Sissy leaned down and I whispered, "Did she see it?"

"Um, yes, damn near the whole park saw it. Get up before we have a crowd around us."

Jaime leaned down. "If you were trying to impress me by showing me what a man you are, it worked. Now get up and go with your friends, Bub. I will be here when you get back."

I jumped up as if there was nothing wrong, but my ankle was throbbing. I was walking without a limp and trying to avoid my mom, who was rushing over to check on me. This was not good because the five sleuths were supposed to fade into the crowd.

Mom's running toward me to check on her fallen baby was more noticeable than me doing a Dick Van Dyke in front of Jaime. "Oh, my baby!" she screamed. "Are you okay?"

There was pretty much no way that I was going to remove the spotlight from my head anytime soon. I knew I wasn't seriously injured but just could not shake the pain right off. I grabbed Sissy's shoulder and pulled her near, gritting my teeth. "You go. Be careful. You will have no problem getting on the boat."

"Yes, Bub. Are you sure you don't want us to wait for you?"

"No, go before Mom and Dad get here." I pushed her away, knowing that for the pact to be carried out, I could not go. For the rest of the day I was branded as "that kid who fell." My enigma status had been revoked.

"Jeez, Mom. A little louder," I said, as she came running up to me. "I don't think I'm embarrassed enough."

She grabbed me and threw me around giving me the quick mom examination. "Looks like you're all right. Why don't you come with me so I can get you some Advil?" Her answer for everything.

Mom was pestering me to go with her to the trailer and to be her patient for the day. The injury was not worth this trouble and I was mad at myself for many reasons. "Dang, Mom! Let's go so I can get back to hanging out." She was so focused on me that Sissy could have been juggling balls of fire.

Sissy hopped on last. "We lost Bub. Mom freaked and started treating him like he was in diapers."

"Damn!" Aaron slammed his fist down on his palm. "Oh well, I doubt there's anything out there anyway."

Staci had been quiet most of the day. The visions were happening frequently as the day progressed, to the point where her body tingled all the time. As long as she kept moving, her hearing wasn't affected. "I have a feeling we're gonna see something."

"Yeah," Aaron challenged. "What do you think we're going to see?"

She sat and stared off the boat to the shore. "A body."

"A body, huh?"

Seth interjected, "Sis, is she okay?"

"I guess, why?"

"Look at how focused she is and she is starting to quiver a little. Have you ever seen her like this?"

Sissy looked confused. "What, are you serious? I only see her for five minutes once a year. So she looks normal to me."

"No, there is something wrong. She is definitely in a trance or something. Try talking to her," Aaron said as he idled away from the dock. "Seth, text Bub and tell him what's going on."

"I realize it may be a little late to ask this," Seth said while pulling out his phone. "Umm, have you ever driven a boat before?"

"No," said Aaron, looking at Seth, "But I have been with my dad on a police boat before. This kinda looks the same."

Seth, watching the dock get farther away, shrugged his shoulders "Works for me," and looked back to his phone.

As Seth was following directions, Staci got up and walked to the front of the boat. Her face clinched tightly as if she was hiding pain. She observed the waters and pointed to the left, "That way!"

Seth was continuing to give Bub a play-by-play via text. A response finally came: "Do what she says." Seth relayed the message. "Do you know where the body is?" he asked Staci.

"Over there." Her head was hanging lower and unable to hold her own weight, she collapsed to the blue fiberglass floor, clearly exhausted by the trance.

"Aaron, you getting this?" Seth yelled back.

"Yeah, but get your ass out of the way so I can watch her."

53

Annissa was packed and ready to go. She had no idea what was going on at the lake and time was standing still. She was restless. The house was immaculate, as cleaning was the only way to keep herself occupied and her mind from wandering. "Please Dave, call me."

No such luck.

The phone rang. "Dave?"

"No, it's not Dave. It's me, Gabe."

"Look Gabe, I came clean with Dave. He knows it is you. Now leave me alone."

"Well, you shouldn't have done that. Now I have to clean up a mess."

"There is no mess to clean up. He said it will just stay between us, if you never contact me again." She was interrupted by laughter.

"Yep, that is exactly what I would do if I were him. Just forget about it and move on. What a wiener. I'm a public figure and now you have to pay."

"Look here, you piece of shit, don't call here again. Leave my family alone. If you do anything to hurt them, so help me God, I will get you." She wanted to say kill you but knew threatening the Governor was probably a bad idea.

He laughed more. "Okay, you aren't even worth getting upset over. Bye."

She hung up the phone. "I want my babies home and this night to be over."

She pulled the drape back with her fingers and saw an unmarked Plymouth sitting down the street from her house.

"Any action?" Samuels asked, as he got in the car and adjusted the seat.

"None," Greta said, looking his way.

"Go get us some coffee," he said, handing Sean a twenty.

"We have full cups," Sean said with a puzzled look.

"Then, go get some doughnuts, son." Samuels was trying to get Sean out of the car so he could talk to Greta.

"Yes, sir." Sean hopped out of the car and drove off in the SUV parked behind them.

"So, Greta, why was it so easy to get the guy to flip? These gangsters, you know they don't rat too easy. I never had any luck, so tell me how did a rookie, like you, do it first try?"

"Beginner's luck, I guess." Greta's nerves overcame her. She was starting to sweat and reached to turn down the heat.

"They say your body temperature rises when you're nervous, uncomfortable or guilt-ridden. Which one are you?"

"None of the above. It's just warm in here," Greta said as she looked around at the exterior of the house.

"Ah, I see. So, I have no reason to suspect that you know that guy and are working on an inside job?" Samuels asked while studying Greta's body language. She was lying. "Are you dirty too?"

"No, and I don't appreciate the accusation," said Greta, rolling her eyes, trying to blow off the question.

"Well, if you have done nothing wrong, then you have nothing to be accused of, do you?" Samuels knew Greta was seeing Bart and was trying to get her to admit it. What Greta did not know was that Samuels and Bart helped each another out.

"I guess not." Greta was not sure where this was going.

"I think that you do, and to top it off, I think you're involved. So, tell me, what's the plan?" Samuels sat back and folded his arms.

Greta rolled her eyes as she conceded to Samuels' question, "The plan is to whack the Chief's wife at dusk, like I told you. Then Bart, my boyfriend, and I, are going to split to the country. He wants out."

"He wants out?"

"Yes, we want to start a life together."

"That will never happen because after we kill the Chief tonight and I become Chief of Police, we can do whatever we want." Samuels smiled and rolled down the window. "We will have a new product supplier soon and we will be back in business in a few weeks."

"We want to raise a family and start a new life together. Please, let us out," Greta pleaded.

"Nope. It's too risky."

"Please!" Tears streamed down her face, "I will do anything."

"Why? So that in a couple of months, when you go through your money, because you haven't changed your lifestyle, you become broke, desperate and decide to whistle-blow, turn us in to the feds? No thanks," Samuels had seen people try to get out before. It never worked.

"Why, we would never..."

"You say that now, but let's see what happens when the money stops."

Greta sat there looking at the house on Pordy Drive. "You know I don't want to do this, but we are stuck, there's no way out. We are going to end up in prison. At this point, it would be a better deal. Why did Gabe put everything at risk by sleeping with this woman?"

"He's not sharp. He couldn't get elected to class screw-up, but he hired the right people who were good at selling him. His charisma did the rest. Otherwise, he would be like us, a working stiff, living for a check." Samuels touched her shoulder. "We just have to figure out how to keep the Chief away until Gabe takes care of him." He sat back. "What about the saint here? Can we get him to work with us?"

Greta was amazed at what she was hearing, "What? Sean? Are you serious? He doesn't know about you?"

"No. I wonder how smart he is. I have been doing goofy shit in front of his nose for a while and two and two don't seem to process for him. I think we should try to keep him in the dark. We lose who we lose. Gabe knows there will be some bodies. It's the only way to keep us clean." Samuels peered into the passenger side mirror as Sean returned with the unneeded doughnuts.

Greta relaxed and sighed. "If I play, I want out after tonight. Deal?"

"We'll see. You know it's not up to me," said Samuels, knowing he would be able to make the decision but was not prepared to give an answer.

Sean hopped in the car with fresh doughnuts, "What's up? Do we have a plan?"

"Wait here and watch that house. Move when they do, try to save lives and put the bad guys in jail." Samuels looked at Greta. "Are you ready?"

Greta sat there. When she decided to become a cop three months prior, and had no clue or desire to be in this position and the guilt was getting to her. "All I have to do is make it through today," she repeated to herself, hoping the time would pass quickly.

54

Sitting on the couch being comforted, I asked, "Dad, where did you all go today? I know it had to do with the shoe we found. It belonged to a thin drug addict didn't it? She was killed by a trailer, near a bonfire?"

Larry's mouth dropped. "Son, who told you that?"

"I saw it in a vision. I thought it was like a mental image or a daydream." I stopped and watched the lake through the front door.

"Visions? What visions, son?" Larry became concerned and knelt in front of me.

"I have been having visions since we left home. They started at Staci's and I saw her here at the campground with us. She has had similar visions and, according to Seth, is having visions right now."

"Where is she?"

"I can't tell you right now, Dad. You have to trust me."

Deciding to play along, he looked at Mom, "You know I trust you, boy. Tell Dad what is going on."

"I can't."

I must be honest I have never talked to my dad that way and usually a response like that would not be tolerated. Patience came through. "Conrad…" He never used my proper name. "I need to know what is going on. Whatever it is, you will not get in trouble. Where is she?"

I started to cry, nestled between my parents with my head in Mom's lap and my feet on Dad's. "I can't. I made a pact."

"A pact? With who?" Mom asked. "We need to know."

"The guys."

"Well son, one of the great things about parents is you can tell us anything. Where is she?"

The screen door was open on the camper. I saw a pontoon in front of me and I pointed, "There."

"Holy shit!" Dad ran out of the trailer hollering back, "I got to find Greg or Jim."

I was crying and could not stop. I let my friends down and I did not know what to do. I just wanted the visions to stop. Until now, they only happened occasionally. Since Staci, Sissy and the guys left on the boat, the visions had been non-stop and the tingling had gotten worse. Staying conscious was a fight and as my vision narrowed, the fight was harder. Staci was in her own hell, and nothing could be done about it.

"Stop!" Staci murmured. "She is in this area, under us."

The water was too murky to see fish, much less a body, which could be at the bottom of the lake. "What do we do now?" asked Seth.

"Here hold this, I'm going in," said Aaron. He handed Sissy his phone and all of his belongings, took off his shoes and shirt, and jumped into the water.

No sooner did he hit the water then his phone rang. "Dad" was displayed on the caller ID. Seth looked at the two girls,."What should I do?"

"Answer it?" Sissy popped.

"Hello?"

"Who is this?"

"Seth."

"Seth, this is Aaron's dad. Where is he?"

Seth shrugged his shoulders, "Um, swimming in the lake."

"What? Where?"

Seth could hear Dad in the background yelling and running to get a boat. Big Jim was yelling, "They have our only one."

"We are in the middle of the lake to the left of the campground." Seth was a bad liar and knew they were busted so there was no point in lying. His nerves were starting to get to him, between Staci being possessed and Aaron in the lake. Adults were needed.

"Stay there boy, we are on our way."

Larry and Greg were jumping from boat to boat looking for keys. "Dammit, these drunks are always leaving keys in boats. The one time I need a boat, no keys." Tiffany walked out on the dock. Greg called to her, "Hey, go in and call Clifton. He needs to get here right away and the state police need to get their dive team here."

"Why? What's going on?"

"Just do it, Tiffany."

"Okay, damn." She went inside and made the calls.

"Here! I got one!" Greg yelled. Dave and Larry were jumping across boats and joined Greg. They sped through the dock area, then past a no-wake sign, leaving white caps in their trail. Boats were slamming against the dock, "Whoops! That's going to do some damage," Greg looked over his shoulder.

"What were these kids thinking?" Dave said.

"They weren't thinking. They're kids. Did we think before doing dopey shit?"

"I never stole a boat to find a body," Larry said. "And, the closest I ever came to water when I was their age was the tub."

Greg threw the throttle in idle and let the boat coast up to the pontoon. Larry jumped over to the pontoon and went to his niece. She was collapsing. "What's wrong with her?"

"I don't know, Dad."

Seth said, "Yeah, she has been like that since we got on the boat."

Staci was faintly murmuring, "We are over her. They killed her. We have to help her."

"Get me those life vests and a blanket or beach towel," Larry said, as he lay her down on the boat deck. "We will sweetie. We will. Just rest." He looked at Sissy and Seth. "You stay right here with her. Don't move. Understand me?"

They both did as directed. Larry went over to Greg and Dave. They were standing on the side, peering into the water, watching Aaron as he exhausted himself swimming under the current, gasping harder each time he returned to the surface for air.

"Get out of the water!" commanded his father. "There is a dive team on their way."

"No, Dad, I can do this. Please, let me prove it."

"Aaron, son, you can't do this. If I thought you had the slightest chance you could, I would let you. Please, come on. Get out of the water. Look, here come divers now."

Aaron nodded his wet head, "All right Dad."

Mom and I were watching from the shore, along with all of the campground visitors. "Wow, I did not mean to cause this much trouble Mom."

"Baby, you did not cause any trouble. Something inside you told you that there was a problem. You listened and reacted. Nothing wrong with that."

As Sheriff Clifton pulled up in the boat, he said, "What's going on, gang?"

"We think there is a body somewhere around these parts. A shoe floated up here this morning and a dog found it. We have a girl…" Greg stopped.

"A girl? What?"

Greg knew Paul well, maybe too well. He really did not want to go further. "Well Paul, a girl who is having visions that the body is here."

"Visions, huh? Maybe I should hire her to solve all of our crimes."

Larry interrupted the two men. "Sheriff, if I may, the girl is here and I am equally as skeptical of stuff like this but come aboard and take a gander for yourself."

"Is that her, under that towel?"

"Yes, sir."

"Okay, I am new to that but I will take your word." The Sheriff looked around at all of the boats. The dive team from the local state police post was there. "Do you have anything on sonar around here?"

"A couple things, sir. It could be a boat, a cooler or a chest. Hell, it could be Captain Hook's treasure. We won't know without going under."

"Go under, but only for an hour. At five grand an hour, that's about all Trigg County can afford."

"Yes, sir. I will get my team ready."

"You better hope your girl is right."

Dad looked at the Sheriff, "She's right. If she's wrong, I'll pay the five grand myself."

"A betting man, I see."

Larry walked over to Greg, Dave and Aaron. "You okay son? You need anything?"

"He's okay, just out of breath. Was the water cold, boy? You're shivering."

"No, I'm just a bit shaken up. We wanted to find the body ourselves. Them two told us it was down here after that dog found the shoe. I thought she was nutty, but the closer we got, the more nuts she got. Hell, I'm convinced."

Chief Davis' phone rang before he could answer Aaron. "Samuels, why do you always call at bad times?"

"Sir, my apologies. I have a hunch. I need your permission to do something."

"What?" Dave excused himself.

"I think Greta might be involved in the hit tonight. The flip in the bathroom went too easy. Why?"

"Luck?"

Samuels laughed, "With all due respect, sir, I have never been that lucky. I would at least like to talk to her. If I am wrong, well, we will deal with that then. If I am right, we may have found our leak."

"Do it."

55

"I can't believe how foolish this has been! I knew there wouldn't be a body. Little girl, you have wasted all of our time. I should lock you up on any charges I can find."

"Sheriff, I think they found something," said Greg, interrupting his lecture.

"What?" Paul raced over to Greg, rocking the pontoon with his movement. "Y'all find something?"

"Yeah, it's a body. Chained. A bad job, too." Paul looked puzzled while listening to Greg and staring down at the water bouncing against the pontoon. "It looks like it has been down here a week or less. It's going to take some work to get her up. How would I know though? You guys are the professionals."

Sheriff Clifton ignored Greg's comments and walked over to Larry. "How is she doing?"

Dad had become impatient with Paul. "Oh, she's great. Can't you tell? All kids act like this." Paul walked back to watch the divers figuring out how to bring up the body. "Staci, come on sweetie. I need you to stay with me." Scared, never having been in this position before, Dad just wanted to keep her talking. "What else do you see?"

The tingling filled her body and Larry's voice became distant as if yelling through a cone. "I can't, I can't do this anymore," she said. "Why is this happening to us?"

"Yes, you can." Dad knelt down. Staci, who was curled up on the deck, picked her head up and rested it on his lap. "Try. Tell me what you see."

Staci's speech was muffled and jumbled, making no sense. "A blue metal building…hidden behind orange flames."

"Greg!" Dad yelled. "You better get over here."

Aaron sat on the bench, watching the divers drop a winch hook beneath the water's surface. "What?" Greg asked as he ran over.

"Get down here!" Dad commanded. "Tell me more. A blue metal building hidden behind orange flames. Then what?"

"Three men."

Greg asked, "Can you tell me what you see the three men doing?"

"Arguing about how to clean a mess up."

"What type mess?" Dad and Greg asked simultaneously.

"Death."

Dave studied Staci, then looked at Larry as she lay there motionless, "Is there any chance she could have been there?"

"No. We picked her up Friday. Her family is three hours away so I know she couldn't have been down here when the alleged murder took place," Larry said while sitting her up. She was starting to become lucid.

"We need more information. Can I ask her some questions?"

"I have never seen this before, I don't know. What can it hurt?" Larry was equally puzzled. "Have you ever seen someone act like this?"

Dave sighed, looked at Larry, and said, "Usually from a junkie. But, I don't think that's the case here." He knelt down to Staci. "Staci, my name is Dave. I'm Aaron's dad." He was trying to use his Dad voice but it was mixed with an authoritative tone. "Tell me what you see."

"A masked man with a secret. He is telling the others what to do and they are afraid of him."

"Tell me about the masked man, what kind of mask?"

"I don't know."

"Clothes?"

"I can't tell. I see overalls."

"Do you see a car?"

"A truck. The thin girl is making fun of the masked man, calling him Ted." She yelled and seized Larry's neck with both hands. Greg had to grab her arms. She was choking Larry.

Dave and Greg pulled her off Larry's neck. "Damn! What was that for?" Larry was rubbing around his neck.

She raised her head up and cocked it towards Dave. "He kilt her."

"Who?"

"Ted."

"What's he doing now?"

"Telling overalls to clean up while he goes to figure out what to do. He started walking through," she jumped awake, startling them and causing Aaron to fall over the side, splashing into the murky lake water. "Ahhhh!!" she yelled, "What's going on?" She looked at Larry, "How did you get here?"

Before responding to her, he answered his ringing phone. It was Mom. "What's going on?"

"Best I can figure, Staci, apparently, knew where a body was in the lake. How is Bub?"

"I didn't think that he hit his head when he fell, but he must have. He is scaring me. He's starting to talk all crazy about walking through the woods to get a truck and gas and…"

"What did you say?" he interrupted, not believing what he was hearing. Walking towards Greg and Dave who were fishing Aaron out of the water again, he shouted, "We've got to go."

"We can't go! This is a police investigation. We still have to be questioned."

Larry started shaking his head while listening to his wife repeat the vision in which their son was involved. He pointed at Staci, and then pointed at the shore. Holding his hand over the mouthpiece, he said, "Bub's doing it now."

"Um, Clifton can question us later," Dave said to Greg, practically yanking his son's arm out of the socket while pulling him aboard. "Untie those boats from the pontoon, discreetly," he said to Aaron. "Larry, keep him talking or get her to keep him talking and take notes." He walked around, making sure the vessel was free, "You didn't anchor anywhere?" he asked Aaron, while starting the pontoon boat.

"No Dad, I didn't."

"Body coming up!" a voice from the water yelled.

"Hey, where are you all going?" cried the Sheriff. "Get back here! Greg, you want me to arrest you?"

The pontoon boat was creeping backward slowly. Dave was hoping no one would see them escape until it was too late. It almost worked.

"For what? Finding a body? See you around, Paul!" Greg snarled as the pontoon floated away.

"Don't leave the campground!" Sherriff Clifton yelled, "At least not until I get a statement from you and those youngins."

The three men went from worrying about dopey Clifton to worrying about Staci and Bub's visions.

"What the hell is going on around here? This type of shit has ever happened before. My kids have always been somewhat normal. I kinda halfway expected some goofy shit like this out of Staci. But, Bub? This is the last time I buy generic breakfast sausages." Dad rolled his eyes trying to make a joke to diffuse the tension in the air.

Greg and Dave could not tell if Larry was rambling to himself or if he was waiting for answer. Seth and Aaron still were unsure as to how much trouble they were in and Staci was immobile with exhaustion. It was a tiring day for everyone and it was just beginning.

Pipe Vision

Dave was driving the pontoon straight towards Mom and Bub. "UGH! Dave, what are you doing?" Larry grabbed a support pole with his hands. "Dave… hey, Dave? The dock is over there. You can't shore this."

"What do I care? It's not my boat. We need to get to Bub."

"Aw shit! This isn't going to be good."

Dave gunned the throttle and tossed it into neutral as the boat aimed toward the trailer while letting go of the wheel. Everyone watched in amazement as he jumped off the boat toward Mom and Bub. The boat was at least 50 feet from the beach.

Aaron looked at Seth. "Now what?"

"We swim," Seth shrugged his shoulders as he got up, stopped at the side of the pontoon and watched Dave swim towards shore.

"Damn, man! I thought we were done with swimming for a while," Aaron said as he got up and followed Seth.

While the two were deciding what to do, the three men were already in the water and on the beach. Thankfully, the water was only knee deep. Everything in their pockets stayed dry.

"What's he doing?" Dad asked.

"Look, he's lethargic and babbling about walking through the woods, something about cleaning up a murder and why did he let this get out of hand. It's a place I have never heard of. Is he okay?"

Dad scratched his head. "I think so. Staci acted the same way and she came out of it. It's the most bizarre thing I've ever seen."

Dave was talking to Bub or, more accurately, the person or thing, which had overtaken Bub's body. Bub felt all tingly, his vision was as if he was looking up through a pipe and his head was pounding. He just wanted it to be over. Dave's voice was faint and muffled.

"Where are you?"

"On a rocky road, not ice cream but hard. I am barefoot and there is orange flickering light behind me in the distance. I am following a man."

Larry snapped his fingers. "Get a truck or something. It is where the girl left off. I think he can take us to the crime scene and maybe to the guy."

"It hurts. It hurts so bad, Mama! Please, make it stop! I can't do this!"

"You are doing good. Keep it up. Be strong and stay with us, Bub," Dad was trying to reassure him.

"Go take care of Staci. We left her alone in the boat. I got Bub," Larry said to Mom.

Mom nodded her head as she started walking away. "Please be safe. You and Connie come back to me in one piece." She ran over to him, then kissed and threw her arms around Larry. "I love you."

Returning the kiss, he said, "I love you too, Babe."

Greg ran around Dad's truck. "I'll drive," he said under his breath. "I am the only one around here who knows his way around."

They had left Staci out on the drifting boat. She was starting to come to reality and was freaking out and starting to cry. No one could hear her cries. The boat was rocking and her knees were wobbling. It was a sure prescription for disaster.

While the one cop and two wannabes were fumbling with Bub to throw his nutty ass in the truck, Mom yelled, "Oh my God!" and pointed to Staci wobbling around.

"Hey, Aaron, Seth!" Dave yelled, "Get out there and help her. She needs help."

Aaron looked at Seth and rolled his eyes. "Damn, back in the water we go."

"We?"

"Yeah, we."

As the truck sped through the grounds, horn honking, Bub was in the back with Dad and Dave, and asked, "Where are we going? Why is the road so bumpy."

Dad asked Greg, "Bub has a good question, where are we going?"

56

A knock at the back door startled Annissa. There was no access from the street; the only access was through the closed garage. She was not expecting anyone and Dave had not called to warn her, as promised. She called him before acknowledging the visitor but no answer. Unsure who to trust, she tried to peek out the window. Whoever knocked was out of view.

"What do I do?" Annissa asked the empty house.

The knocks persisted, becoming louder. Her heart was racing. Nervousness consumed her exhausted body. Grabbing the phone, she headed down to the basement to escape.

"Knock again," said Samuels, cocking his head upwards. "She is in there. We have been watching the house all day."

Samuels knew she would open the door for him, but he wanted Greta to knock and form a trusting female bond. "Identify yourself."

"Mrs. Davis, my name is Greta Uthens. I work with your husband. He told me to come get you and the 1937 Ford."

Many years ago, Chief Davis, then working in an undercover drug operation, warned her that he might have to send someone to get her if she was in danger. They used an old parent-child technique, the secret word. Their phrase: "1937 Ford." It was in a movie they watched on one of his weekends off. In their 20 years of marriage, the secret word having never been used, she knew it was safe. He had also given her a small, .22-caliber pistol to put in her purse if the word was ever used.

Annissa yelled, from mid-staircase, "Give me one second. I need to finish getting dressed." She headed for her gun.

"Why didn't Dave call me? I hope he is safe." In all of the excitement with Staci, Chief Davis had sat his phone down on the boat and had forgotten about it. "Wow. Something must be up if he isn't calling me." She grabbed the gun out of her safe and buried it in her purse. The knocking persisted. She ran her hands through her hair in front of the mirror before finally opening the door.

Annissa came face to face with Samuels standing in jeans with an un-tucked T-shirt dangling over his waistband and Greta in a jogging suit and baseball cap with her ponytail hanging out. Samuels was pacing around the porch, occasionally peering in the kitchen window. Greta stood still with her hand on the doorknob waiting for it to be unlocked. Impatiently waiting for Annissa to open the door, she said, "Mrs. Davis, I am Greta Uthens and this is Sargent Samuels. We are here to take you to a safe house. We know three men are watching your house. If you look out your front window, you can see we are in the process of arresting them. We need you to grab your necessary belongings and come with us. Your husband is on his way back and will meet us at the safe house."

Annissa stood in shocked silence. She always knew this day might come, but she never dreamed it would be due to her actions. She left the door between the kitchen and the family room open to walk over to the front window. What appeared to be two undercover cop cars were surrounding a Town Car with three men being questioned. "Guess this is legit," she thought.

"What do I need to bring with me?" Annissa yelled, walking from the living room to the kitchen and opening the door. "Please come in."

"As little as possible, ma'am," Greta said as she walked in. "Thank you for finally letting us in."

Samuels, passing the two ladies, went into the living room and walked through the house. After making his scan of Dave and Annissa's home, he returned to the kitchen and sat silently at the kitchen bar leaving his sunglasses on. His silence was intimidating and caused Annissa to be nervous. She was always friendly and talkative with everyone, but not with this guy. She had only met folks from the department a few times, but with it being a small department, it was a stepping-stone for rookies to get their feet wet before pursuing better jobs at bigger departments. That was her husband's plan, but then he fell in love with the community and he advanced his way through the department.

"I'm ready." she grabbed her purse and a small overnight bag. "Where are we going?"

"Don't worry about that right now. Let's just get you out of here safely. Now, your house is surrounded by suspects. So we pulled into your neighbor's garage and we are going to cut through the fenced yard so that no one sees you leave."

Annissa nodded her head in agreement.

Samuels silently led the way to a hole in the fence separating the yards. Cedar planks were lying on the ground next to a hammer. They were walking swiftly and, the Davises' neighbor, Mrs. Gfander, was waiting for them at her back door.

Annissa was close to Mrs. Gfander. She had been widowed for six months and had no family. During her husband's lost battle with cancer, she used Annissa's shoulder to cry on and her home as a place to escape her painful reality. The two women had grown closer as Mrs. Gfander healed from losing her husband.

"Oh, Mrs. Gfander, I am so sorry to bother you." Annissa greeted her with a hug.

"It's never a bother, dear."

"Mrs. Gfander, I need you to do as I say." Samuels cleared his throat and sat his sunglasses down on the table, and stared at her, waiting for a response.

Mrs. Gfander was in her late 80s and stood about five feet tall, with white curly hair. The grocery store, the drug store and the Davises' house were her only destinations when out of her nest. She spent her days in front of the TV and nights reading herself to sleep in her recliner. She was never scared and always willing to do a good deed. Annissa looked forward to spending her later years in such a manner.

"Yes, anything you need," said Mrs. Gfander, extending her shaky arm and raising a teapot to make a friendly offer.

"No," he tilted his cap. "Here's the plan. I'm going to leave in my car. The three of you are going to wait 20 minutes after I've gone and then, you leave. There's a Minute Mart four blocks up, on Main. We will meet there and switch cars. Got it?"

"Yes, sir," Greta responded. "See you there."

As Samuels exited the neighborhood, he stopped where the men were being taken into custody. "We got her," he coolly stated to Sean before he speeded off.

57

Aaron and Seth returned to shore with Staci's arms hanging around their necks. Mom and Cosby rushed to help. The three kids were exhausted. Aaron was spent. He needed food and rest.

As they came out of the water, Seth heard, "Hey text buddy!" It was Samantha. They had texted non-stop since their meeting at the diner. A friendship had blossomed. Seth discovered that she lived less than five miles from Jeff, but she was still recovering from an ex who had treated her badly.

Neglecting Staci, due to the sight of Samantha, Seth let her arm slip from his hand. Staci fell halfway to the ground and he didn't even flinch. "Hey there! I didn't think you were coming?"

"What, and miss seeing you?" Samantha knew it was a cheesy line but couldn't stop the words.

Blushing, he said, "Wow," and then he was speechless. He was feeling faint. The crowd was thick around the shore, as the spectators watched the police pull Mollie's lifeless body out of the water.

Samantha could tell Seth was struggling to stand and rushed to his side, grabbing a towel off the canopy-covered picnic table. "Sit down and rest. I'll be right back. Here, let me help you get her inside." Her motherly instincts piqued Seth's interest further. She turned to Bub's mother and said, "Let me help you get her inside. I'm Samantha. Are you Seth's mom?"

Mom was supporting Staci's limp body. "Oh thank you honey, these kids have had quite an ordeal. I'm not Seth's mother but he and my son are very close and I know him well. My daughter is somewhere around here. She has an amazing ability to make herself scarce when needed."

Pipe Vision

Samantha laughed, "Well I am here now. Let's get her inside and into bed. Seth, stay there 'til I get back and I'll take care of you."

A stranger, who was a fellow guest of the campground and saw Samatha and mom having trouble, walked up to them offering to help and took Staci into his arms. "Go get the door. I have her," He instructed the ladies. Walking into the camper, he laid her on the bed.

"Thank you so much, both of you," Mom said to Samantha and waved to the neighborly guest as he walked off.

Larry's phone call interrupted her conversation. "Hi. Where are you all going with Bub?"

"We think Bub's visions have taken over where Staci left off. This is peculiar but they seem to know what happened to this girl and, from what I have been told, no one would have ever found the girl in the lake. Anyway, is Seth near you? I need to find his dad."

"Yeah, he is outside. These kids are just wiped out." She jumped out of the camper. "Seth, where is your father?"

"I don't know. I thought he was here. What's up?"

"Larry needs you to find him. They need his help."

"Great, once again my dad is not around when he is needed." Seth dragged his tired body up the side of the hill to the pavilion and looked for anything with a skirt and four kids because he had a feeling that is where his dad would be. His dad couldn't keep the charade up and probably had very little interest in floating bodies on the lake. He knew the bar was the best place to start since his father was not answering his phone. Seth had unintentionally ditched Samantha at the camper and decided to send her a text that he would be back as soon as possible. Her reply: "take your time, I'll wait," closing with a smile.

Sure enough, his dad was sweet-talking a girl who might have been pushing 25. He had been so used to his dating in the past that he wasn't even fazed. He stood at the door, watching the master of scuzzy sweet talk lure an innocent victim into thinking he was a wealthy playboy. This was the part Seth enjoyed.

"Hi, Dad!"

"Dad?" She looked at him with rosy cheeks and a tightly held body, which started to sag with her disappointment. Every baby-mama around these parts wants an older single man with no children and no baggage.

"Yeah, um, well, a few weeks out of the year, then he goes back to his mama." Jeff crossed his arms. "What do you want, boy?"

"Bub's dad needs you. A body was found in the lake and Bub knows the details of the crime. He is taking them to the place where the murder supposedly happened." Seth made it sound as dramatic as possible, hoping he might be taken seriously.

"For real?"

Seth thought, "What a juvenile thing to say, 'for real,'" but he repeated the words of his father before continuing. "He said to call him." He concluded the conversation by giving Larry's number to Jeff and saying, "I don't care. Do what you want."

Seth was on to better things. Yeah, seeing a body being pulled out of the lake was cool, but the feeling he experienced around Samantha was more important to him. He had heard all of the clichés his whole life about love. How, when someone just knows as soon as they meet a person, they are the one. His love life was immature, young, well let's be truthful, it was nonexistent. He was trying to play it cool. He had seen his mom and dad burn through relationships by being smothering, overbearing and needy. He did not want this. His plan was to spend the day with Samantha and make her feel special. If she dug him, great. If not, well, he was a pro at the "if not."

He sashayed through the crowd, which had returned to the stage area. His hands were in his pockets and his head down. He was being careful not to rush back to Samantha's side. It was tempting to be overbearing.

After walking aimlessly around the pavilion, he felt a tap on his shoulder. "Are you avoiding me or something?" It was Samantha.

"Far from it. I couldn't wait to get back to you, but I want to be cool and not look like an overbearing dweeb." The words were uncontrollable as his face flushed with embarrassment.

She stood back and smiled, "You don't have to worry about that with me. What you see is what you get and I would like to know everything about you, the kid from California."

"Well, we could not have picked a better day for a first date." Everyone appreciates a little sarcasm, he thought.

Seth decided to ditch Aaron, Sissy, Staci and Bub. After all, he had a pretty girl who wanted to spend time with him and he did not care about anything else.

Seth and Samantha walked through the pavilion and ended up in front of our trailer when Mom stuck her head out. "Seth, are you okay? I don't want to leave Staci, but can I fix you and Samantha something to eat?"

Samantha beat him to the answer. "I'll take care of him. I'm going to take him for a bite."

"I must be the luckiest guy in the world," he thought. As they walked back toward the pavilion, she gently put her hands around his arm and her head on his shoulder. It was a feeling he had never experienced but was willing to walk around all day so that it wouldn't end. The feeling was mutual.

58

"**W**here are you going?"

"Back to where we were this morning. How's he doing?" Greg asked as he was speeding down the country road traveled earlier in the day.

Larry was a strong man who never showed much emotion, but this day was getting to him. Staci was not as bad, but seeing his son in this state, was a little too much. "He is okay. Just get there." His voice cracked from holding back tears.

"Man, I am getting there."

Completely sidetracked from the events of his own life, Dave snapped his head up. "Damn, I need to check on my wife." Reaching in his pocket, "Man! I left my phone with the girl on the boat. Can I borrow your phone, brother?"

Greg tossed his phone to Dave, who caught it between his forearm and stomach. "Thanks!" He immediately dialed Annissa and asked, "Hey, where are you?"

"Mrs. Gfander's."

Sitting there trying to think of a situation that would put her next door, he asked, "Umm, what? What are you doing there?"

"Well, I was waiting for you to call me. You said you would, to give me a plan." She was trying to hold back tears.

"I know, sweetie. I actually have been caught up in a case."

"So, you finally had to bring out the 1937 Ford, huh?" Annissa laughed.

Dave laughed with his wife. "Finally had to use it, Babe."

Annissa was validating his use of the word to make sure Samuels and Greta were actually sent by him. "What is the plan now? Is everything okay there? When can you come home? Oh, Dave, I am so scared."

He was too, but kept his concerns to himself. "I will be home tomorrow. I have to help Greg with something and then I will be heading that way." He gulped. "Do what they say until I get there. They will keep you safe." Or so he hoped. "I need to call you back, okay."

"Dave." Her tone was serious. "I love you. Please come home safe to me."

"I will. I promise." Putting the phone on the seat, he looked at his brother in the rearview mirror, "What are the chances of me getting a helicopter or private plane home tonight?"

"I don't know. I have never had that request," he laughed but noticed the lack of a smile on Dave's face. "What's up?"

"I think Annissa is in trouble. I can only handle one situation at a time. I am here, now."

Bub let out a loud scream from pain as they turned in the rocky road, "There Daddy! There's the man! He just killed her! He is walking towards us."

"Do you all see anything?" Larry asked Greg and Dave.

Both men shook their heads.

"No." Dave looked out the window. "Stop."

Bub was in a place he had never been before, tracing the steps of a man he had never met, solving an unknown crime and giving them directions to a place they never knew about. Bub took them to the hideout.

Jeff had caught up to the group and knew the property they were on. But, according to his notes, it belonged to a guy who had died a few years ago. The guy had no family and the estate never probated. The property was considered abandoned.

Dave kept asking Bub questions about the man, his clothes and the car he was driving. Bub knew all of the answers, but the trance was coming to a close and he was exhausted.

Putting his head down Bub said. "I need to rest. I can't do anymore."

"Bub, is there anything else?" Dave was trying to keep him talking and keep the vision alive in his head.

The last words Bub said were, "He lives, up north, near cars and water."

"Detroit?" Dave snapped.

"Yeah." Bub was out.

"There is no way this world and my world could be connected. It doesn't make sense. It is too convenient. What is this? A sewer, out here? With a padlock?" The Chief knelt down to examine the padlock, "This isn't a sewer." The sun was starting to set and the shadows of the trees created darkness around the men. "I want in there, open it up."

Greg looked, "How do you propose we do that?"

"I don't know?"

"Shoot it?"

"Trust me, that only works in movies. You have anything in that rig of yours?" Dave innocently asked. "Better yet, let's call Clifton and get a warrant and a Crime Team down here."

"Crime Team," Jeff laughed. "Boy, you are downtown. You think anyone around here is going to lose sleep or expend any efforts on finding out who killed that crack whore? Whoever did it did a service and deserves to be praised."

"Greg, call Clifton." Dave stared coldly at Jeff. "You see sir, where I come from a life is a life. If people chose to destroy their lives with drugs or being a whore, that is their choice. But, law enforcement has a responsibility, no, a duty, to protect it. Now, I suggest you leave here."

Jeff stared back at them as he walked down the dirt-covered road. Dad yelled to him, "Your boy deserves better than you, and I will call his mother and ask she pursue revoking your visitation rights."

Jeff stopped and said, "Go ahead. Taking care of him two weeks a year is more stress than it is worth." He continued down the road, never looking back.

"There is no damn cell coverage here. What are we going to do? You know, I hate to say this, he's right. As much as I disagree, Clifton is going to say the same."

"This is unbelievable. I am in the redneck court of law where guilty until proven innocent and a life is only important if you are not a druggie." He sighed and looked around. The moon had not risen yet, and only silhouettes of bodies could be seen, except for the dome light on the truck. "Well, if that's the case, this crime won't even get prosecuted. So, why get a warrant? So, I ask again, is there anything in your truck we can pry this cap off with?"

Larry looked toward the sky in thought and walked over to the rear of the truck. He only had simple tools. After digging around the bed of his truck, he found a two-foot crowbar. He hopped down from the bed, walked over, turned the headlights on and checked on me. I was still dazed.

"Where is Brookside? Or Pordy? Bub is in the back saying the man is on Pordy."

Greg looked at Dave, "Isn't that . . . ?"

"Yep."

"That what?" Larry wanted to be included in the brother-ease. "Umm, what's going on?"

"My house in Michigan is on Pordy," said Dave. He told Larry and Greg the true situation of his wife and her affair. He knew there was no way that the two could be connected. It was illogical and too convenient. Honestly, it was too frightening. He was here now, that was his focus.

"Don't you need to get home to your wife?" Larry asked, as he started working on getting the padlock off. It was a fruitless effort. The lock and loops it closed were high-gauge steel and there was no play was in the grated cover. "This isn't going to work."

"I have mixed emotions," said Dave. "The nice guy, in me wants to rush home and protect her and the asshole in me is saying 'fuck her, she made her bed, let her lie in it.'"

"This isn't going to work." Larry, out of breath from swinging a sparking crowbar, threw it down and sat Indian-style, as headlights appeared in the distance. "Who could that be?"

Checking his gun and looking down the sight, loading it and then placing back in his hip holster, he said, "Hopefully, it isn't the guy who hides here."

"No, that's Jim. I recognize the sound of the car. How did he find us here?" Greg walked up the road a spell and waited for the truck to finish pulling toward the trees.

"Hey Jim, what brings you out this way?" Greg asked as Jim shut the door to his truck.

"Well," Jim said, spitting on the ground, "I heard about the kids finding Mollie's body and stopped by your campsite, Larry, to check on your young-uns and your wife said Bub was having more visions."

"But how did you know we were here?" Dave asked.

"Well, I knew you were headed to where we was earlier and I saw something moving back here and thought I would scope it out," he smiled, spitting. "And here you guys are."

Larry pointed at the truck. "My boy had a vision that led us here," he said. Never in his dreams did he imagine uttering those words.

"Ahh, I see. Well whatcha doin' now?"

"We want to get this cover open," Greg was pointing. "No luck though, we came unprepared."

Jim hobbled over to the target that the three men wanted open and walked back to his truck.

"What's he doing?" Dave quietly asked Greg.

"I don't know." Greg studied Jim as he dug through a toolbox on his truck.

Jim was digging and throwing some stuff in a five-gallon bucket, which was browned with faded blood from hunting. When he returned, he said, "I think we can get that open with a little C-4."

"What?" Dave's eyes shot open.

"Plastic explosives, you know?"

"Yeah, I know. But, what're you doing with it?"

Larry sat there silently, "This is bad. This is really bad. No good can come from this. What the hell are we doing, Greg? We aren't cops. Your brother is, but he isn't part of the good ol' boy club down here. For all we know, this could be run by the local authorities."

Jim looked at me as he started to prepare the cap for the blast. "I like your thinking. But, nah. The boys around here, they ain't that smart. They ain't this smart," he laughed, while launching his dip into the woods.

They sat silently, while Big Jim studied the cover and the lock he was attempting to blow open. Dave knew nothing about explosives but he did know how to ask questions and get information.

"Where did you get that stuff?"

"Does it really matter?"

"No, I suppose not."

Greg started wondering what else might be brought onto his campground without his knowledge.

"Do you know how much to use?"

Big Jim stopped and looked up, "Not really. I am just using a little to snap the lock. I think we're ready." He grabbed the roll of detonator cord. "Let's go over there, behind those trees."

The three walked over to a row of big locust trees. Each man being blocked, Dad shut the car door to protect my sleeping body.

"Ready?" Jim asked as he positioned himself with the detonator in his hand.

Three non-confident men agreed. Jim counted down from three and flipped the switch. Nothing happened.

Chief Davis, who had had a little experience with plastic explosives, walked over to Jim, "Is there a delay?"

"No, it should have gone off. I don't know what happened." He got up from his stoop and started to walk over to the cover. Before he was halfway there, he heard a click. "Whoops!" he said, as he dived behind our truck.

The explosives ignited, and then a monstrous bang. They watched as a raincloud of dirt and debris sailed into the air and returned to earth. The three rushed over to the cover and it was gone.

"Where's the cover?" Dad asked.

The three men jumped to a loud bang. The cover landed on the hood of Larry's truck, leaving what appeared to be large quarter slot for a pop machine.

"Holy shit," Dad ran over to inspect the damage. "That could have killed one of us. Are you a moron?"

Big Jim got nervous. "I'm sorry. I had no idea it would do that. I . . . I just used a little. Looking at the crater it made in the earth, I guess a little goes a long way."

Greg wasn't interested in their conversation. "Look, there are stairs down. Give me that flashlight."

He looked at his brother, standing on soft earth. Chief Davis stepped back to control his slipping feet. "Wait here! I am going in to look around. Wait five minutes. If I am not back, well, I guess, come after me." He sat down, placed his feet in the hole and shined the light in.

59

"I guess we should be leaving now," Mrs. Gfander said, as she walked toward her purse sitting on the counter. "I don't want to be late."

"We're leaving, but you're not." Greta pulled out her gun and shot Mrs. Gfander in one motion. Annissa ran in from the garage, where she was putting her bags in the car.

"Oh my God! What did you do?" She dropped to her knees, putting her ear on Mrs. Gfander's lifeless body, listening and feeling for a heartbeat or breath. There were neither. "You...why did you do this?"

"She was in our way. Now get up and go to the car!" Greta yanked Annissa up by her hair. "You have been nothing but a problem for me. I want the problem to go away. Now go!" She shoved Annissa down the stairs, where she landed on the garage floor.

"There is no reason to treat me this way." Annissa was on her knees looking at her torn running suit.

"Shut up!"

Watching the gun that was pointed at her face, Annissa said, "All right! Whatever you want. Please, just don't hurt me."

"We'll see." Greta opened the car door. "Get the fuck in the car and don't say another word. My 'sweet and nice' routine is over. I have you now and you are my ticket. Dead or alive."

Annissa sat there silently, waiting for Greta. Her purse was on the back-seat floorboard on the driver's side, just beyond arm's reach. As much as she hated it, being friendly was her only option until she could devise a plan, "So," she said, jumping in her seat with enthusiasm and reaching for her seatbelt, "where are we going?" Realizing after saying this that she disobeyed her order to be silent,

she said, "I'm sorry. You told me to shut up. You'd think being the wife of a cop I'd know how to follow directions while being kidnapped."

Greta turned and looked at Annissa, who was still babbling nervously in the back seat, "HEY! You wanna stop talking? We are going for a ride." Greta pulled her phone out of her pocket. "Now shut up."

Samuels answered her phone call. All Annissa could hear was the side next to her. Greta told him that everything was being taken care of and that they were on their way to meet him. She was hurrying and driving recklessly. Annissa did not know who to trust anymore. These were cops, the good guys, and the ones who her husband had said would help her. Was he behind this? Could she trust him? So many questions without answers and her only feeling was fear, which had to be hidden and not exposed as a weakness. Samuels and Greta talked a while, but Annissa was lost in her own thoughts.

When Greta finally ended the conversation, Annissa looked at her and asked, "Where are we going, and what is this plan you kept referring to? My husband told me that you would keep me safe until his return."

"Don't worry about it. We do not work for him. We work for Gabe and you are his property now. Just sit there and shut up."

Annissa did as she was told. It was her only option for staying alive.

60

Zake knew he was screwed. The body was found and he was sure he would never see Houston again. After Greg, Dave and Larry left his place, he began to pack and figure out an exit plan. Zake did not have enough money to go far. He needed leverage because once Mollie's body was found, the local cops would come after him. He would be the scapegoat and everyone else would remain free to make drugs and money.

He had a plan.

Showering and cleaning up, he transposed himself from a country redneck to a clean-cut Southerner and headed out to blend in at the campground, thinking he could ditch his truck there, steal a boat and go someplace where no one knew him.

Zake parked his truck on a dirt road that ran beside the grounds and walked through the woods to the pavilion, where people were gathered waiting for the ceremonial bonfire lighting. Families were huddled together talking and getting to know their chair neighbors.

Jaime, Betta and Joe were together and appeared to be a family. Jaime was not used to being in the crowd; she was usually an observer. Music was blaring, grills smoking and parents drinking while the kids ran back and forth, checking in between riding bikes, fishing or swimming.

Zake saw this as the perfect opportunity to grab a boat and go, until he saw Jaime sitting there with Joe. She stuck out as the type whose parents would do anything to protect her. He noticed Sheriff Clifton at the docks signing a clipboard, wrapping up paperwork with the State Police.

Everyone thought Clifton was dirty, but it was an act he used to get the crooks in Trigg County to trust him and keep the honest citizens,

well, honest. It had worked all through his tenure as Sheriff, but it was an accidental plan. His main goal when he took office was to keep the children out of the drug scene. Since he had taken office, drug use among minors had been cut in half.

"Hey kid, want to make a quick sixty?"

The nerdy kid, who was at the campsite only for one night, looked at Zake cautiously. "Um, what do I have to do?"

"See that girl over there in the jeans and white shirt?"

"Blonde hair?"

"Yep."

"The one I don't have a prayer with," the kid said smugly.

"Yep, that would be the one." Zake was beginning to wonder if he chose the wrong kid. Out of a hundred to bribe, he was here and he decided to roll with it. "I want you to take this sixty bucks and go buy her something at the snack bar."

"Mister," the kid was snorting and was impossible to understand through his hyena laugh, "You must be joking! There is no way that girl would spit on me if I was on fire, much less let me take her to the snack bar for a treat."

"I tell you what, here's the sixty," he handed the kid the money. "If she shoots you down, keep it."

"Man if you want to waste your money, I'll try," he grabbed the money and took off, "Thanks mister!"

The little guy could hardly walk, he was so nervous. Jaime was beautiful. "You can do this," he thought.

Walking up to her, trying to use an intelligent tongue, like old-time movie stars, the boy said, "Good evening, madam. Would you like to accompany me to the snack bar?" He looked at Joe. "With your permission, sir."

"You have my permission, young man," Joe said, extending his hand.

Jaime contemplated while the two shook hands. She looked at Betta, who nodded and winked at her.

Smiling at the kid, Jaime replied, "I would be honored."

The kid didn't know how to react. He wanted to jump up and scream, "Hell yes!!" But, knowing he had to play it cool, he offered his hand to help her up.

As the two walked off, Betta yelled, "You have your phone? Don't be gone too long. Your father might worry." Betta was laughing and Jaime was trying not to.

This poor kid had no idea what to say. Never being in this position before, he stuck to the basics. After simple introductions, they made it to the snack bar quicker than he cared. Everyone was looking at them. They were looking at him and he loved it.

"How may I help you?" Tiffany asked before they arrived at the counter.

The kid paused and looked up at the illuminated menu, "Um, give us one minute."

"Okay." Tiffany went back to playing with her cell phone.

"Do you know what you would like?"

"Um, I think just a dog and a soda."

He looked at Tiffany and held up two fingers, she responded, "That'll be eight bucks."

Handing her a ten and wanting to look like a big shot, he said, "Keep the change."

Unimpressed, Tiffany said, "Thanks, I will bring the food right out."

Jaime and the kid sat down at a booth and talked about everything. The kid could not believe how much they had in common. The time and the meal went by too quickly. Full from pop, he excused himself to go to the restroom and when he returned, Jaime was gone.

Thinking she may have run to the restroom herself, he sat down and waited. Thirty minutes passed, then an hour. He felt sure she would come back at least to get her cell phone and purse. No such luck.

Finally, giving up, gathering her belongings, he walked up to the counter, "Did you see which way the girl I was with went?"

"No."

Saddened and holding back his tears, he said, "Do you have a lost and found? She left her purse and crap here."

His tears were easy to hide, but not his anger.

"Yes."

He threw the stuff up on the counter, stuffed his hand in the pockets of his shorts and disappeared into the crowd.

61

Betta was starting to get concerned, calling Jaime's cell and scanning the crowd for her. She did not see her anywhere. This was not like Jaime. She does not run off, she knows the danger. "Joe, I think we should look for her."

"She's fine. You know how puppy love is … they're probably somewhere talking or making out. Just give her some space." Joe stood up to scan the crowd.

"You know, we are in deep shit if anything happens to her."

"Very," he said, continuing his crowd-watching and puffing on his pipe.

Betta said, "I am going to the restroom and to look around for her."

Betta walked toward the restroom just as the crowd roared during the lighting of the bonfire. Halfway to the restroom she saw the nerdy, zit-covered kid sitting on a park bench in the dark. He looked up as she approached, "What's wrong?"

He did not recognize her at first and then remembered Betta's face. "I went to the restroom and when I came back . . . " He was fighting a losing battle with tears. "She was gone." He took a deep breath and tried to compose himself. "I guess I said something wrong."

Betta sat down beside the boy and took him in her arms, "No baby, Jaime is not like that. At least, I have never seen her act that way. Come, let's go look for her together. I am sure she is here somewhere. Where did you see her last?"

"The snack bar."

"Let's go there," she was starting to worry. "You know, not many people would have the nerve to ask a girl like Jaime out."

"Yeah, neither would I, if this guy hadn't paid me."

Betta interrupted him and spun him around, "What are you talking about?"

"This guy gave me sixty dollars to ask her to go with me to the snack bar. I told him he was wasting his money, that she wouldn't want anything to do with a geek like me and I was right." The boy started crying again.

"No. Oh my God, no! I can't believe this." she hugged him tightly. "You did nothing wrong, it was a setup. Come on, we have to hurry." They ran toward Joe. Betta forgot about having to use the restroom and was out of breath when they reached him. "Joe, Joe, my God! She's been taken."

"What?

Betta repeated the story that she had just heard from the kid. "We need to find a cop or Clifton." She felt a wave of anxiety wash over her.

62

"**D**o you think we should go look for Greg?"

"How, Dave? He has the only flashlight, my truck is about dead from having the headlights on and, to be honest, I want to get Bub home." Larry sighed. "These kids have been through a lot today." He put his hands on his knees as he rose, flannel shirt flapping in the wind. "Hell, we all have."

Big Jim stared down at the hole he blew in the ground, "Think there is anything down there?"

"Nope, a waste of time." Greg's phone rang and Dave answered it. "Now we have a signal. Hello?"

It was Betta, frantic. "Someone took Jaime from the campground and she is gone."

"What, who is this?" Dave didn't recognize the voice.

"Betta, Greg is that you?"

"No. It's Dave, Greg's brother, what's going on? Do you need help?"

"Yes! I need your help! We got to find her. Otherwise, we are all fucked."

"Find who?" Dave wasn't sure who Betta was, meeting so many new people over the last few days.

Betta's voice filled with cell phone static. "Jaime Anderson."

"No shit! I will be there as soon as I…" The call was dropped.. "Damn these cell phones." He looked at Jim, his eyes blank. "Someone has kidnapped Jaime Anderson."

"Who … who would do such a thing?"

"Well, let's see here. A Congressman who isn't really liked, a good-looking teenager. We're in poor redneck country, who wouldn't?"

"Jesus. We got to hurry up and get back. Come on!" Jim said, "Can you wait for Greg?" Jim was throwing stuff in his bucket and looking around frantically.

"Yeah," a flickering light appeared from the woods.

"Nothing here," Greg was unable to finish.

"We need to get back. Jaime Anderson has been kidnapped...the daughter of a Congressman."

Greg was out of breath and leaning against a tree. "Man, Dave, I don't have time for your jokes right now." He reached and slapped the shoulder of his unsmiling brother. "Oh shit."

"Yes."

"Hey Greg, I'm going to head back, I have a funny feeling our friend Zake might be involved in this." Jim excitedly tossed his bucket in the back of his truck.

"No, wait, don't throw that, Jim." Watching the bucket sail through the air with a slow-motion feeling, Greg ducked to the ground, covering his head. "Oh shit!"

"What?" Jim looked at Greg as he opened his truck door.

"You . . . " Greg said, getting up and brushing off his jeans, "you just threw a bucket with C-4 like it was no big deal. That could have blown us all to smithereens."

Jim shrugged as he got in his truck, turned it around and sped down the gravel road.

Dad stopped and looked at his hood. "Uh, um," he said, rubbing his forehead, "I really hope my truck starts. Otherwise, it's gonna be a long walk with a spaced-out kid with visions."

"Have faith man," Greg grabbed the keys from Larry. "I'll drive. I can get us there in half the time."

"Hope one of these kids can find that girl," Dave said, rolling his eyes and stepping into the truck.

As the truck doors slammed shut, Bub popped up, "What girl? Jaime?"

Greg stopped midway through starting the truck and turned around. "How did you know her name?"

"Geez, guys it doesn't take a rocket scientist to figure that out. She's famous and mingling with the crowd. They may as well put a 'kidnap me' sign on her back. We gotta get back."

"Please, please, visions come back, let me be a hero," I thought. Catching a plague could be more fun than visions returning, but I have to find her. I had been dreaming about her since last year and I knew in my heart we would hit it off. Finding her was my chance to get to know Jaime better.

Greg started the truck and threw it in drive, taking off so fast he fishtailed and hit a tree with the bed. "Damn man, I'm sorry."

Larry shrugged, "This truck can't look any worse."

Remembering his own issues, Dave said, "Yeah, tell me about it. I got to call Annissa." After impatiently waiting, a signal was reached, but there was no answer at home or on her cell. "Damn, I told her to take the cell into the crapper if she had to go."

"No answer?"

"No, Dad. He thought he would say that after she answered and found out she was okay. Anyway, she's not home," I said sarcastically, looking out the window.

All three of them, Dad, Dave and Greg turned and looked at me as a car was heading towards us. Greg was still looking at me and was completely unaware he was drifting into oncoming traffic. All I could do was lean back in my seat and bring my knees up to my chest.

"What's he doing? Is it happening again?" Dave asked Larry.

While the three adults were trying to decide if I was nuts or not, I finally mustered a double-barrel point: "We are going to die!"

Puzzled, Dad studied me. "We are?"

Dave finally turned around and saw the headlights of the car barreling toward us. "Jesus! Greg, get on your side."

"What?" Greg looked at his brother.

A horn started to blow. He swerved the truck just in time. "Whoops!"

"Yeah, whoops," said Dave, staring at Greg who apparently was trying not to laugh. "apparently my dipshit brother can't drive," Dave turned back to Dad and I sitting in the backseat. "You said my wife wasn't home. How do you know and where is she?"

My body was tingling and Dad's voice was becoming faint. "I see her with cops, bad cops. San... Sad... no, no, that's not it."

"Samuels?" Chief Davis was baffled.

"Samuels! That's it. He is a bad guy, I think he is holding a gun." I could feel myself start to pass out.

"Oh, God! He's one of my best guys."

"No he isn't," I said, laying my head on the vinyl bench seat. "He is actually a pretty bad guy and really doesn't like you very much." I started to scream, "Chief Davis does nothing but suck ass!"

Chief Davis sat with a blank look on his face, strategizing on what his next move would be. "Do I call him? Do I call the department?" This was a new experience for him and he only knew how to respond when other lives were affected. This was his life, his family, his problem. No one was going to help.

The campground was already barricaded and the state police were not letting anyone in or out. Greg had to get out of the car and explain who he was.

"Look, man, you got to let us in. That man needs to be with his son, who is in there and the kid in the truck needs his medication." He was lying, saying whatever he had to say, to get them into the campground. "Just let me in, I can help you from the inside. This is my campground and I can help, but only from in there."

The police trainee, who was following direct orders, was not yielding. Dave became impatient. "This is stupid," he said, fumbling around the front seat and leaning out the window. "Hey get the fuck out of the way," he said, showing the trainee his badge and gun. "Come on Greg, get in the car."

As Greg got in the car, Dave yelled, "Ain't this your campground? Why the hell are they hassling you?"

"He's a new kid, that's all. A new kid." Greg waved as they drove by the trainee.

Dave hung up the phone. "Fucking son-of-a-bitch," he said, kicking the dirt and slamming the phone on the ground. "All of my hard work fucking gone." He threw his hands up. "Poof! Just like that."

"Get that boy under control!" Clifton said, pointing at Dave. "We got enough chaos going on here."

"Dad, what's going on? What's wrong with Mom? I swear, if you don't tell me I will call her myself," said Aaron. He reached into his pocket, but before he could withdraw his phone, Dave grabbed his hand.

"Stop, I'll tell you later. Mom is in trouble and I am running out of options." He had to change focus. "Where are we here?"

"According to Clifton, we have nothing," Greg said as he walked back over to Dave and Aaron.

"Great, a dead girl, a kidnapped girl and my wife has been kidnapped. What's next?"

Aaron, amazed, jumped up, "What? Mom has been kidnapped?"

"Yeah, but don't worry. It's a setup to rob the department. It's gonna be all right. I was just overreacting." He wanted to reassure Aaron, even though he wasn't sure.

Staci and I were together for the first time since our visions began and we were revisiting the events of the day with my folks. The party had essentially died since Jaime's kidnapping. I was so tired and my head was killing me. I just wanted to sleep. Staci and Sissy, in typical girl fashion, wanted us to get in touch with our feelings and discuss. I had no desire.

Dad, looking in my eyes, said, "Conrad." Whoops, he called me Conrad, which only means one thing, seriousness. "Has this ever happened? Do you see visions often?"

"Not until this trip," I said, rolling my eyes.

"Staci?" You could hear the concern in his voice. Mom sat there quietly.

"Not away from our house. It's haunted. My mom denies it, but I know it is. I have, like, seen ghosts and weird stuff happen."

"Well, you all did a good job, they think."

I interrupted my father, "Oh, no, not again. Please, no, I can't do this right now."

"Do what, Bub?" Dad grabbed my hand.

"Jaime, where is she?" I asked Dad as my body tensed up and the tingling started. Voices became muffled and I could see Jaime sitting at the end of the tube.

"Look, man, you got to let us in. That man needs to be with his son, who is in there and the kid in the truck needs his medication." He was lying, saying whatever he had to say, to get them into the campground. "Just let me in, I can help you from the inside. This is my campground and I can help, but only from in there."

The police trainee, who was following direct orders, was not yielding. Dave became impatient. "This is stupid," he said, fumbling around the front seat and leaning out the window. "Hey get the fuck out of the way," he said, showing the trainee his badge and gun. "Come on Greg, get in the car."

As Greg got in the car, Dave yelled, "Ain't this your campground? Why the hell are they hassling you?"

"He's a new kid, that's all. A new kid." Greg waved as they drove by the trainee.

63

Enjoying a quiet dinner with his wife was a thing of the past. Agents and the flashing lights of the press corps had ruined any chance of romantic dinners in public.

"Mitch, Mitch, I have the plane ready for you sir." Alex was running and screaming through the restaurant.

"Why?"

"You haven't heard?" Alex dropped his head, pulled his phone out and showed him a news video streaming live from the campground.

"Oh my God! Get your coat," Mitch gasped, looking at his wife.

"What?"

"She has been kidnapped."

"Jaime?"

"Yes, let's go." He grabbed Jessie's hand and they scurried out of the restaurant, ignoring questions from reporters.

The waiter handed Alex the check, saying, "Sorry, sir, but I can't afford to have this taken out of my wages."

"I'll get the check!" Alex yelled. "Here." He handed him a few hundred-dollar bills, ran out the door and was barely in the limo when it squealed off.

"What do we know?"

"Nothing." Alex cleared his throat. "I am trying to reach local officials, but I am having no luck. Betta and Joe are being held and questioned. No one will let me talk to them."

"Give me the phone." Mitch dialed Greg. "We'll get to the bottom of this. I'm sure she is fine."

"I've been waiting for your call, sir. Give me one second." Greg walked away from the crowd and told him what he knew. "We are pulling all of the boats on the lake and searching them. It has only been a few hours. I am sure she is fine. When I get news, I will report in to you."

"We are on our way now. You are my eyes and ears."

64

The metal door rolled up after Greta released three horn blasts into the night air. Annissa was unsure what area of town they were in. The streets and the air were damp from the day's cold rain. As the car pulled into the smoke-filled warehouse, three men in leather coats and black shirts greeted them.

"What is this?" Annissa asked.

"Home." Greta opened the door. "Wait here." She got out of the car. The only person Annissa recognized was Samuels and it seemed he was giving the orders. "What do you want me to do with this mouthy bitch?," asked Greta. "I think she and her dumb cop husband are plotting something."

"You're a dumb cop, too. Did she get any calls or make any?"

Ignoring the comment and laughing at Samuels, who was also a cop, Greta said, "No."

"Damn." Samuels walked over to the passenger door and opened it. "Get out."

She did as directed, knowing the best action was to be submissive. Her gut told her to fight but they each had big guns, Glocks, .357's, AK-47's and sawed-off shotguns. She was armed with her mind and a rinky-dink, .22 purse gun. If she were to pull it out, everyone but her would get a shot off.

"Where is he?" Annissa asked.

"Dave? That stupid ass isn't here, nor will he help you," he laughed, "Well, at least not until he finds your body here or wherever it ends up."

"You son-of-a-bitch! Not him. Gabe." Tears, impossible to hide, streamed down her face.

"Yes, I am that. Gabe will not be here either. You are useless to him."

Samuels grabbed a chair and told Annissa to sit down. He spun a chair around and sat in front of her, brushing her hair out of her eyes.

"You see, you are our ticket out of this here," he said. "You have met Greta. Now, meet Bart, Frank and Timmy. We all work for Gabe and he has us by the balls. But by kidnapping and possibly killing you, we can get out of this racket, go down to Kentucky and start a new life, away from a political gangster who has the decision capability and IQ of a pig. Oh yeah, pig. That's where your husband comes in."

"Dave would rather let me die right now than help a handful of thugs, like you," Annissa said.

He backhanded her. "Shut up!" He composed his thoughts and lowered his tone. "You are going to help us. Just do what I say and we will all get what we want."

She sat there quietly and looked at the black muck-stained floor. "Why, why did this happen to me? I was a housewife. I had it all and I had to fuck shit up by having a useless affair with a people-user."

"Yeah. Yeah, you did, but now you can fix it. Are you in?"

Annissa sighed, having no other choice. "Yeah, I guess I am."

"Good, shall we call him?" Samuels pulled out his phone, flipping it in his hand to face the keypad toward her. "Here you go."

Annissa keyed in the number while her upset stomach and hands trembled with waiting for the phone to ring, mumbling, "This is crazy."

Dave answered, "Samuels, do you have my wife safe?"

"Well, Dave, you could say that."

"Annissa?"

"Yep."

"What's going on?"

"Gabe."

"What do you mean, Gabe?"

"Apparently, these morons are cops. I think I am pretty well fucked. They tell me that if I . . . well . . . we, cooperate, they won't hurt us."

"Son-of-a-bitch. Where are you?"

"Got no clue."

"Give me Samuels, that slimy son-of-a-bitch."

Annissa gave Samuels a cold stare while silently handing off the phone.

"Here's the deal," said Samuels. "You know that two hundred fifty thousand we took in the drug bust a few weeks ago? Well, Gabe's wants it back."

"It's locked up in evidence."

"Yeah, he cares about that," said Samuels sarcastically.

Chief Davis sighed in frustration, "Let me see what I can do. We'll be in touch."

"You got two hours."

Dave hung up the phone. "Fucking son-of-a-bitch," he said, kicking the dirt and slamming the phone on the ground. "All of my hard work fucking gone." He threw his hands up. "Poof! Just like that."

"Get that boy under control!" Clifton said, pointing at Dave. "We got enough chaos going on here."

"Dad, what's going on? What's wrong with Mom? I swear, if you don't tell me I will call her myself," said Aaron. He reached into his pocket, but before he could withdraw his phone, Dave grabbed his hand.

"Stop, I'll tell you later. Mom is in trouble and I am running out of options." He had to change focus. "Where are we here?"

"According to Clifton, we have nothing," Greg said as he walked back over to Dave and Aaron.

"Great, a dead girl, a kidnapped girl and my wife has been kidnapped. What's next?"

Aaron, amazed, jumped up, "What? Mom has been kidnapped?"

"Yeah, but don't worry. It's a setup to rob the department. It's gonna be all right. I was just overreacting." He wanted to reassure Aaron, even though he wasn't sure.

Staci and I were together for the first time since our visions began and we were revisiting the events of the day with my folks. The party had essentially died since Jaime's kidnapping. I was so tired and my head was killing me. I just wanted to sleep. Staci and Sissy, in typical girl fashion, wanted us to get in touch with our feelings and discuss. I had no desire.

Dad, looking in my eyes, said, "Conrad." Whoops, he called me Conrad, which only means one thing, seriousness. "Has this ever happened? Do you see visions often?"

"Not until this trip," I said, rolling my eyes.

"Staci?" You could hear the concern in his voice. Mom sat there quietly.

"Not away from our house. It's haunted. My mom denies it, but I know it is. I have, like, seen ghosts and weird stuff happen."

"Well, you all did a good job, they think."

I interrupted my father, "Oh, no, not again. Please, no, I can't do this right now."

"Do what, Bub?" Dad grabbed my hand.

"Jaime, where is she?" I asked Dad as my body tensed up and the tingling started. Voices became muffled and I could see Jaime sitting at the end of the tube.

"I don't know, Bub. Why are you asking me?"

"I'm not, Dad." The pipe vision came back. "Staci, do you see that?"

Staci nodded. "It is a warehouse with a bunch of guys and a black lady with her hands tied behind her back."

"No, it's Jaime with the guy we saw earlier. They are at The Waffle Iron. She is acting like his wife or daughter and she is scared. They're sitting and he is trying to get phone numbers from her. She's so scared."

Dad shot out the door, Cosby barking after him. Only his white shirt was visible in the night air. "Greg, Dave, Clifton!" he screamed, running toward the blue and red flashing lights.

"Over here," Dad heard through the speakers of the PA system.

Dad was out of breath by the time he got there. He couldn't talk and Cosby was running toward Dave and Greg, barking, running toward our trailer, then back to Dad, Greg and Dave, as if to say, "Come on guys, you need to see this!"

"Do we need to go to your place? Is something wrong?" Greg asked.

Dad was shaking from adrenalin going through his veins. All he could do was nod and let out a faint, "Yes."

The two brothers dropped what they were doing and ran to us.

"What's going on?" Greg asked as he was running.

Mom and Sissy were with us. Mom was listening to me, and Sissy to Staci.

"Well, this one apparently knows where that kidnapped girl, Jaime, is, and this one," Dad said, pointing to Staci, "knows about some black lady in a warehouse up by a big lake?"

"Lake Michigan?" Dave asked.

"I don't know, she just said a big lake."

Mom shook her head in confusion.

"Staci, can you hear me?" asked Dave, as he snapped his fingers in front of her face.

We were both on the couch leaning opposite ways, and mumbling gibberish.

"Yeah, Daddy. I can hear you."

Playing along, Dave said in a soft voice, "Tell me what you see," while placing his hand on her knee, consoling her, attempting to elicit the images in her mind.

"Not much, a big warehouse, five men, a lady who is scared. They are talking about plans, if the money doesn't come through."

Dave pulled his notepad out of his back pocket. He reached behind his ear for a pen or pencil that was not there. He searched all over his person for one. Aaron, who had just arrived, saw a pencil by the TV and grabbed it. "Here," he said. "Thanks." Dave squatted to the previous position. "Do you see anything outside? Any signs or numbers?"

"Let me go outside." She got up and walked out the trailer door. He followed her and she began to rub her fingertips along the shell of the trailer until reaching the end and turning with the trailer, said, "Here."

Dave studied her and waited with eyebrows raised. The commotion from the pavilion wasn't upsetting his focus on her. "Here, what?"

"See, Peterson's Metal Shop." Dave examined where she was looking and could see nothing. She stopped and waited for direction. "If you want to know more you better start asking." She jumped and turned around, "No, no don't shoot me."

"What, Staci? Who's going to shoot you?"

She fell to the ground. Dave ran to her side, gently slapping her face. "Come on girl. Stay with me. I need your help." It was no use, she was out cold. He scooped her up and took her to the couch.

While Dave was with Staci, Greg and Dad were grilling me about Jaime's location. We must have been pretty convincing, because when I look back and reflect, I wonder what my reaction would be with my son.

"Tell me what you see, Bub?"

This hurt so badly. Jaime was my girl and she was, literally, in my dreams and I was the only link to her. They interviewed the nerdy kid and he was so scared and upset they had to sedate him and take him to the hospital.

"I don't know."

"Focus! You can do this." This was the first time I have ever seen my parents positively reinforce my goofiness.

"It's a little Waffle Iron with grease on the yellow and blue walls and windows. White, dirty tiles on the floor. Yellowed ceiling tiles and floor-to-ceiling glass in front. They are sitting in the corner. He is playing with a phone, I think but can't figure it out. She is refusing to help him. He looks like the guy we saw today, but he is cleaned up with laundered clothes."

"How did they get there?" Dad asked calmly.

Aaron was standing by the front door of the camper, watching in amazement as he transcribed what was before his eyes. He was writing everything down while he listened. Sissy was sitting beside him. She asked, "Why doesn't this happen to me?"

"Shh, Sissy. I need to write this down." She was trying to regain possession of the spotlight.

"A boat, then a car…I think. I can see them leaving here in a John boat. I don't see the route. Sorry. It's starting to fade."

"Quick, look around! Do you see anything else? Are there people there, anything?" Dad was screaming trying to keep my vision going.

I joined Staci in sleep.

65

Jessie ignored Mitch the entire trip to the airport. When he tried to hold her hand or comfort her, she jerked her body away from him. Knowing her and feeling her pain, he did not push her or try to talk until they were in the air, midway through the flight.

He gulped, knowing that no matter what he said, it would be the wrong thing. However, the silence was too much for him. "We will find her," he said. They were facing each other by the window. He put his hand on her knee.

"I never should have let her go," Jessie muttered. "Not with the crazy people we have surrounding us. Why did I ever let you talk me into this?"

"She's a teenager who sees normality everywhere except in her own world. To us, her life is normal. We have been in this lifestyle for 20 years. Hell, I've forgotten what it was like to go to the store and buy a gallon of milk, or drive, for that matter."

Jessie looked at her husband. Mitch always had a way of putting her mind at ease. "I know but this wouldn't have happened if she was with us."

"How do you know?"

She looked out the window. "I don't. I just have a feeling."

He sat back in his seat. He realized why he fell in love with her. Even when she was upset, she was gorgeous, sexy. "Look at all of the people we know who grew up like her. They have no sense of reality, no clue about hard work. Their lives are just handed to them."

"I know," Jessie said, without making eye contact.

"Most of them end up disasters, either on drugs or following in the footsteps of their parents. They are out of touch with reality, fighting for lost causes they don't believe in but are play acting for the public eye and to win the next election."

He paused, crossed his legs, loosened his tie and unbuttoned his collar. "Most parents are honored when their kids follow in their footsteps. They want their kids to be just like them. Not me. If I had it to do all over, I don't know that I would have gotten into politics. There's no room to raise children."

She was in no mood to have this conversation. She was worried about her baby, but hearing his voice made the flight seem to go faster. It took her mind off the hell her daughter was suffering. "You know, if you win your bid for the presidency, it will only get worse."

He hadn't really thought about that. In his mind, their lives would be easier, more stable. "How so?"

She looked at him squarely.

"Are you serious?" Jessie said, starting to cry. "I thought that you had worked all of this out. You know what that job entails. You will be on call all of the time, be involved in life-threatening situations, constantly traveling. You think that you don't see us now. Well, that will get worse."

He sat and thought. As much as he didn't want to admit she was right, he hadn't truly thought of his family, just the self-inflating thought of being the Commander in Chief. He leaned over and kissed his wife. "Let's find our baby. Then, we will make our decision. If we decide the best thing for us is to drop out of the public eye, we will."

Alex walked up and interrupted their embrace. "Sir, you have a call. It's a Mr. Davis."

"Clive?"

Alex wasn't sure how to respond. Who could joke at a time like this? He stood there and glared at his boss.

Mitch waved his hand and motioned for the phone.

"Relax," he said. "We need to keep our sense of humor. It will keep us positive."

He grabbed the phone and felt the plane start to descend. "Mitch Anderson."

"Sir, Greg Davis. I wanted to give you an update." Greg cleared his throat. "We still do not have much to go on."

"What do you have?"

Greg told him about Bub and Staci's story and how it had led them to the body and to Zake's trailer, and about the second round of visions, regarding Annissa. He told them that the two were also claiming to be able to see Jaime in a vision but, as of yet, they were unable to confirm this..

"Do you think this is valid?" Mitch sat in his chair with his elbow resting on the armrest and striped tie lying on his chest.

"It's all we have, sir. At this point we need all the help we can get."

"What about Betta and Joe?"

"Their story checks out and they are at the police station."

"I'll call you when we land." He paused. "And Greg, not a word to the press or the authorities. You go check it out."

"Yes, sir."

Handing the phone to Alex, Mitch updated him and Jessie about the conversation and what Greg knew, concluding with, "And not a word of this to the press, got me?" He pointed at Alex.

"Yes, sir."

The couple sat silently for the remainder of the flight.

66

"**W**ho are you?"

"Shut up," said Zake. He was getting frustrated with her badgering. "I know a cute little girl like you has to have a daddy who loves her. Now, give me his number." He rolled his eyes. "Hell, give me any number to call."

"Well, moron, I would if I could, but because you told me not to take my phone, I don't know any numbers." Jaime wasn't lying. Since she had a cell phone, she did not remember any numbers, except their house in Indiana and no one was there. "Have you any clue who I am?"

"Yeah, you are that Senator's daughter."

"Congressman."

"Whatever."

"Speaker of the House, to be exact."

"Yeah, well, without Daddy's numbers, that don't get you shit." The gun he kidnapped her with was hanging out of his jacket pocket. He had told her that if she made any movements or tried to attract attention to them, he would kill her.

Jaime learned from her Secret Service classes that if she were ever in this position then she should always do what she was told, but keep eyes open for weakness. She noticed, as time went by, that he was starting to shake and sweat from what seemed to be withdrawal. He was jonesing. The mystery was withdrawal from what? Jaime knew that as people detox, their minds and bodies do weird things and they had no desire to become a victim.

"What's your name?"

"Zake."

"Seriously?"

"Yes. Why would I lie?" His heart was racing and his plan was falling apart. She was a yakky paycheck with no phone numbers and he needed to contact her parents. "You got to know some numbers I can call for the ransom."

"Ransom?" She leaned forward and put her chin on her fist supported by an elbow on the table. "They won't give you any money. They are going to issue an Amber Alert, put my cute little picture on the TV up there and wait for tips."

"Amber Alert?" He scratched his head and was puzzled. "What's that?"

"Seriously, do you live in a cave?"

"Don't watch TV." He motioned to the waitress. "More soda please."

"Then how do you know who I am?" Jaime was truly mystified by this creature and wanted to get as far from him as possible.

"Seen your picture with some people in the paper." This sounded good to him, not really remembering how he knew who she was.

"Ahh, I see." She spun her hair around as if to flirt. "They say I have a face to never be forgotten."

She had no desire to be around this guy but she had seen in the past that a false flirt could get women what they wanted. Why not try?

The waitress brought their sodas and did not wait for another request. She was more interested in watching the USA Idol, on the snow-covered TV. Jaime was praying for a special bulletin to pop up, hoping one of the bar people would see her and help. Zake could not see the TV from his angle.

"Do you even have a plan?"

"No."

"Then why did you take me?"

"It was an afterthought."

"To?"

"All I was going to do was steal a boat to get over here," he laughed. "Then, I saw you and you just looked like a paycheck. I never would have dreamed you would agree to letting that geek take you to the snack bar," he said, wiping his brow with a red bandana.

"You were behind that?"

"Yes." He grabbed her hand and put a knife up to her wrist. The waitress was fidgeting around in the back. "Now, if you want that pretty, little young body of yours to remain unharmed, give me some numbers."

She yanked her hand back. "I truly don't know any." She was thinking and she had no clue. Did he want her to guess a number? She had an idea. She turned her face to look out the window, sighing and rolling her eyes. "Ask for a phone book."

"What?"

Pipe Vision

"Ask for a phone book. We'll call the campground and ask for a guy named Greg," she stated, looking down. "He knows how to get hold of my father. He'll get a message to him."

Impatient with her games, Zake asked, "You lying to me?"

"No. I swear."

Jaime could not hide her trembling.

67

"**C**ome on Dave, we gotta go check out Bub's story."

"Shouldn't we tell the police and let them do it?" Dave really needed to figure out how to rescue Annissa.

"No," said Greg. "I promised the girl's father we would investigate this on the down low. He wants to protect everyone before the press gets a hold of this vision story. I feel sure, based on today, it's a good lead, but Mitch made a request and I have to honor it. Besides," he said, walking to the car, "if it's true, he will help you. Give me the key."

"Okay," Dave shrugged as he hopped in the car. "We should at least tell Clifton we'll be back. If we leave without checking in, it could be suspicious."

"Good point." Greg started the car and threw it into gear.

Larry ran behind the car. "Wait, wait I'll go with you."

"No, stay here with your family," Greg yelled back from the rolling car. "They need you." He sped off, stopping to interrupt Clifton's meeting. He told Paul they had to run into town and meet Mitch to bring him back. Greg declined their offer of an escort.

Speeding through the dark, two-lane country road, Dave finally broke the silence: "Did you ever think about forgiveness?"

"Huh?"

"With your ex? Did you ever think to forgive her?"

"Yeah, lots of times." Greg was not sure where the conversation was going. "Divorce isn't for everyone. In my case, no kids were involved and it wasn't a whoops situation."

"Explain."

"Well, let's just say she went out one night and had a one-night stand, came clean the next day or soon after and never saw the guy again."

Greg sniffed and cleared the crying voice away. "We could have gone to counseling and probably recovered fine. However, once I found out about it, she smeared my nose in it, told me that she had to give the guy a chance and see where it went. I was tossed to the curb like rancid meat. I tried to make it work, but after being shoved aside so much I … I left."

The two men sat silently in the car as the night passed them by. After several miles of quiet, deep thoughts, Dave scratched his head.

"I'm torn," he said. "I don't know what to do. I want to just leave her to get even for the pain she has caused me, but all that would do is hurt Aaron."

"I don't know. The pain never goes away. It becomes a matter of if you truly love her or not. I was misguided by hurt. It is in the past now and it took two years to get over her."

"How did you get over her?" asked Dave, turning his head and looking at his brother.

Greg coldly stared into the oncoming night.

"I killed her," he said.

Dave started laughing deeply. "Yeah right, that's hilarious. Like, in your head, you killed her in your head."

Greg glanced silently at his brother.

Dave's smile began to fade. "No, man. You can't be telling me shit like that. You know, I am a law man. Tell me you're kidding."

"Yeah, man of course I'm kidding." He wasn't. The truth is that they went on vacation. He came back, she didn't.

"So, did she stay with this guy?"

"Yes, and what a piece of shit he was," he laughed. "She got what she deserved."

"Why didn't you ever find someone else?"

"Tired of getting hurt."

Greg sighed deeply and changed the subject. "I hope this girl is here. You ready?" Greg asked while they pulled into the lot behind the dumpster with his headlights off.

They checked their guns and exited the car. There were windows on two sides of the building; the remaining sides were brick.

They hid their guns as they slid in the door and saw Jaime and Zake sitting alone in a booth. Zake was starting to fade from withdrawal, his body feeling weak and quivery, unaware of them sliding into the booth beside him.

"Hands on the table." Dave poked Zake in the ribs with the gun. "Greg, get her out of here."

Greg grabbed her arm. "Come on Jaime, your parents are on their way." He escorted the girl out of the restaurant and to his car.

Once safely outside the restaurant, he began dialing. "Mitch?" Greg screamed into his phone, "I got her! She's safe!" He followed the news with the Waffle Iron's address. "How long until you get here?" He waited for an answer and then ended the call with, "See you then."

Jaime was in tears. Her once clean white shirt was now wrinkled and smudged. "Thank God! How did you ever find me? That kid he used to coax me in, is he dead? He told me he was. My parents are going to kill me and fire Joe and Betta." She started pacing up and down the side of the car in the glow of the neon lights. "It's all my fault. I'm the one who wanted to go to the party so Betta could meet you."

"Me?"

She dropped her hands and smacked them on her leg, "Yeah, she's kinda got a thing for you." She raised her hands and slid them down her face while sighing.

"Really?" Greg had no clue and his mouth gaped open with surprise.

Blue and red flashing lights, accompanied by sirens, invaded the night sky as the police sped into view. Before the unmarked Secret Service vehicle could halt, Mitch was out of the car screaming, "Jaime, baby, are you okay?"

Jaime was crying and grabbing her dad for dear life. Jessie was right behind him, trying not to fall over in her high heels. "Oh my God, oh my God," she said, pushing her husband out of the way. "Let me see my baby." She spun Jaime around and ran her hands down Jaime's body looking for blemishes or marks.

"She's fine. What the hell happened?" Mitch asked, looking to Greg for an answer.

"He saw her at the campground with Joe and Betta."

Mitch shook his head and squinted, "What? Where?"

"Dad, don't be mad. It's all my fault," said Jaime. She told her father of the plan she had to fix up Greg and Betta and that she just wanted to be around some kids her age.

"Well, how did you know to come here?" He was looking around at all of the chaos going on. They could hear Zake in the background saying, "He made a deal with me! He told me I wasn't going to be arrested."

Dave sashayed out the door behind Zake, with one hand grasping Zake's hand-cuffed arm and the other twirling his index finger around his shaking head. "Got me. Oh, and ask him about his meth recipe. Tell that to the school kids. I guarantee they'll never do drugs again."

Zake was still screaming profanities at Dave. The officers who had taken Zake from Dave were trying to put him in the car and yelling "Shut up and get in the car."

Wandering over to Mitch and Greg, Dave said, "You're Mitch. Excuse me, Congressman Anderson, right?"

"Yes," said Mitch, holding out his hand. "Why?"

Dave returned the gesture and showed his badge, "I need to borrow your plane, to bust some bad guys."

"Okay, where?"

"Near Detroit."

"Done," he pulled his phone out. "When do we leave?"

"Soon. Like, now. I know who the drug lord is for this area and he sounds a lot like Gabe Maddox."

"Ah, shit," said Mitch, and stormed off to make the arrangements.

"Gabe Maddox?"

"He is the Governor of Michigan and apparently likes to supply this guy with products." Dave pointed at Zake, who was resting his head on the side of the police car as he screamed and resisted the confinement of the vehicle and the fate that awaited him. Officers, laughing at the attention-getting technique surrounded him. "Then he takes all the money, leaving him with free dope."

"What was that about a deal?" Greg scratched his head and walked over to the car door.

"Oh, I told him, he would have immunity if he told me how Mollie died and who it was," said Dave. "Houston killed her three days ago. Apparently, he asked this guy to tie her up. Which explains the floating shoe. No pro would leave shoes on a body about to get sunk. Let's go get Bub."

68

The gang was sitting around the table playing gin and passing time. Annissa was tied to a chair, head hung low from exhaustion. The execution order had not been given and all were becoming impatient.

The overhead door opened, guns were cocked. A black Town Car pulled in. "Where is she?" Gabe stepped out of the car and shut the door.

Bart nodded his head toward Annissa.

"Get lost!" commanded Gabe and everyone scattered to the back of the warehouse. "Wait for my signal. Give me that," he grabbed Bart's Glock from him. Walking over to Annissa, he nudged her with the barrel. "Wake up, you slut."

"It's over, Gabe. I want to go back to my husband. I love him. He has given me a great life and my son and I belong with him."

"No way. Sorry, you are mine and I won't let you go back."

"You won't let me?" She started fighting with the ropes that bound her. "I decide who I go with."

"Not any more. If I can't have you, I will kill you myself." He laughed as he grabbed a beer from the table and popped it open. "Usually, you women are nothing to me, but you are different. You make me, and I want to be with you for the rest of my life."

"Gabe, we were only together once!"

"Funny."

"What's funny?"

"How we were only together one night and I know we will spend the rest of our lives together."

He drank the beer in one gulp and grabbed another. "He'll learn to live without you. He'll have to."

"What about my son?"

"Kids are strong. He'll learn to adapt. Besides, the little bastard is only 16. I'll make it so miserable for him that he'll want to move out or I'll just throw him out." He hated kids but he hid it when the cameras were rolling.

"I don't know, Gabe. I love my family and the life my husband has given me. He doesn't deserve to be treated this way."

"He loves you, huh?" He snapped his fingers and his driver handed him a folder. "If he loves you so much, then why is he talking with, and meeting, these women?"

"Look, he isn't perfect. None of us are. But, he never did anything to me and I'm not going to leave him."

"Yeah," he sighed, sat back and nodded, "you are. If you don't, I'm going to start exposing everything. Telling all of your family and friends about the minute your husband left town with your kid, you couldn't wait to hop in the sack with me. And look here," Gabe said, tossing a stack of photos at her. "Pictures of you going in and out of hotels while he is at work, Let's see how much he wants you then."

Annissa started to cry. She had been confused for so long that she didn't want to hurt anyone. This was all a fantasy and was never supposed to become part of twisted reality. "Please, just let me go."

"No, you are mine now and always will be. Nothing will ever get in our way. You will do as I say or suffer dire consequences."

"No, Gabe," she was fighting the ropes and losing. They were beginning to break her skin.

"Wait here." He leaned over and kissed her. "I'll be right back."

As she sat there, she started to cry. All she wanted was her husband, who made her smile and always seemed to take away her tears.

69

"How far out are we?" Dave was stewing. He did not know how the night would end.

"I don't know, maybe an hour or so. Relax dude, it will all be good," Greg said, reassuring his brother. "She's alive and fine. We'll get her back."

"I hope so." Dave turned to Mitch. "I need your help, Congressman."

He rubbed his forehead and ran his fingers through his hair. "It looks as if I have a dirty police department, a crooked Governor and God knows what else. I need some backing. This could get ugly or go easy, but I need help."

"You got it. Let me make some calls." Mitch rose out of his seat and walked back to his office on the plane.

Greg started to get worried and doubted this positive attitude. "Damn man, are we going to die?"

"I don't want my son getting hurt," Larry popped in, "but I'll be glad to help you take these guys down. I was an M.P. back in the day."

"Really?"

Larry didn't want to tell them that he was in the reserves and the closest he came to police duty was torturing a kid who stole a candy bar. He wasn't Barney Fife, but he wasn't a slick TV cop either. He liked the thought of bringing down bad guys. "Yes sir."

"Bub will be safe once he leads us there, if he can. He will stay with the Congressman," he turned and looked at his sleeping son. "Can you try to wake him up? We need to see if he knows any more than what he told us. We need to see if he can visualize the location."

"Bub," Dad gently shook me, "Bubba, you need to wake up."

Pipe
Vision

———— ◆◆◆ ————

Dad was rubbing my chest and pressing down.

I yawned and stretched out my body. "What?" I did not know where I was. I looked at Dad with fearful eyes and started crying.

"Hey, hey, it's okay," Dad said in a soft voice. "We are on a plane headed to Detroit. We are looking for the warehouse you told us about."

"The girl, Dad…did you find her?"

"Yes, she is safe at her house. We couldn't have done it without your help, son."

Mitch walked back in from his office on the airplane. "Done," he said looking at Dave.

"This is Congressman Anderson, Jaime's father."

The Congressman walked over to me and extended his hand, "Thank you, young man. I don't know how you helped me, but I am very grateful."

"Yes sir, you're welcome. I just wish these visions would quit and leave me alone."

Dave took over the conversation. "Do you have anymore visions, besides what you told us? We think we know the area but we could use more detail."

70

The engines started to hum louder as the plane made its descent. The pilot's voice came over the speaker: "Sir, we will be on the ground in 15 minutes."

Alex walked up the aisle from the office. "Sir, I think we have everything in order. Don't we need search warrants or something?"

"Probably. Chief?" asked Mitch.

"My wife is with dirty cops and a Governor who we have found to be the leader of a drug operation in Kentucky. Right now, all I care about is getting her back. My suspicions are that there are dirty judges, as well. So, we just have to see how it goes."

"I agree," Alex said, while sipping his water. "You're the leader of this operation," he said to Mitch.

Mitch studied Alex for a minute. "No, actually. No, I am not. This is Chief Davis' family and town. He is the one in charge."

"Thank you, sir," the Chief said.

The plane landed and they were greeted by National Guard Reserves and SUVs. "Guys, this is Chief Davis. He is in charge," said Mitch, turning to Dave. "How do you want to do this?"

Dave looked his notes over and scanned the available vehicles. "We all ride together in that one," he pointed to the second vehicle, a big black Suburban.

"Oh man, not again!" I felt the vision feeling come over me again and I fell to the ground.

"Quick, get the boy in the car so we can start driving." Dad draped me across his shoulders and ran over to the Suburban. Chief Davis grabbed the door as Dad tossed me in.

There was a Secret Service agent driving, wearing a tan suit and striped tie, a second-generation agent who knew Detroit well. "Where are we going?"

"Toward the lake," Dave snapped. "Is he saying anything, Larry?"

"Nothing that makes sense. Just what we have heard," he paused and listened. "What Bub, what do you see?"

"The warehouse, it's behind a deli. There is a theatre in front of the deli."

Dave interrupted me. "What kind of theatre?"

"One with plays."

"Can you see what is playing?" The Chief looked at the driver. "Can you call your office and ask for a theatre search with delis nearby?"

The driver grabbed his phone. "I am sure that will narrow it down," his tone was sarcastic.

"There are rolls of metal all over the place with big machines with levers on them."

"Wait, didn't Staci say something about metal?" Dave flipped through his notes, "Yeah, she said Peterson's Metal Shop. Ask your office where that is and if there is a deli and a theatre near it."

"Yes, sir!"

"We need to hurry," I said. "She's in trouble and she wants you, Dave. I see her being tied to a chair and the ropes are starting to mark her wrists. This guy is saying that she can never go back to her family — it's him or death. There are guns everywhere and cans, like soda cans. I can't tell what is in them but they are everywhere."

"Probably beer cans," Dad said, holding me tight, I was quivering with fear. "Just what you need. Drunks with guns."

"They are blue and silver with red writing."

"Chappy's."

"Chappy's?" Dad didn't know what Dave was talking about. "What is that?"

"It is a local brewery here in town. They make really cheap, good beer. Hangover of death, though. But, if you need to drink cheap, it's the beer of choice in these parts." Dave started laughing. "Great, well we got a room full of drunks in a metal shop with guns, if he is right. If he isn't, I don't know what we'll do."

"We will find her," said Mitch. "I will have every agent I can muster on this. Your wife will be safe. It's the least I can do. Whatever you need, it's covered." Mitch untied his tie, slid it through the collar and tossed it in the back.

"What are you doing, sir?" the agent driving asked, looking at Mitch through the rearview mirror.

"Getting ready to help take down some bad guys. You got a gun up there for me, Dave?"

"Sir, I can't let you do this. I know you want to help my wife because we found your daughter, but you have an important job and a wife and daughter who need you. We should be close. Why don't you pull over and let's put vests and gear on, if we have them."

I started rocking back and forth in the seat looking at the warehouse through pipe vision. "No time, no time, we got to get there, Daddy. They're going to kill her."

"Who's going to kill who?" Aaron asked.

"A man, standing over a black woman tied to a chair. He is standing over her with a gun." All I could see was the vision, my body tingled and my head hurt so badly. "Please stop!"

"Step on it. The place is right around the corner. Kill the lights. Here's the plan, guys, when we get there, Congressman Anderson, I want you to wait in the truck with Bub and Aaron. It's important."

Mitch nodded in agreement. "Just leave Bub and me in the truck. It's bullet proof. So, take the driver as backup."

"Sir, I can't leave you. I will get fired," said the driver.

"You will get fired if you stay."

"Hey, Greg!" He had been in deep thought, fearing what the night might bring since leaving the airport. "You okay? You gonna be able to help us with some bad guys?"

"I am," Aaron said with his hand on the door handle and answering before his uncle. "I'm going to help you get Mom back."

"No, it's too dangerous," Dave sternly said, looking at his only child. "I can't afford the chance of losing you and Mom if this thing gets ugly."

"Dad, I need to do this. I am a man now. I left here a boy who didn't see the good in the world. You're a good cop and these are bad cops," he paused, putting his hand on his dad's shoulder. "Dad, we are the only people you can trust. Now get outta the car and give me a gun."

The Chief sat in the front seat, smiling. He had no idea what lay ahead, but in three days, his son has become a man. Was it an act? He did not know, but he knew one thing. He never dreamt he would say these words to his 15-year-old as he handed him a gun: "Here, don't shoot yourself."

Aaron was tempted to start spinning the gun around on his finger and act like they did in movies, but knowing the serious trust placed in his hands and the situation, this wasn't the time.

"Chief, what's the plan?" Greg was using his red bandana to absorb the sweat off his palms.

They were walking down a partially lit, damp alley, stopping at the main door, which was next to the overhead door. "Shall we let them know we are here?" Chief Davis asked, tilting his head toward the door.

The National Guard caved in the door, using a battering ram. As soon as they were through the door, the only sound was guns cocking and screams of, "DROP YOUR WEAPONS! DON'T SHOOT! FREEZE!" The guards cleared the warehouse rooms and gathered the suspects at the table, disarming them and cuffing their hands behind their backs and tossing them in chairs.

Bang! A single shot was fired by a Guardsman. "Bet you wish you would have dropped your gun now."

Dave ran over to the puff of smoke. "Who is it?" he yelled, as he ran across the floor thinking, please don't be Gabe, he is mine.

"I don't know there is no name tag on his shoulder," the young private was shaking and looking at the blood-soaked corpse on the floor. "He raised on me, sir. I never had to shoot no one before."

"You did good son, put your weapon down until you quit shaking."

Dave motioned another private over. "Take him and let him calm down." As the two men walked away, Dave added, "Oh, and get his statement while it's fresh." He mumbled under his breath, "God knows we are going to need a good paper trail." He kicked the gun away from the lifeless body as he saw his wife.

Staff Sergeant Michaels yelled, "Secure?"

One by one, each man yelled, "Secure."

Chief Davis held up his badge to show the men in custody who he was, showing his authority. "Sit still, Annissa. You are safe now," he walked over, kissed his wife and untied her. "Aaron, come here." He helped his wife onto her feet. "Take your mom to the car."

Annissa put her arm around Aaron's neck and they walked toward the battered door. Her body was numb and stiff from being tied to a wooden chair for most of the evening. "Come on Mama, you are safe now. No one will hurt you."

Mitch saw the two walking out the door and got out to help them. "Mrs. Davis, I am glad to see you are safe. Your guys were worried about you," he said with a smile. "Here, take my arm and we will walk slowly to that truck. Do you need an ambulance?"

"No, thank you. I am fine. Hey, aren't you…?"

"Mitch Anderson? Yes ma'am, I am. Your husband and his friends found my kidnapped daughter this evening and I had no choice but to return the favor by helping to find you. You are very lucky." He opened the back door and helped her in. "If it weren't for these kids, we probably would have never discovered your location."

Annissa looked in the backseat at Staci and Bub, sleeping, "Aaron, who are these kids?"

Aaron pointed and said, "Bub," then pointing at Staci, "This is Staci. They had visions which led Dad and everyone here."

He accompanied his mother in the car and told her the story of how they met. "Everything was cool, then they started freaking out and seeing stuff that no one else could see." He paused and looked at Bub and Staci, still sleeping. "But everything they said turned out to be true. How did you get here, Mama?"

"Baby, it is a long story, one with many turns, twists and sins. I hope one day your father forgives me and we laugh about it."

"Dad loves you and I am sure he will forgive you. He has forgiven me, and Mama, I hope you will too."

She grabbed her baby and held him tightly to her, rocking him as if he was an infant. "Baby, there is nothing you can do that I won't forgive.

"So, guys what's up?" Dave grabbed the chair his wife had been tied to, flipped it around and sat on it, "Who's the dead guy?"

"Never seen him before," Frank said. "I was lost and needed directions. I was on my way out when I came back here to take a piss. I didn't know that lady was tied up. The way they had her sitting at the table, it appeared as if she was eating. I was about to call the police about all of the guns when the damn door was busted in."

"I see, when you noticed two, no wait, three cops in here, you weren't suspicious, Gabe?"

Bart looked across the table at his partner, "Dammit."

Gabe's face grew pale as he glared into Dave's eyes: "What are you talking about?"

"Zake," the Chief looked around at the group of five sitting around the table, three of them his own cops, "So here's the deal: full immunity, you walk out that door tonight after signing a statement disclosing everything you know about Gabe Maddox." He got up and turned the chair around and sat, propping his feet up on the table, causing all of his change to fall out of his pocket.

"You dropped something," Bart said laughing. "Why should we believe you? No attorneys are here, either for us or for the state. For all we know, you could be trapping us."

Dave sat there and thought. He rubbed his forehead, placing his feet on the floor then rested his elbows on the table. He sighed and extended his arms on the table. "Wait here."

"What's your name?" Chief Davis said, as he grabbed a young Private.

"Michaels, sir." The boy stood proud and at attention as this was his first assignment since enlisting in the National Guard.

"Glad to meet you." Dave tossed his notes and radio into his other hand as he shook Michaels' hand, "I want you to start taking these suspects and putting them in the vans out front so we can transport them to the station."

"Yes sir." The Private stood at attention and saluted Dave.

"Easy son, as far as that one," Dave said, pointed at Gabe Maddox. "We'll need to make special transportation arrangements for him, since he is our Governor. Why don't you take him over there?" Dave pointed to an empty break room.

"Yes, Sir!"

Chief Davis headed out the back door to talk to Mitch Anderson and see if he could offer deals to the others to close a case against Gabe.

Everyone in the SUV was sleeping or quiet, except for Mitch. He was on his phone checking in with Jaime and Jessie. Larry and Greg were standing outside of the vehicle, just killing time until Dave concluded his business.

"Everything cool, man?" Greg asked his brother as Dave walked up to the SUV to talk to Mitch.

"Yeah, hang out here," Dave said, as he hopped in the front seat. "I want to give anyone who will sign a statement against Gabe a pass. Can you make that happen?"

"I don't know who you have or what they have done and I know you are vested emotionally, so we should probably get a DA or State Attorney here to work that out."

Dave interrupted him. "With all due respect, sir, I got three cops and a Governor of the state in there, and a witness in Kentucky, saying Gabe was the supplier and benefactor of a meth operation. Whatever they did, it was on his behalf. Now I want to get this guy." He looked in the back. "Where's Aaron?"

"He said he had to pee, sweetie," Annissa wearily replied.

"Shit!" Dave grabbed the door handle and flung it open. "Make some calls!" he commanded Mitch, slamming the door and ran towards the building, "Did you see Aaron go by?"

"No." Greg and Larry followed him as he ran.

"Stop, Aaron!" Dave walked into the room where his son had Gabe on his knees. Both of Aaron's hands were on the butt of the revolver and his finger trembled on the trigger. "How did you let this happen? Fifteen of you, I leave for three minutes and come back to my kid with a suspect at gunpoint!"

"He walked in to grab a pop from the machine and the next thing we know he has a gun drawn on Maddox," Staff Sergeant Michaels said.

"Stop Michaels, I don't need a report right now! Give me the gun, son," he walked up behind him. "Give me the gun," he grabbed the barrel.

"No, Dad. He told Mom that she was his property and she could never have us back." Tears rolled down Aaron's face. "He has to die, so Mom can have us back."

"No, son, Mom isn't going anywhere. He, however, is going to jail and if I can trace the body in the lake to him then he will die. Kentucky is a death-penalty state."

"Kill me boy! Show your wimpy dad what men are made of and how men solve problems. They do it with guns, not hide behind their badges and power. Be a man."

"Shut up!" Aaron screamed.

"Aaron, relax. I will take care of this guy, give me the gun," Dave wanted to get the gun out of his son's hands as fast as possible.

"No."

"Hey, give me the gun. You don't want this on your conscience."

"Sure he does. Killing makes you a man. Shoot me." Gabe was laughing at Aaron's indecisiveness.

Aaron pressed the barrel harder against Gabe's head.

"No," said Dave. He knelt beside his boy, spun him around and removed the gun from his trembling hands. Holding him, Dave said, "Come on."

"No. Boss," a voice from the crowd yelled.

A gunshot echoed through the warehouse. Dave tossed Aaron down and shielded him. Gabe's lifeless body landed on them.

They laid there on the ground for a minute and waited for the shock to pass. "Someone want to get this fat, dead prick off me?"

Rising to his knees, Dave scanned his boy, finding no wounds. "You, take him out to his mother," he said, pointing to a Private who was standing there with a gaping hole for a mouth. "Hey, can you do that, pal?"

He snapped to attention, saluted Dave, and replied, "Yes, sir!" He walked to Aaron and put his hand on his shoulder. "Come, let's get out of here." He nodded to Dave as he pulled away from his son.

Mitch flew into the warehouse. He saw his friend Gabe's lifeless body on the floor. "What happened?" Annissa ran in behind him.

"Oh my God!" She yelled, grabbing her son in her arms and continuing to walk out to the SUV. "Please, tell me you didn't do that?"

"No."

Larry was standing still as a stone, holding the gun he fired, not believing that he had killed a man. Dave walked up to him and he passed his palm in front of Larry's face. "You there man?" Snapping his fingers, he said, "Larry, let go of the gun." Then, yelling at the crowd of guardsman and agents, "I need a bag!" He shook Larry's hand until the gun dropped into the evidence bag.

Mitch looked at the chaos-filled room and his friend laying there on the ground. "What the hell happened?"

Larry, shaking, sat down on a nearby metal chair. "His cuffs were off and he had a leg holster." Larry heaved a big sigh. "When you turned with Aaron, he reached and pulled the gun on you. I shot him."

The four new friends sat there. Dave took an official statement from Larry. When the statement was finished, Dave said, "I think we need to get you guys back to Kentucky and I need to get my family home." He paused and looked over at Larry. "I might need you to come back next week and testify or answer questions," he sighed. "State Internal Affairs will be all over my office, especially after word gets out that dirty cops were in my house. Ey, I guess it is all part of the job."

Mitch handed Dave a card. "You need anything, you call me. I might not be in politics much longer, but I will help anyway I can."

They started walking toward the door. "You know this has been the strangest week of my life, but I'm glad I met you guys and reconnected with my brother," said Dave. He stopped walking. "Maybe we can get together without dead bodies."

They shook hands, which turned into hugs and goodbyes. As they piled in to the SUVs, Dave stood there with his hands in his pockets watching the black SUV fade into the night. Annissa and Aaron were standing next to an unmarked police car waiting to drive them home. Dave raised his eyes with pleasure when he saw them and ran and hugged them both, "I love you guys more than anything. I hope you know." He opened the door and followed them into the car, "Let's get the hell out of here and go home."